STEELTOWN

A NOVEL BY
RICHARD E. MOUSSEAU

MOOSE HIDE BOOKS
imprint of
MOOSE ENTERPRISE PUBLISHING
PRINCE TOWNSHIP
ONTARIO, CANADA

cover illustration by Richard Mousseau

STEELTOWN
By Richard E. Mousseau
Copyright March 1, 1981

Published September 1, 1998
BY

MOOSE HIDE BOOKS
imprint of
MOOSE ENTERPRISE PUBLISHING
PRINCE TOWNSHIP
ONTARIO, CANADA
P6A 6K4
web site www.moosehidebooks.com

NO VENTURE UNATTAINABLE

CREATED IN CANADA

Library and Archives Canada Cataloguing in Publication

Mousseau, Richard E., author
        Steeltown / Richard Mousseau
        2nd Ed.

ISBN 978-0-969831-98-3 (PBK.).—ISBN 978-1-927393-42-0 (PDF)

    I. Title.

PS8576.O977S74 1997   C813'.54   C96-901063-X
PR9199.3.M69S74 1997
PS8576.O977S74 2017   C813'.54   C2017-901663-6

STEELTOWN

CHAPTER ONE
Fade Back#

"Plug her up! Plug her up!" Reese yelled repeatedly while the crimson red iron oozed freely from the furnace. "Plug up the damn thing!"

A devilish grin came to Boo's lips. From across the cast-house floor, Tommy Jenkins watched the commotion.

"Pull it out," yelled Reese to the operator. "The tip of the clay gun is melting. Refill it and try again!" Reese looked around for the clay-man who was suppose to pull the release chain so that the operator could bring back the gun. "Pull the damn chain Boo." Boo just grinned at a fuming Reese. "Boo you bastard!!!"

Gobs of melting cast iron fell from the clay gun's nozzle. Reese pulled the chain several times before the gun released. Unexpectedly the iron exploded in the hole. No-one was safe on the open cast-house floor. Tommy dropped to the floor as sparks shot over him. Boo grinned like a Cheshire cat as the sparks exploded past the opening. Unlike others, he was protected by the operating room. Tommy shielded himself and listened to the shrill of the emergency sirens ringing as everyone evacuated the area. Tommy counted heads and found that one was missing. Tommy could only see Boo on the far side of the trough. Was it an accident? Had Boo something to do with it? These questions raced through his mind. He had witnessed the whole thing, he had not seen anything out of the ordinary, and most of his suspicions and evidence was melting away. Was Boo the only survivor?

. . . . . .

The dark black sky filled the night as grey smoke and steam billowed upward from the factory blast-furnace. Red hot slag flowing from one of the four blast-furnaces illuminated the night sky. The road past the railroad tracks along number five furnace was brightened as if it had been daytime. A steady stream of men walked the half mile distance from number 4 gate. It was the shift change, and along the pathway somewhere between number seven and number five furnaces, workers walked to the welfare building nestled amongst smaller factory shops.

Tonight, the air possessed a certain burden as men brushed silvery graphite off their already dingy clothes. Others coughed sporadically, an industrial cough, the kind that never seems to go away. Men on the graveyard shift walked up the brick stairway on their way to the locker room. Rows and rows of lockers, painted repeatedly with the company's dark green colour stood like soldiers all in a row. Sweat permeated the air as steam filled the shower room. Work clothes filled the baskets that hung over the lockers throughout the room. Men; young, old and middle age chattered in English and Italian. Of the two, Italian was the more common language of most workers that had settled in this steel town.

The level of chatter increased as men of different proportions milled around the locker room. Men clad only in towels walked to and from the showers. As the number of men increased so did the chatter. For about an hour and a half, between the three to eleven shift and eleven to seven shift, the room full of bodies seemed to be in a state of chaos. In a short period of time the aisles would be empty and the lockers would be silent. But for now, the smell of human sweat still filled the air. In a short while the men would be heading home or to their jobs.

As the last man left the welfare room, only silence remained. A cool September wind blew through the open window above the lockers. It would not be long before the impending winter would bring its cold blast of arctic air. The summer had been eventful, but as the fall of 1979 arrived it was obvious that events had changed. The times would never be the same again.

A stream of light filled with dirt beamed down upon the shoulders of a lone man sitting silently on a hard bench worn with age and use. Dressed in work clothes and with boot laces untied, his eyes glanced at the concrete floor. He reflected on a different place and a different time. Raising his head, an expressionless face glanced from locker to locker. His eyes seemed to anticipate something that was there, but it was not. Closing eyes, he gently rested a heavy head back against the locker behind.

Longish brown hair, cut in a shag style, rested on the shoulders of his six foot one inch body, weighing 170 pounds. A clean-cut face and deep brown eyes were accented by a moustache which extended down to the corners of thin lips, giving him the essence of a loner. He sat alone. Calloused hands resting on his lap, facing upward in a questioning manner. He opened glossy wet eyes and scanned the entire length of the lockers, as the smell of sweat disappeared. A smile came to lips, but faded as quickly as it had come.

His thoughts seemed to depart from his body. No longer were there lockers, or the clanking of the steel mill.

Lowering eyes, he bowed a weary head. Above him a beam of light rested gently on his shoulders. He sat on the green painted bench and felt the cool September wind whispering above. Clothes moved in rhythm with the wind blowing gently above the lockers. Around him the empty lockers stood waiting to be occupied.

There was a time before this, a good time. His thoughts gravitated toward those times as the cool wind above the lockers gently caressed the darkening night sky. He wished for the wind to carry him away.

CHAPTER TWO
The Boys

The auditorium was bright against an empty and dark stage. People milled looking for the seats with the best view. On this evening, everyone was dressed for the occasion. Mothers, fathers, sisters, brothers and even grandparents were here to share the upcoming spectacle. Another hour elapsed before all would arrive to take their seats. June 19, 1979's graduation class would be the last graduating class of the seventies. Disco was dying and rock was being resurrected from its ashes. The fads of country music were becoming the new trend-setters. Faint sounds of a whispering voice were desperately trying to be heard over the sounds of people chattering. Yet commands went totally unnoticed, and as her voice died, she gasped for air. Miss. Cradock was clad in her usual below the knees skirt. She was wearing her old-fashioned shoes and her half moon specs. She waddled amongst the inattentive and disorderly assembly. Most thought that she was in her eighties, and she looked it! With a walking-stick in hand, she poked and herded the graduation group into formation as she had done over the years. Her eyes were stern and voice was harsh. She was both hated and loved. Underneath, she was soft hearted, but not today, for today was Graduation day. Her students had to be just perfect! With one wrinkled hand, she patted a tied back-bun of white hair on a small head. She looked up and down the rows of devilish angels. The rows were not just right. Someone was Miss.ing!

Towards the back of the gym, in a corner, moaning voices could be heard coming from two people wrapped in the same graduation gown, no doubt his hands were caressing her ample bosom. Inside the gown a young colt of a stallion held a young beautiful girl. She was just one of many in a long line of girls who had fallen victim to his spell. She had not been the first and certainly would not be the last to fall under his spell. His ability to enter and exit one affair after another had earned him the nick-name 'Ziggy'. Ziggy would never let himself be caught, or be tied down by any one girl! He dressed stylish and was always a trend-setter. Blessed with good looks, which included the bluest eyes, he always seemed to mesmerize all the girls that fell under his spell. He was never seen without some girl at his side. Ziggy was what everyone wanted to be. And everyone wanted to be with him.

"Mr. Motonovich," yelled Miss. Cradock's squeaky voice. "We would like to have your presence over here! You too, Miss. Simpson." Her stern eyes and harsh voice caused the blonde to scramble out from beneath the gown.

All eyes were fixed on Ziggy and the blonde. Girls giggled and boys praised their leader.

"Now Miss. Simpson!" Miss. Cradock's voice crackled.

"Yes . . .," whimpered the blonde. "Yes, Miss. Cradock. I'm coming."

Laughter filled the entire gym as the embarrassed young girl emerged from Ziggy's graduation gown.

"You came just in time," yelled the graduating group in unison. "Did both of you come at the same time?"

"That's enough now, everyone take your places." Miss. Cradock waved the walking cane as if herding sheep. "Hurry up, Mr. Motonovich."

Ziggy took his time walking nonchalantly past the rows of students. As he walked down towards the stage, he left each girl swooning breathlessly. Miss. Cradock waited, her foot tapping, a scornful look covered her face. Her cane poised ready to strike at the source of this delay. Stopping in front of Miss. Cradock, Ziggy cast flirting charms upon her. Then bending close planted a kiss on her flushed cheeks. For a moment, the room fell silent. Eyes stared and mouths fell open in disbelief. Miss. Cradock stood motionless. Slowly a faint smile came to her lips. She patted the hair bun in a childish manner. Her pale cheeks suddenly turned into a blushing pink. Her heart beat feverishly, as any young girl's heart would in a situation such as this!

"You may take your place now, Ziggy," stammered Miss. Cradock. Her typical harshness seemed to have suddenly evaporated. Regained composure, she walked daintily down the aisle and took her place at the head of the group.

And so, it seemed to Ziggy, that he had now added yet another conquest to his long list of conquests. With a sense of accomplishment, Ziggy took his place among the other disbelieving fellow students.

Miss. Cradock started to speak again now having everyone's attention. "Now ladies, and gentleman; when you walk out into that auditorium, please stand tall and walk straight. Please act like young ladies and gentlemen."

Everyone was paying attention to Miss. Cradock as she explained the procedures for the graduation ceremony. Back in amongst the rows of students, two boys who were not paying attention to Miss. Cradock, instead were whispering to each other. To all those that knew these two, everyone knew that they were usually behind any shenanigans that went on around the school. One who seemed to be standing out of line as usual, wearing his ever so prevalent sneakers, grinned devilishly, with curly blonde hair, had to be Salami. Salami had not been blessed with an awful lot of height for his age, but he was not as short as many of the other boys. It was typical for Salami to be the first into any ploy and usually the last one out. Most girls liked him, but he just wanted to love them and leave them. Only one girl, Anita, managed to forgive and forget his wayward ways, she loved Salami. The kid's name? Well it came from the food that he would bring everyday. Italian salami, hot and tasty. He would not bring anything else, so the name suited him to a tee.

His usual dress included sneakers with untied laces, and pant cuffs that dragged on the floor. Salami was speaking with a sense of intrigue to his buddy, Boo. Whenever these two got together there was bound to be something amiss. Most times, they were usually up to something.

Boo, as the name implies, was mysterious. No one knew that much about him. Not even closest friends, Salami and Ziggy.

Even Frog, who was the butt of most of Boo's and Salami's jokes, had no knowledge of Boo's past. School girls usually ooed and aahed about Boo's shaggy hair and droopy moustache, but that is as far as they went. The girls that were usually considered nice girls were the ones that usually ended up with him. Boo was slim, tall and just as good looking as Ziggy but somewhat withdrawn. His world seemed to revolve around his chums and only his chums.

Dragging his feet, as the line of students filed forward, Salami gave final details to Boo. His words had barely left his lips when a crackling sound echoed throughout the gym and echoing inside of his head.

"I told you to get in line." Miss. Cradock swung the cane at his head of curly hair. "I said walk straight and tall."

"I am. I am!" Salami ducked behind the girls for protection.

Miss. Cradock began to speak again, but stopped in disgust. Looking at the dishevelled attire of Salami, she shook a discontented head in disgust. Not until Ziggy passed did she blush a rosy pink like a little girl who had just discovered a first love.

A hushed silence filled the auditorium. Teary-eyed mothers ooed, uninvited children giggled uncontrollable. It was a splendid sight to behold, to see the line of gowned students proudly walking towards a new beginning.

When everyone was seated, the auditorium lights were dimmed. Only one spot light shone brilliantly on a small figure. Miss. Cradock walked slowly across the stage, almost with an air of nobility. She took a seat among the distinguished guests, a tear of joy in the corner of an eye.

With a smile, as broad as a barn and a body to match, the Principal sat next to her. In between the jolly Principal and the scornful little Vice-Principal, sat the school's Valedictorian, Penelope Snidermost. She was a vision of primness and properness, sitting stiffly in a pink fluffy dress with her knees pressed tightly together. No-one was the least interested, though thinking that someone was looking, she pulled at the ends of the dress with dainty white gloved hands.

At the end of the row of distinguished quests, slightly nervous, and wearing his big brother's suit, sat Frog. He was constantly fidgeting with required horn-rimmed glasses. How he ended up on stage as Master of Ceremonies, only Boo, Salami and Ziggy knew. Though he did not want the job, he had inherited it. With slicked back hair, and in a slightly outdated over-sized suit, a nervous Frog undertook this job with vengeance! He was going to show the rest of the school students and faculty who he was!

Growing progressively larger, the spot light followed the hobbling Miss. Cradock to the podium. Unsure of new-fangled gadgets, she tested the mike, tapping it with angry fingers. Hearing the thudding sounds echoing from the darkness, she began to speak in a voice loud enough to be effectively heard without the mike.

"Ladies and gentlemen, and this year's graduating class. I would like to welcome you to our 1979 convocation".

Most of the audience listened respectfully, except two scheming figures cloaked in the darkness of the auditorium. When all were seated, the seats assigned to Boo and Salami were empty. Amongst the rows of seats, crawling along the floor, Boo and Salami scrambled quickly.

"Boo, have you found it yet?"

"No! You sure you put it in this row?"

Boo checked the end seat for the row's number. "Row seven, Salami"

"That's not the one, it's row eight . . ., I think".

"Well hurry, before it's too late".

"And now," Continued Miss. Cradock. "I would like to introduce our Principal, Mr. Finlay."

The applause was thunderous as the roly-poly man waddled clumsily to the mike. "Thank you. Thank you. It's so nice to be here today, with all these fine young boys and girls. I've enjoyed their company over the past four years. It was just a pleasure . . .,"

"Crap!"

"Ziggy!"

"Ok, I'm sorry. It's not crap!"

"No not that! Get your hands away. There might be someone looking." The blonde squirmed in the chair, pulling at her cape. Even in the darkness of the auditorium, and covered by a graduation gown, her large breasts were silhouetted like two luscious melons. The finest set of hooters, Ziggy had ever seen!

"No-one's going to see," his voice whispered soft and passionate. "The gown covers my hands."

"Ehhhh!"

With a slight gesture of Ziggy's hands, the blonde let out a shrilling shriek. Silence fell over the auditorium. The words on the Principal's lips stopped in mid-air. Miss. Cradock perked up; her cane ready to strike.

"Ah! There must be a mouse among us." The jolly man recovered the attention of the bewildered mass. "Ha! Ha! Ha! I hope the little thing did not bite anyone," his cheeks and belly rolled in laughter as he spoke.

"Can't you wait until tonight?" She resisted Ziggy's advances, just a little.

"No," Ziggy's voice was soft and irresistible as he whispered in her ear and nibbled on her neck.

"Thank you. Thank you. It has been a pleasure talking to you, and I would like to express the best to all of you fine students. Now my right-hand man, Vice- Principal Lawford would like to say a few words."

The applause was only polite, not as thunderous as it had been given for Principal Finlay. Mixed with the applause for Principal Finlay, cat calls could be heard throughout the auditorium.

"All right that's enough!" spoke Mr. Lawford. His face was shallow and lips tight. Often his eyes could burn fear into the students, like a red-hot iron. "I'm here to do a job. This is my job. Despite your booing, I'm really not that bad within."

Some parents laughed at the intended humour, but the students knew better. Their boos continued throughout the Vice-Principal's speech.

Without paying any attention to anything or anyone around them, Salami and Boo weaved in-between rows. They scrambled in-between legs, searching the floor for something that was very, very crucial!

"Boo, have you found it yet?"

"Not yet! Are you sure it's here? No one could have found it? Could they?"

"Naa . . ., it's here."

"Well, whatever it is . . .," whispered a long-legged girl, "It's not up my leg!"

"Salami! Look for it. We're losing time."

"And remember, that without my strictness and good judgement, some of you might have ended up as juvenile delinquents. Now, I will introduce our Master of Ceremonies, who will outline the social events, name the various awards and introduce this year's valedictorian . . .,"

"Boo, I've got it!" Salami pulled slightly, getting the object into position as Boo worked his way down the rows of tangled legs.

"You've got the camera ready?"

"Yeah!" Salami replied as he headed into the darkness towards the back of the stage.

"Tonight, our Master of Ceremonies will be . . .,"

In a chorus of voices, the students helped the forgetful Vice-Principal. "Frog!"

"Yes, Mr. Frog."

A roar of laughter filled the auditorium. Both parents and students laughed more at Mr. Lawford than at the somewhat nervous Frog. Hurrying for his seat, Mr. Lawford eluded the spotlight searching for the still seated Mr. Frog. There he sat, fumbling with

14

written notes, pulling at a tie and hoping that this was all a dream. With cheers urging him on, Frog shuffled clumsily up to the podium.

"Good evening," In a cracking voice not yet changed for his age, Frog mimicked a poor imitation of Alfred Hitchcock's famous opening line from the Alfred Hitchcock Show.

"Good evening fellow students and guests."

With a stern look from Boo, a student quickly gave up his seat. Getting into position Boo pulled ever so slightly on a silver wire. Pulling, then easing back, a sinister grin covered his face when realizing that the wire was in working order. No-one chose to question his actions. If possible, all would have moved, yet knowing Boo and Salami, they would stick around for whatever was going to unfold.

From back stage, Salami dragged himself along the stage floor towards the curtains. Lifting the bottom of the curtains, he positioned himself. Salami felt that this was not quite right. He needed to position himself a little more to the left, so that he would have a great view. At least so he thought! With a camera and flash in hand, Salami squirmed to a better vantage point. He hoped to have enough time to set up, but, he was not sure how long Frog was going to speak. He set up as quickly as possible with the flash. Salami knew that the camera, the one with the telephoto lens, was going to give him some great shots. As Frog's speech came to an end, Salami made one more check to make sure that the camera was loaded.

". . ., and the student council invites everyone to tonight's events," spoke Frog. "Also, there's a big party tonight, so check around to find out where and when. And now, I'd like to introduce our class Valedictorian, Penelope Snidermost."

"Miss. Goody-two shoes," mumbled a few students.

Out of politeness, everyone applauded. Accompanying the applauding, there was also some hooting, louder than anyone, louder than the applauding by Penelope Snidermost's parents who sat proud as peacocks. In the darkness of the audience, Boo gave out a loud whistle.

"I've been waiting all night for her," Boo said to all near him as a grin grew larger. "She's the most!"

While Penelope Snidermost, in her pink fluffy dress, waddled to the podium, Boo slowly let the silver wire slip through fingers. While fluffing the pink dress for all to see, Penelope stepped behind the podium and placed dainty white gloved hands neatly on the podium.

Parting the curtains, Salami focussed the camera and adjusted the flash. In this huge auditorium with people taking pictures, no-one would notice the flash from Salami's camera. Patiently waiting on the floor, he focussed the camera. Salami waited for the moment to take the perfect shot!

The wire eased through Boo's fingers, and under the rug to a pulley at the edge of the stage. Boo concentrated on the thin wire, unaware of Penelope Snidermost rambling on about something unimportant. Along the lower edge of the stage, the wire ran unnoticeable though the orchestra pit to another pulley waiting at the upper stage rigging that lead the wire directly over the podium.

Miss. Cradock, because of her age or because of the speech, closed her eyes and started to slowly rock back and forth in the darkness. Lawford stared ahead into the darkness, straining eyes to focus on someone that was doing something questionable at the far end of the stage. Principal Finlay, with a smile that covered most of his face, shook with laughter at non-funny things Miss. Snidermost said. He laughed so hard that he had to remove eye glasses to stop them from fogging up.

There at the end of the row, Frog sat, a bit more relaxed now. He straightened a crooked tie and adjusted the glasses on his nose. Unable to see anything else but Penelope Snidermost, Frog watched her fluffy dress sway back and forth behind the podium. With every emphasized word, the dress would sway back and forth, giving him all kinds seducing ideas. He was forgetting who he was, and who she was, because the body under that dress was certainly causing him to generate some wild fantasies about what he and Penelope could be doing together.

Salami gave some final adjustment to the camera and then looking above the stage tried to locate the almost sightless wire. Inch by inch the wire passed through Boo's fingers. His eyes were focussed just above the spotlight. There was plenty of time, for Penelope Snidermost knew how to ramble on at the mouth. At first glance, a kind of sparkle caught Boo's eye. The wire now loomed in mid-air.

". . ., We're young and have a lifetime ahead of us," Penelope said. "We must take advantage of opportunities." Her hands rested on the podium, but her fluffy dress, and whatever caused it to move, swayed from side to side. As if fixated, Frog's eyes were glued to the swaying motion of the pink dress. The back-stage curtain parted as Salami zoomed in on the target with the camera. Boo lowered the wire down into the spotlight. So far, the silver wire was only noticeable to himself. Miss. Snidermost carried on with her speech, unaware of torturing the audience.

"We are now entering the adult world as young ladies and gentlemen," she spoke. A large boastful smile covered most of her face as if she had said something worth remembering.

Down the back of Penelope's pink fluffy dress, Salami noticed the hook shaped wire. At the same time, Frog instantly caught a glimpse of a shadowy wire against the dress. Not sure of what he saw, Frog adjusted horn-rimmed glasses to make sure he was seeing clearly. It looked like something was sliding down the swaying frame of Penelope's dress. Frog gazed upward, and then around as far as eyes could see. No-one else on the stage had seen it, and Penelope Snidermost certainly did not feel it. Frog was tempted to rush up and grab it. He started to move, then hesitated, thinking that everyone would think he was attacking her.

'Was she a Damsel in distress, worth saving?' he thought, or would he just sit tight and watch? And so, watch he did as the wire moved further downward. Assuming that the wire was down far enough, Boo began to raise it slowly. Salami's trigger finger was itching to take the climatic picture. But, he would have to wait! He watched the wire slip limply upward.

Frog sighed quietly, and Lawford turned to glance sternly. Frog started to look away as if nothing was happening, while keeping eyes on Penelope Snidermost. Down came the wire for a second try. Frog glanced around and saw that no-one was looking. He looked back at the dress and then at the wire. He had to remove glasses to stop the mist fogging up the lenses. Salami pressed an eye to the camera. He was ready to try again. The wire slipped through Boo's fingers and then he felt the tension on the wire. It had caught! Salami pressed lightly on the shutter button. Frog's eyes widened unbelievingly, as his mouth fell open. Boo pulled very slowly. A beaming grin appeared to cover his entire face.

Penelope Snidermost swayed as she spoke, smiling as cameras flashed in the darkness of the auditorium.

"Gone are the games and pranks of adolescence," she stressed. "We must leave that all behind and face life seriously!" Gesturing,

Penelope raised an arm with a finger pointing skyward. Smiling as her parent's camera flashed, she continued to hold a pose.

Filled with excitement, Salami began to click the shutters on the camera. Frog watched the wire with amazement. His eyes bulged, and mouth dropped open. Frog was dumbfounded! The wire crawled up further and further, bringing with it the fluffy pink dress of Penelope Snidermost, still swaying side to side.

"Now, Ziggy!" Boo whispered into the darkness. He then raised his voice slightly. "Now!"

With arms still wrapped around a girl, Ziggy began to sneeze and cough loud enough to be heard by all in the auditorium. In the darkness, all eyes were focussed on the sound somewhere to the left of the stage. Lawford leaned forward in his chair, blocking the view of all except Frog whose eyes were still transfixed on the fluffy pink dress. Salami's camera flashed repeatedly as Boo pulled the wire upward.

Penelope Snidermost continued to speak despite the interruption. She was so involved with the speech that she did not feel anything as her dress and slip crawled slowly up her back. Grabbing the seat of the chair, Frog swayed with excitement. Her dress and slip crawled up past her nylons and past the white clips that held them up. Salami focussed the telephoto lens and clicked endlessly, picture after picture after picture!

Penelope's legs caressed each other. Frog adjusted his glasses to see better. This was something he did not want to miss, no matter what! Pulling his legs together, he pressed his hands hard between legs. A tidal wave of sexual arousal swept over him. Salami clicked away as Boo continued to pull the wire further and further up.

'There isn't any . . .,' Frog moaned. The camera behind the curtains clicked rapidly as Penelope's pink fluffy dress rose higher and higher. The speech continued never letting up. Frog watched with the greatest enjoyment of his life, as eyes devoured Penelope's white and pinkish buttock. Penelope Snidermost, so prim and proper, had nothing on. There she was as bare as the day she was born! Naked, firm and inviting; her buttocks swaying back and forth as Frog savoured every second.

Finally, it ended, Penelope Snidermost stamped a foot and the hook slipped. The camera stopped clicking, and Frog slid from the chair, panting and gasping for air. He was in love, or just plain horny, he did not know which!

The sneezing stopped, and Salami rolled away from the curtain, camera in hand. All eyes were focussed on Frog. The stern piercing look from Lawford seemed to burn into Frog's neck. Principal Finlay just chuckled at the boy's display.

"I told you to behave like young gentlemen!" whispered Miss. Cradock sternly, as she tapped the cane for attention.

Frog scrambled into the seat, trying not to sit up straight for obvious reasons! Stopping her speech, Penelope Snidermost faced Frog and began to tap her foot in disgust.

"More . . ., More . . .," moaned Frog as he bent over praying that the dress would go up. "Up! Up! Up!"

"Mr. Frog!" Miss. Cradock scolded. "Let her get the speech over with."

"Up! Up! Shit!" Boo lowered the silver wire then tried to raise it. It would seem, that another successful attempt was all over.

The voice of Penelope Snidermost blared over the P.A. as she continued her speech. Everything was back to normal . . ., almost. Salami, with photograph pictures of the century, raced down the back hallway to the Graphic Arts Department. Boo retrieved in the silver wire and sneaked away from the rows of honourable students. He was off to join his partner in crime. As for Ziggy, he returned to his main preoccupation. Ziggy slid a hand up under the gown of the girl he was with.

While the speech continued, Penelope Snidermost swayed back and forth. Frog moaned and groaned in lost ecstasy. The convocation would continue with more speeches, the awarding of certificates, and a guest speaker. Salami and Boo had time to develop the negative. Frog would be left on the stage; eyes wide and mind reeling with what wishes might happen if he and Penelope were together.

"Martha Mowman, Simon Monario . . ., Simon Monario . . ., Salami!" Vice-Principal Lawford raised his voice speaking into the mike. "Salami Monario!"

"Here! Here! I'm coming." Rushing from the back of the line Salami panted to a stop in front of Lawford. "I came as fast as I could."

"It was not fast enough," grinned Lawford. Principal Finlay handed Salami his diploma and congratulated him.

From the stage, Salami waved the diploma in the air and at the same time patted his chest. "I've got it! I've got it!" Salami shouted above Lawford's voice.

Raising his voice some-what in anger, Lawford continued to call out the names of the graduating class. Rushing to a seat behind Ziggy, Salami began to fill him in on the details. The blonde beside Ziggy pulled away pushing his hand from her gown.

"Salami, can't you see I'm busy."

"Yeah, but this is more important."

Handing Ziggy a pen-light, Salami revealed the pictures one at a time.

"Great! Great! What an ass!"

"I even got some of Frog and Snidermost together."

"Any more, Salami?"

"Lots. Boo is going to run off as many pictures as he can. I'm going back to keep watch."

Calling to Salami as he headed for the door, Ziggy spoke loud enough that all would hear. "I'll make the necessary promotion and take care of sales."

All at once everyone's ears perked up and the whispering began. Rumours began to circulate thanks to Ziggy. The price of just one picture doubled as the word spread.

CHAPTER THREE
Party Time

"I'm in love," Frog moaned, as he kissed the picture of Penelope Snidermost. "I want her! I've got to get laid!"

Ziggy's Baby Blue '52 Hudson pulled up to a quick stop at a set of lights. A flat bed Ford loaded with sex starved animals screeched to a dead stop along-side the Hudson. In the front seat, Boo, Ziggy and Salami stared at the enlargements of Penelope Snidermost's butt. Frog, alone in the back, pressed an eight by ten to his lips, then drooled in ecstasy.

"Hey Boo, we want to buy some of those pictures."

"Yea!" the rest of the animals echoed in anticipation.

"No way!" yelled Frog between kisses. "She's all mine. I ain't sharing her with anybody."

"All yours! Suck ass Frog! She would not let you do her laundry even if you paid her, let alone kiss her ass."

"Yea! You moron!" the rest hooted in unison.

Frog paid them no mind. His eyes were focussed on Penelope's pink inviting ass.

"How much you willing to pay?" Boo held up a couple to show the animals.

As the light changed, Ziggy peeled away, turning left at the last moment.

"They don't come cheap," Salami hollered.

With car horns blaring, the flat-bed cut through the intersection, ignoring the oncoming traffic. Wheels squealed as the chase began to the next set of lights.

The Baby Blue came to a quick stop at the yellow light, giving the animals a chance to pull up alongside.

"Frog, get up off the floor. Wait till you have those big, firm, pink ravishing cheeks in your hands before you make a fool of yourself!"

"I've got to get laid Ziggy! It ain't no joke! I'll bust!"

Boo held an eight-by-ten out through the window. "Take a good look animals. The price just goes up every minute."

"This could be your last chance to get a piece of history from the seventies," Salami bragged as he held a few in his hands. "The money up front boys."

"Ok! Ok! Back off you jerks. How much for the pictures?"

"Ten for a long shot and . . ., and . . .,"

"And how much?"

"Don't rush me children. Let's say twenty for a close-up of the prettiest pink ass in town."

"Twenty bucks!"

"Take it or leave it."

"Ok, we'll take it."

"Too late animals," Ziggy yelled as the Baby Blue Hudson pulled away. "You still on the floor Frog? You're going to get your suit all mussed up."

"How in the hell did you stall this truck?" A fat boy hollered while he pounded fists on the cab roof. "Get going!"

"Stuff it Pudden Face!" The driver said as he ground the gears and spit out the window. Porky seemed to be the leader of the gang, known to everyone as 'Animals.' It was not a fraternity, but the name suited their personalities. Wherever Porky went, the rest of the hungry vultures followed. Whenever Porky had his nose into something, Pudden had his two-hundred-and-fifty-pound body as close as he could get.

Once the flat-bed Ford was into third, Porky pulled a mickey from his suit pocket and gulped an eighth of it down. He was bound to get one of those pictures of the bitchy Snidermost. Whatever was on his mind, only he knew, but it would not be a pleasant talk about flowers. Porky's Ford pulled beside the slowing Hudson. "Ok. Give me one of those pictures. A close-up one."

"Twenty bucks Pork," Boo's voice was low, cool and resonated with authority.

Pudden dished out twenty, and Boo handed him the photo. The Baby Blue Hudson eased on through the intersection, leaving the animals to drool over a facsimile Penelope Snidermost. The lights changed from red to green then back to red as horns blared in unison from other cars behind the flat-bed Ford.

"I paid the twenty bucks," yelled Pudden, hanging over the side window, dangling puffy hands in Porky's face. "I should be the first to see Snidermost's ass!"

"Wait your turn." With one motion Porky pulled, then pushed the arm away and jerked the truck forward at the changing of the light. Pudden quivered like Jell-O on the edge of a bowl as he slid and shook to the pavement below. Reminiscent of an old Laurel and Hardy movie, Pudden waddled like Hardy after the jerking truck.

"I'm hurting! I've got to get laid!" moaned Frog from the back seat.

Three voices from the front echoed with confidence. "You will tonight, don't worry."

"Now I'm worried."

. . . . .

Penelope Snidermost was busy talking to all the teachers. She talked to them whether they wanted her to or not, and at the same time was trying to get everybody organized as to what they should be doing for the dance. Never ending, her mouth was flapping away unaware of what was taking place behind her back. As she talked to one aging teacher, he was paying more attention to a picture he had received anonymously. He adjusted specs to focus on the picture, then readjusted them to gaze at the back side of Miss. Snidermost.

"Is something the matter with my dress, Mr. Finch?" She glanced back and fluffed the pink dress with a hand.

"Oh . . ., Oh . . ., not at all my dear. It's just . . ., just that I don't remember my high school days as being as intriguing as your generation might find theirs to be." Mr. Finch adjusted glasses to focus on the picture.

Continuing, without really understanding Mr. Finch, Penelope Snidermost rambled on about something totally uninteresting to the aging teacher.

"If I knew then what I know now. If I only had the guts to do it," mumbled Mr. Finch, but Penelope's words drowned his out.

"I've got my own way to rock, I've got my own way to roll." The music of the band echoed the music of Burton Cummings throughout the gym. Slowly the dance floor heaved with dancing bodies, leaving only the Wall-Flowers standing against the gym wall, waiting for someone to ask them to dance. Finch peered over glasses and surveyed the array of Wall-Flowers. He glanced at Miss. Cradock, then quickly changed his mind about asking her to dance. Tapping the floor with the cane, Miss. Cradock was trying to keep time with the music. 'There is just no hope,' thought Mr. Finch as he quickly walked over to the punch bowl. One way to keep Miss. Cradock's mind off dancing was to bring her a drink of punch. Taking a sip, he realized that the punch had yet to be spiked.

People were dancing as more couples arrived. The atmosphere was beginning to lighten up. Principal Finlay, Vice-Principal Lawford and some other teachers, and of course Penelope

Snidermost, were chattering about something. Brushing the greying hair from his eyes, Mr. Finch casually eyed the surroundings. As usual, the animals were hanging around the girls' washroom. They would obviously spike the punch when they could. The other three should be close by. Stretching his neck, he noticed the three handing, or rather exchanging something with their fellow students. He felt for the picture in a vest pocket and smiled reverently. 'Back to the punch,' he thought. Those three would spike the punch, but, yet, no-one had.

Miss. Cradock continued to tap to the music. She smiled innocently when catching Mr. Finch's eye. Finch turned away abruptly, thinking to himself. 'It's now or never!' Putting the glass down, he reached deep into the outdated suit-coat and retrieved a flask. He always wanted to do this, and now finally, he had a chance to do it! He emptied the flask into the punch bowl and with dipper in hand, he stirred the punch as if nothing unusual was happening. "Not bad," he whispered after sampling the mixture.

"This stuff should really set old lady Cradock flying." It was school policy that there should never be any alcohol on school property, but like anything else, rules were meant to be broken!

As the evening progressed, Mr. Finch would no-longer be fetching drinks for Miss. Cradock. She insisted on retrieving her own. That way, she could have one at the punch bowl and bring one back to her seat to be sociable.

As Porky was spiking the punch bowl, Boo was standing before it with both hands stretched out over it. Miss. Cradock, with specs a little off balance, came up for a refill. Without moving, Boo smiled and winked delightfully at Miss. Cradock. "Mr. . . ., Mr., what-ever your name is," Miss. Cradock slurred. Her glass moved unsteadily beneath the dipper. "Whatever you're putting into this punch should be bottled for madicmal . . ., midicmal . . ., medicinal purposes."

As the night wore on, it seemed that everyone had a picture of Penelope Snidermost's butt. Even Mr. Finch glanced at his copy every now and then. He showed it to an inebriated Miss. Cradock, who roared with uncontrollable laughter. Finch vacated the area, wanting nothing to do with what was happening. Each time Penelope Snidermost walked by, Miss. Cradock would laugh louder and longer.

Penelope sensed that there was something a-miss, but she could not put a finger on it! Every time one of the animals hit on her for a dance, being a lady, she politely refused. After all, she had an image to maintain!

"You've still got the negatives on you, Salami?"

"Yea, Boo, why?"

"I've got an idea, let's go." Boo pulled Salami away from his girlfriend.

"Girls, if only for a moment," Ziggy's voice was smooth and captivating. "Would you excuse my friend and I." Several girls looked puzzled. "I think your noses need powdering."

The girls parted, leaving only Frog drooling in his punch. "When's it going to happen, Ziggy?"

"Now's as good a time as any."

Frog perked up lifting his head from the table.

"Go ask her to dance Frog."

"Dance! She ain't going to dance with me. She would not even dance with any of the animals."

"Ah, but you're better than any of these animals. So, make your move and go and ask her to dance."

"I will." A bit shaky, Frog stood up, he was afraid to let go of the table. Finding balance, he adjusted large glasses and looked for Penelope. He made himself as presentable as possible as he walked straight and tall towards Penelope. At least he thought he was walking straight and tall!

"Penelope, may I have this dance?" Frog smiled as he teetered in front of her.

"No." She turned and quickly left, leaving Frog as if it was no big deal.

Plopping back into a seat, Frog felt the pains of love. Grabbing everyone else's drink one at a time, he gulped them all down. He had to drink away his sorrow. This was all that he could do, because he truly felt like dying!

"Be more forceful, Frog. Don't ask her to dance, just take her by the hand and drag her onto the dance floor. That way she can't leave you."

"You're absolutely right, Ziggy." Gulping another punch, he once again searched for the love of his life. The band was playing a fast song, and the stage lights were flashing. 'No one would notice them,' he thought. Frog approached Penelope who was still talking to several teachers. Frog grabbed her arm and dragged the startled girl onto the dance floor.

"You, repulsive little runt! What do you think you're doing?"

Paying her no mind, Frog began to dance. He was just getting into the music when having a strange feeling that he was being stared at. Pushing glasses into place, Frog noticed everyone staring at him. Worse than that, Penelope was no longer dancing with him! Straightening himself, he casually put hands into pockets he strolled back to a seat, as nonchalantly as possible.

"One more time Frog. This time have confidence, and don't let go of her."

"You're right, Zig. I'll wait for a slow dance and hang onto her. Then she'll have to dance with me."

. . . .

A silent click sounded as the door locked behind them. Only a dim yellow light illuminated the small room. Looking through the cupboards, Boo found what he was searching for.

"O.K. Salami, here it is, the highlight of the dance."

"You're going to . . ., out there?"

"That's right."

"All . . ., right!"

"Tape all the negative strips together in the order that you took them. Then, when the time is right, I'll just put them through this little machine and . . ., voila!"

The noise in the gym faded as the lights went dim. The band played an old rock and roll song by the Platters. Frog knew this may be his last chance. This was going to be their song! Without hesitation, Frog headed for Penelope. The words of the song rang in his mind.

"Only you . . ., can make the darkness bright. Only you . . ., and you alone, can thrill me like you do . . ., you're my dream come true . . ., my one and only you."

Penelope Snidermost downed a second glass of punch just in time. Frog literally swept her off her feet and held on as tight as possible, remembering a past mistake. To Frog's surprise, she was not fighting back, and the more relaxed he became the more relaxed she was. "Was it the music? Or the drinks of punch? Or was it Frog?"

"Only you can thrill me like you do. You're my one and only love."

The music played on and Frog could not believe what was happening.

Hurry up, Salami, there's only a couple more songs left."

"One more, then it's ready." Salami taped the last negative to the end of the strip. Salami rolled the negatives onto the machine.

Boo focussed the machine against the wall to test it. "It's ready. Now when the dance is over and you-know-who makes her speech, we'll roll the still shots."

"Great, Boo, fantastic!"

The leader of the band yelled into the mike. "What do you want to hear? Three fast songs or three slow ones for the lovers and the perverts?"

"Three slow ones." everyone hollered in unison!

One lone voice trailed on the echo of the others. "For us perverts!"

A soft melody filled the air as couples gathered on the floor. Everyone held their partners close, wishing that this night would never end! Ziggy had no problems with having a girl to dance with. Sometimes it was a problem selecting one!

Standing by the entrance, a dark-haired girl scanned the dancing crowd. Then she scanned all the tables surrounding the dance floor. Rita slowly tapped a foot as she searched for her boyfriend. At least Salami had been her boyfriend when they arrived tonight.

Frog once again led Penelope to the dance floor. He was not going to miss anymore chances. He had her and he was going to keep her! Penelope downed another punch and handed the glass to Frog, who quickly stuffed it into the large pocket of his suit. A romantic quietness filled the gym, but a strangeness also loomed in the air. Everyone felt that something was going to happen. Miss. Cradock had entrapped Mr. Finch, who was no-longer able to fend off her determination to dance with him. Miss. Snidermost leaned warmly against Frog.

Was it the music, Frog, or was it that she had more than her share of the punch?

Frog, dancing near the stage, motioned to one of the band members. Leaning closer to Frog, the lead guitarist listened to his request. Passing the word to the other guys, the song faded into the last song of the evening. Frog held Penelope close, his arms wrapped tightly around her. She was no longer resisting. With the start of the song, Penelope sighed. An arousal overcame Frog, an arousal no one could see, but surely Penelope felt, as Frog pressed closer.

"Only you . . ., can make this dream come true. Only you . . ., and you alone, can thrill me like you do. Only you . . .,"

The lights in the small room went out. Boo flipped the lens port open and adjusted the single frame projector at the opening. Pressing the start button, Salami waited for the order to switch on the lamp.

"Any minute now," Boo said anxiously, opening another port. Boo focussed the spotlight into position.

To most, the song did not last long enough, even though the band played it twice. Excitement filled the gym. Applause, hooting and the stamping of feet and clinking of glasses filled the gym. Penelope Snidermost made her way to the stage. She thanked the band and all who helped to make this dance a success. As usual, she rambled on and on and on . . ., followed only by boos and cat calls.

"Now Salami!" Boo switched on the spot light focussing it on Penelope Snidermost. Salami shut the main light switch, throwing the entire gym into pitch black darkness. With the other hand, he switched the projector on, flooding the wall behind Penelope with a yellowish brightness. A shot of her back-side, from earlier that day, filled the wall. All the hooting and booing suddenly changed to applause and appreciation. Thanking everyone, she began to speak into the mike. She thanked the band, and everyone that helped. At every pause the crowd roared and applauded. Behind her the scene changed, showing what Frog had seen from the stage. Even now, Frog's eyes were glued to the pictures on the wall.

Mr. Finch's mouth fell open in disbelief. He adjusted specs. "Why was not my high school days like this?"

"What's that you said, Finch?" asked Miss. Cradock in a slurred speech.

Penelope continued talking about who knows what. Other teachers whispered in disgust, but their eyes were focussed upon the ten by ten-foot section of wall. Boo and Salami rolled with laugher, knowing they had done something that all would remember for a long time to come.

"I don't know how to thank you enough," Penelope said in a choking tearful state. The band's music faded in with the song of the night. "Only you . . ., only you . . ., can thrill me like you do . . ., only . . ., you."

Fading slowly, the music came to an end, yet on the dance floor couples embraced each other hoping this night would never end. The main doors opened and a cool night breeze filled the gym. Outside everyone gathered in a group and asked Ziggy where the party was. The last to join the crowd was Frog, and a reluctant Miss. Snidermost.

"Well, where's the party, Ziggy?" Frog asked as coolly as could be expected. All eyes and ears were on Ziggy.

"Well," he started. "whose parents have the biggest house around here?"

All thought as Penelope spoke up arrogantly. "Our house is the biggest." She smiled, swaying silently.

"And who has a pool that's indoors and outdoors at the same time? And who has the biggest collection of liquor and wine around?"

"My father," Penelope said proudly.

"Now Penelope, one question. Are your parents home tonight?" All ears were anticipating the right answer.

"No, tonight they're not home," Penelope smiled broadly, knowing she was the centre of attention.

"Need I say more," Ziggy waved his hand forward speaking in a John Wayne dialect. "Forward ho pilgrims!"

Frog and Penelope pulled up the rear of the flowing crowd. "Where are we going?"

"With them," Frog answered reluctantly.

"Hey, wait for us!" Down the stairs bounced Boo and Salami. From both sides of the car, the two clambered into the back seat with Frog and Penelope.

Snidermost's eyes met Boo's with caution. Boo slowly slid an arm to the back of the seat. "Cozy situation we have here."

"Where have you been all night, Mr. Salami?" Sitting in the front seat with Ziggy and his girlfriend, Rita was about to climb over it to grab Salami. "Some date you are! Leaving me all alone. I should have picked up some guy and had a good time! But no! I had to wait till you came back after the dance is over. Some nerve you have! I should . . .,"

Car horns blared in the night air as the car's headlights beamed towards the highway, heading towards the Snidermost house. Straggling behind was the animal's truck following the parade.

"Am I right in saying that this party is going to take place at my parent's house? I do get the feeling that I am correct, but to be sure, I would like a second opinion."

Boo looked deeply into Penelope's eyes, almost passionately. He spoke softly in a sort of disappointed voice, "I thought that you would invite us all to share in your good fortunes. You know that we are underprivileged."

Penelope was taken aback by Boo. She listened without understanding. The old Hudson's back seat was not very large and it seemed quite crowded. Frog was not complaining. He was enjoying the situation. Salami continued nudging him closer to Penelope's heaving breasts.

"We don't have pools or big houses . . .," Boo wiped an imaginary tear from his eye. "Or, like . . ., some of us who don't even have parents."

Penelope gave a big sigh, Frog grinned happily. "Well, I guess I . . ., I mean, it would be alright if the party was at my house . . ., If nothing is broken." Boo slid an arm around her shoulders between Frog's face and Penelope's heaving breasts. "Hey, all right! You just might fit in with the rest of us. If you work at it."

Frog cleared his voice. "Oh, sorry Frog, I did not mean to interrupt anything important." Boo pushed Frog's head closer to Penelope's breast.

"Ahhh . . .,"

Cars parked on the road, on the sidewalk, and on the lawn. Any place that looked flat was as good a place as any to park. The house had an unwelcoming look to it, a look stating that not everyone was welcome. It did not bother Ziggy. He wheeled the car to the front of the house and parked it as close as he possibly could to the front door. As soon as the lights went on and the pool was lit up, it seemed that everyone wanted to make a move on Penelope. Once she stopped babbling, that is!

"This stuff taste's like piss!" Porky spit the wine onto the floor. Pudden reached for another bottle in the bar. Slamming it on the bar, he slid it down to Porky. Popping the cork on another bottle, he tried it for himself. "Well this one's better, Pudden Face. Let me try another."

"What are you going to do, Porky?" Pudden opened another bottle.

"You've been looking at that picture of Snidermost all night."

"I don't know . . ., but why should the likes of Frog, be the first to christen a puss like that." Porky slammed the bottle down on the picture of Snidermost's butt.

"Well do something before Frog does."

"I will! I will, when I'm ready. Give me another bottle Pudden."

With his sweating hands, Porky rubbed the picture over and over. Loud window shattering music echoed across the pool area. Couples that could stand, swayed together. Others headed for darker corners, and whatever empty room they could find. The only one that seemed to be talking was Penelope. Frog was not, or did not seem to be listening. Frog's thoughts were on a different matter.

"Frog! Frog!"

"Uh . . .,"

"Have you been listening to what I've been saying?"

"Yeah, . . ., kind of."

She sucked back on a beer. "Do you like me? I mean like you like everybody else?"

"Sure," Frog swallowed, looking about hoping no one heard him."

"I'm not that different from anybody else . . ., I have certain feelings. Feelings I could share with someone." She took another mouth full of beer. "Do you like me? I mean like you like everybody else? You know what I mean?"

Frog thought, trying to figure out her meaning. "No not really."

"Heck! Do I have to spell it out for you? Don't you think I know what people have been saying behind my back, making fun of me. The butt of their jokes!"

Frog choked on the beer. "Butt."

"Yes, people have been talking about my butt all evening. I don't think mine is any different than anyone else's."

"It's not," Frog was beginning to feel sorry for her. He wanted to explain, but the other guys, they would not understand. "Well, yes, it is, I mean . . .,"

"Go on! Tell me what they've been talking about."

Hesitating Frog fumbled in a coat pocket, a crumpled picture he handed to Penelope.

"What's this?" Her eyes focussed closer on the picture.

"That's me, you . . .,"

Before the scream left her lips, Frog wrestled Penelope to the ground. His hand held tightly over a wide mouth. "Don't scream, please, please."

It took awhile before Penelope relaxed. With a nod, she agreed not to scream. Cautiously, Frog took the hand away and helped her to her feet. As he wiped the dirt from the fluffy dress, Penelope gave a quick knee to Frog's groin.

"You jerk! Who was behind this? Who took these pictures?"

Wincing in pain, Frog clutched family jewels and hobbled to a chair. "I can't tell you that. If . . ., If everyone finds out, you'll . . ., you'll be laughed at more. It'll just be worse."

Slapping the picture back into his hand, she thought for a moment. There was only silence, as her face fumed with vicious anger.

"Right now, you're the most popular girl in school," Frog's voice spoke an octave higher than normal.

"Yes, I think you're right. I'll be remembered for a long time to come." The fuming face slowly relaxed. "My image could be changing. Maybe, everybody will think of me as one of the gang."

Frog seemed uncertain. "Well, maybe, anyway, you're immortalized in print."

"It's not my best side."

Frog sighed, and pulled at tight pants.

"Your best . . ., side?" croaked Frog.

Penelope picked up a beer and downed the rest of the liquid strength. "Well, if I'm going to be like the rest of the gang, we might as well do what everybody else is doing." Grabbing Frog by the collar, she dragged the limping boy across the lawn.

"Where are we going?"

Penelope made her way through the dancing couples, up the curving stair-way to the upstairs of the house with Frog in tow. Frog did not know what to expect, but just in case wiped lips and straightened fussed hair. If it is going to be heaven, he wanted to be ready.

"Come on! Quit dilly-dallying." Penelope opened the first bedroom door. The bed seemed to be moving, and moans filled the room. "Not this room." She quickly closed the door.

They moved down the hall, trying two other doors with the same results. Standing at the last door, they listened for sounds. They pressed their ears to the door.

"Sounds like the whole cheerleading squad." Frog pressed closer to the door.

Quickly the door opened, and Penelope and Frog stumbled in on Ziggy and several girls. Sitting on the bed with a girl on either side, like a king, Ziggy welcomed his guests.

"Nice of you to join us. The fun's just beginning."

"No, we can't." Frog helped Penelope to her feet. "We were looking for . . ., a closet . . ., the bathroom . . .,"

"Really, we were trying to find the change room, the girls, the boys, ah one for her and one for me."

"Yes, that's right," Penelope agreed with Frog. A reddish blush covered her cheeks.

"Penelope," Ziggy slowly questioned. "You live here. Don't you know where the change rooms are?"

"Well, ah yes, but, you don't understand."

As Penelope continued to talk, Ziggy reached into a pocket then tossed car keys to Frog. "I understand. Here take the Baby Blue."

Giggles filled the room. Turning, Penelope ushered Frog from the room.

"Thanks Ziggy," Frog hollered back.

"Porky, look who's heading out of the door."

Looking over, Porky caught a glimpse of Penelope and Frog heading out through the front door.

Pudden had excitement in his eyes. "What are you going to do, Porky?" Pudden leaned over the bar. "Are we going after them?"

"Give them a minute, then we'll tail them." Porky poured another drink, his lips sneering with a look of mischief. Hearing the Baby Blue Hudson's wheels squeal out of the driveway, Porky and Pudden quickly headed for the door. Porky's old truck roared to a start. Snidermost's picture was pinned over the sun visor.

"Let's go Porky!" Pudden bounced in the seat. This late at night, it was not hard to keep the car in sight. The roads were traffic free and this road leading to lover's lane was deserted. Porky pushed the headlight switch off.

"Smart Porky. They'll never know we're following them."

The only noise in the Baby Blue was the music from the radio. While driving, Frog fidgeted with glasses and moved around in in the seat. At this point, he did not know what to expect. Penelope stared straight ahead and pressed down on the fluffy dress. She was noticeably nervous as well!

"We're almost . . .,"

"What!" they both jumped, each startling the other.

"We're almost there."

"Oh . . .,"

Slowly the Hudson slowed to stop. Then silence! The sounds of the wilderness filtered into the car. Each stayed on their side of the seat, waiting for the other to make the first move.

Porky and Pudden parked their truck at the entrance and waited for the right time to make their move.

"Wait until they just get into it, then we'll have our turn at the tight little ass."

Pudden bounced in the seat, rubbing anxious hands together. A sneer was back on Porky's lips.

Like the first time for anybody, Frog and Penelope had their awkward moments. The first move was mutual, clumsy, but the ball was rolling.   The front seat of the Hudson was not the most comfortable location. Frog's leg became stuck in the steering wheel as Penelope wiggled beneath him. At least she was trying to get beneath him. Her fluffy dress was everywhere except where it was supposed to be. Glasses were not meant to be kissed with and soon Frog ditched them on the floor. Moans and groans that echoed from the car for the first time were of pain not passion. Penelope reached for Frog's shirt, pulling it up. There would be a lot more room if Penelope had gotten into Frog's large suit, rather than trying to get it off! Making do with what knowledge, Frog had to work with, he bit off the buttons on the front of Penelope's dress. Paradise by the dash board lights was in sight.

Bang . . ., Bang . . ., piercing sounds shivered throughout the car. Bang . . ., Bang . . ..   "Ahhh . . .!" Penelope screamed as she pulled legs together. "Lock the doors."

"Roll up the windows too." Forcing the window up, Frog sat with legs still stuck in the steering wheel.

"What's going on? What's out there?" Penelope tried to close the front of the dress. Her beautiful abundance over-came the odds and the dress stayed open.

"That's enough Frog. You've had your fun. Now be a good boy and share, share with your friends." Porky pulled at the door handles.

"It's Porky and Pudden," Frog said as he reached hopelessly for lost glasses.

"They're your friends? Those animals?"

"Of course, not!" Frog pulled a leg free. "I've more class than that."

"Come on Snidermost," yelled Pudden, smashing fists against the window. "You know you want it, and we can give it to you."

"You would not want Frog to be the first. You should have a man." Porky gave a quick kick to the window.

Penelope screamed at the top of her lungs and shook Frog. "Start the car, and let's get out of here!"

Roaring to a start, the Hudson kicked into gear. Spewing gravel all around, the Baby Blue squealed away.

"I can't see without my glasses!" Frog wheeled the car around and headed for the road. His foot was to the floor, and he hoped that nothing was in the way. Behind, Porky and Pudden picked themselves up from the ground. Dusting their clothes off, they headed for their truck.

"I'm going to get that jerk, and Snidermost is going to have her moment too." Grabbing the picture of Snidermost, Porky crumpled it with a crushing grip.

"Me too," Pudden pounded fists on the dash.

Both vehicles picked up speed once on the pavement. There was a lot of room to manoeuvre with most of the highway being straight.

The hum of tires broke the silent night air. Behind the Hudson, the roar of the old truck's engine sounded like a demon breathing down Frog's neck. Frog pressed harder on the gas pedal, but was not able to pick up any speed. Closing in fast, Porky pulled over to pass, with Pudden bouncing with joy. Now beside the Baby Blue, Pudden hung out of the window and beat upon the roof of the car with his fist.

Inside, Penelope's screaming became louder, "Stop the car!"

"Stop? If I stop the car, they'll get us."

"I don't care! He's going to run us off the road."

With both feet, Frog jumped on the brakes. In agony, the Hudson's tires skidded to a stop.

"They've stopped Porky," Pudden said, hanging out the window and looking back. "Hurry up and turn."

Without gearing down, Porky hit the brakes and pulled hard on the wheel. A one-eighty-degree turn and hard on the gas would put them right in front of the Baby Blue. The truck swayed at the start of the turn, while the light ass end bounced and slid on the pavement. Heating up and with the touch of the brakes the tires grabbed the smooth surface of the highway.

An unbearable scream and the reflection of lights from metal was all Frog and Penelope saw as the truck flipped ass end first then rolled over with Pudden still hanging from the open window. Silence prevailed. The humming of the Hudson's engine was the only audible sound on the highway.

Penelope could not scream. She could not breathe or say anything. Her eyes stared at the truck laying on its side with a body pinned beneath it.

"Go to a house for help," Frog said in a shaky voice.

Penelope opened the door and began to run to the nearest house. Frog walked hurriedly but cautiously towards the truck. As Frog approached closer, Porky had already lifted himself from the driver's side. He was breathing hard, blood running from a cut on his forehead. In a tearful voice, he mumbled, "Pudden, Pudden, you ok, Pudden?"

Frog stood by the cab looking down at the grave face of Pudden. His eyes were open. His chest was rising and falling slowly. Porky dropped to his knees, his hands reaching to touch the lifeless face.

"Pudden, you ok? Hang on, you'll be ok." Porky stripped off his jacket and slowly placed it beneath Pudden's head.

Pudden's eyes rolled and blinked. His lips moved, but not a sound was uttered. Porky stroked dirt from Pudden's pudgy face. Frog watched helplessly. Pudden's chest rose and fell one last time.

"Pudden . . .," Porky's cracking voice echoed aimlessly. "Pudden Face."

Helpful sounds came too late. Lights on the street lit up. Sounds of parading cars left the Snidermost's house. Ears perked up and bodies gathered, questioning. Piling into cars and vans, the party goers followed the wailing sounds of the shrieking police and ambulance sirens. Boo, Ziggy, Salami and others gathered quickly around Frog and Penelope. On the ground, still pinned, lay the lifeless body of Pudden. Friendless, Porky swayed on knees rubbing tormented hands along legs, trying to wipe his guilt away.

While the police began pushing back the mounting crowd, Ziggy put an arm around Frog and began to walk away. Rita, Penelope and Salami followed. Only Boo stayed a moment longer, sending a piercing vengeful look that caught Porky's eye for a brief moment.

"Frog," Ziggy said softly. "you should pull up your fly and tuck your shirt tails in."

CHAPTER FOUR
Jobs#

After the fatal accident, the days seemed to pass quickly. Once the funeral was over, Porky somehow seemed to vanish from sight. The old truck was still parked on the road, in front of Porky's house. It seemed to sit there as a reminder. As a kind of memorial to Pudden. For most of the crowd that had known Porky and Pudden, the incident seemed to just fade into the past. It was the summer and the odd jobs that many of them had seemed to occupy most of the gang's time. For Ziggy, it would be a summer job. His parents had wanted him to go to college. For Boo, Salami and Frog, the summer job would end up as permanent careers. They had no future plans beyond their present summer jobs. For Ziggy, he did not like the idea of going back to the everyday grind of school, day after day after day.

It was a week later when the four headed off to the employment office at All Steel, the local steel mill. The plant had always been in the habit of hiring summer workers in large numbers, knowing that most would return to school in the fall. The idea of this visit to the employment office at All Steel was to fill out a summer employment application, not a full-time application. And then, when summer was over, and if you had a good job, you just stayed on. Not returning to school. It was a ploy used often by students wanting to land permanent employment with THE STEEL MILL.

"Thank you," said the secretary politely. Her body was dynamite to look at, and Ziggy, as usual, was taking in an eyeful. His mind too preoccupied with what she looked like, to really be listening to what she was saying!

"Take this to medical . . ., sir."

"Uh, yes."

"Take this to medical, and when you're finished there, come back here please."

"You bet," replied Ziggy.

The boys all headed down towards the medical wing and upon arriving, each of them reported to the front receptionist. They were each told to wait and take a seat, and they would be examined shortly.

The neatly dressed nurse, behind the receptionist's glass, spoke to them all at once. "You're in here! You're in here and you're in there!" She stated, pointing to three examining rooms at the end of the hall. "Strip to your shorts and wait for the doctor please." The nurse behind the glass reminded the boys of an army type nurse. Once she had given them their instructions, she turned abruptly and marched away. Without turning around again she shouted, "Don't touch anything in the rooms please."

Frog was the first to respond in a voice that was filled with tension. "I won't, I promise." After which the army nurse turned around and cast a convicting eye towards Frog.

Standing in the examining room, Boo stood with arms folded. He patiently waited until hearing a slight knock on the door, and watched as the door opened slowly. A woman walked in with a clipboard in hand, which she seemed to be examining. Boo gave her his typical once over and nodded. He thought to himself, 'For a woman in her apparent thirties, she isn't too bad looking.' His eyes glanced at her fingers to see if she had any rings on, and there did not seem to be any.

She lowered the clipboard and looked up at him. For some reason, her face blushed a slight pink colour.

"You were supposed to strip to your shorts," she said trying to look directly into his eyes.

I don't wear shorts," replied Boo.

"What . . .."

"They restrict my movements, so I don't wear them."

"Oh . . ., ah . . .." She seemed to be at a loss of words by Boo's explanation of why he did not wear shorts. Boo noticed that her face was a much brighter pink then previously. Apparently, she was trying very hard to concentrate on the work.

"Are you a Doctor or just a nur . . .."

"I am a Doctor," she interrupted. "I have been for several years." 'This is no way to act,' she thought to herself. 'I've seen men before.'

Boo changed his position suddenly, startling the Doctor. She quickly placed the clipboard on the table and began going over it with a pen. She turned around and facing Boo asked, "Have you ever had . . .,"

Boo listened as she rambled off all of the so-called diseases that apparently were on the clipboard. She began to check them off as Boo responded by either a yes or no.

Boo leaned against the table slightly, glancing over her shoulder to peek at the papers. Boo seemed very curious to know what she was writing on that clipboard. It caused the doctor to tense up even more, and Boo noticed, again her face was turning a bright red.

"Ok! Everything here seems fine. You can get dressed now," she responded and quickly headed for the door.

"What about the physical part?" Boo asked, as the doctor was heading out through the door. Turning around she took a good look at Boo's entire body, "You're physically ok," she responded.

Leaning against the outside of the closed door, she began to fan a warm face with the clipboard. She thought about the kid before this one, the one that would not come out from behind the table until a male doctor came instead.

When all the boys had their medical examinations, they gathered at the employment counter, and the main topic of discussion seemed to be the female doctor. The stories that they told were, that not one of them was given the physical by the female doctor, and Frog, in particular, ended up with a male doctor. It seemed that they were all medically fit, and that they were all ready for work. Ziggy glanced at the secretary behind the desk and cast a smile. She in turn, smiled and gave him a little wink.

"These are your cards," she said handing one to each of them. "It will tell you when and where to report."

Ziggy noticed that along with his card, the secretary had slipped him another piece of paper as well. Heading out the door, Ziggy glanced at the piece of paper and to his surprise there was an address and telephone number. But tonight, he would not be able to call because the four of them had been told that they would be working the eleven to seven shift at the number 6 blast furnace.

. . . .

It seemed that Frog was the first to arrive at the number 4 gate. A steady stream of workers filed past Frog, and as they did, they eyed him up and down. Each of them, as they passed Frog, seemed to give a little smirk. They watched Frog standing there in his new clothes, new boots, shiny new hat and little red lunch pail. The kind that kids in grade school seemed to carry with them. They could not help but find themselves laughing at him. Ziggy and Salami scuffed up their clothes to make them look more used. Only Boo came in looking like he would been there for the past few years.

All Steel stood like a monolith, with its massive buildings and billowing smoke stacks rising endlessly into the night sky. The pouring of red hot molten steel illuminated the blackness of the night sky with a crimson glow, being cast in the nearby blast furnaces.

The roar of furnaces burning gases, and the clanking and pounding of the rolling mills could be heard by the four boys standing there. It sent shivers up and down their spines. Spines of the weak and scared. After a time, a body becomes accustom to the sounds. But what about the mind? Could the mind ever become accustom to the sounds?

The factory seemed to engulf its workers. Seemingly holding on to them, until their very last breath of life was extracted. Before anyone entered that gate, their minds should have been made up. Each should have known what they wanted to do with the rest of their lives, before it was snatched from them by this hungry steel mill. Boo punched the time clock without thinking, and Salami was right behind him. Finally, Ziggy and Frog caught up to them by breaking out of the line of workers streaming into the mill. They did not seem to have any time to think, or to change their minds. For the most part, the lure of money, cars and nights on the town with the girls of their choices was beckoning them to move forward.

Everything in this place was new to them. A kind of adventure at times, and they seemed like tourists, each one being caught up in the amazement and glitter of their new surroundings. Wherever there's excitement, there always seems to be a little bit of danger. For now, they were not concerned with the potential dangers that they might be facing.

They walked past number 7 blast furnace, paying particular attention to the green glow and heat of the slag pouring from the blast furnace. It seemed to warm the cool evening air. The way the hot summer sun warmed an early morning's dawn. The boys were reminded of red molten lava flowing from an erupting volcano. It seemed like that as red molten slag poured freely into the open pit. Huge earth movers hauled the cooling slag away, while another incredibly huge loader broke up the mounds of slag. There was something almost unbelievable about what was happening. It seemed reminiscent of a science fiction movie. As if this was some distant planet somewhere in the universe with flowing molten rock, ready to engulf anything that stood in its way.

The number 6 furnace was at the extreme end of the line of furnaces past number 4 and 5. Like a humongous pot, the Blast Furnace stood an incredible ten stories high. From the lower levels the raw material was brought to the very top of the furnace and fed in. Burning gases melted the new ore and almost magically turned it into iron. It was on the main floor of the casting level where all the excitement seemed to be, and where all the new workers would get their first experience of working in the Blast Furnace.

"So, these are the new girls!" a short blubbery man sitting back in his chair blurted out. "New little girls we have to take by the hand and kick their butts to get moving." Reese was an old-fashioned thinker that believed women could never work in a steel mill, only men worked their way up to the good jobs and positions in the mill. Very few people got close to Reese except Brown nose-ers. There seemed to be a chip on his shoulder. The kind that Boo had an inkling to knock off.

From the mouth that blended like the cigar he was chewing on, Reese spat out, "Well girls you ready to work?"

Boo did not like the labelling he was given, he inched forward. Two of Reese's flunkies stepped back from the table in anticipation. Ziggy held fast to Boo's jacket, Frog stepped in front, only to come face to face with Reese's soggy cigar.

"Can you . . .," Frog's voice cracked. "tell me where the closest washroom is?"

"You'll find it when you have time. Right now, you go to work."

Frog backed away as Reese pushed the cigar closer to Frog's face." Frank, show these new girls what to do, and make sure you give the shittiest job to that female." A finger pointed to the only female.

Out on the cast floor the new workers seemed to be putting their backs into it. After the cast was poured, other workers seemed to take it easy while the labourers, shovels in hand, bent over to clear the troughs from the excess slag that had built up.

"What's with that foreman anyway?" spoke the only girl worker.

"What has he got against us anyway?"

Boo leaned on a shovel, in the kind of position Ken Dryden used when leaning on his hockey stick when playing for the Montreal Canadiens.

Salami, who was working closest to the fair-haired girl piped up, "Ah don't let the guy bother you. Stick with us and you'll have nothing to worry about."

Boo gave a slight nod of his head, and thought that this was his type of girl. She was not overly abundantly stacked, as far as breasts were concerned, but she seemed to have a natural look that he liked.

The rest period did not seem to last very long, after seeing the foreman walk by and recalling that this was their first night on the new job, Boo continued digging the shovel into the already hardened slag that covered the troughs.

The floor of the cast house was covered with bricks and sand piles. Throughout the entire length and width of the floor, clay and sand troughs meandered from the furnace along the floor to ladles and pots waiting beneath the cast house floor. Towards the back of the cast house floor was an open pit where sand and materials were constantly being brought in. There was a large twenty by twenty-foot opening in the floor with about a thirty-foot drop to the ground below. Inadvertently touching the flimsy railing, the girl suddenly seemed to freeze on the spot as she caught Boo watching her. Without paying him any further attention, she mustered the strength and went back to digging.

"I think we're finished." Frog wiped the grimy dirt from his new clothes, now covered with silvery graphite from head to toe. "What do we do now?"

"Well we sure as hell don't stick around here," no sooner had Boo said this, when all dropped their shovels and headed towards the shack where other workers had gathered.

As they headed towards the welfare room, a new boy named William tagged slowly behind.

"This sure is a long night," Frog chattered on as he brushed every bit of grimy dirt from work clothes. "You think we'll be able to sleep . . .,"

"Where the hell do you think you're all going?" Reese barged past waving a hand for all to follow him. "The show is just about to start."

The Blast Furnace floor seemed to come alive again! The pots were checked. The gates on the troughs were checked and finally with a signal from the foreman everything exploded into action. A large drill began boring into the furnace at the main trough. The new workers gathered together near the make shift bench and took a deserving rest.

This was more fantastic than any Canada Day fireworks they had ever seen. The dimly lit mill became an extravaganza of sparks, bursting from the furnace hole. An almost too brilliant fountain of molten iron oozed down the main trough. Sparks flew precariously close to the benches, yet everyone in their own way seemed overly impressed. Even that guy William seemed particularly more mystified. In a hastened scamper, he headed across the floor, dropping gloves and helmet in one motion before leaping over the railing. Unbelieving eyes watched him sink from sight as the whole crew scurried to the railing just in time to see a body in motion leaving the scene as fast as his legs could carry him.

"One gone five more to go," Reese laughed, taking a bite from the cigar.

The cast seemed to continue without excitement. Ladle after ladle was filled with iron and pot after pot was filled with slag. Boo, leaning against a wall slept through the cast, while the others had been watching what was going on for the past two hours.

Reese approached the new workers and kicked Boo's feet, giving his authoritative orders, "Ok, now girls, our work is finished. It's your turn. When the slag cools down in about five minutes, start cleaning out the slag, then we can cast all over again." Tobacco dripped down his chin below a sinister smile. Boo reacted by assuming a sleeping position and giving the finger to the retreating foreman.

This was just the first night, but every night it seemed would be like this one. Cast, clean up, cast, clean up and then if there was time before the end of the shift, cast again. This job seemed like a proverbial nightmare, it never would change, it would always be the same. This would be their particular type of hell. Boo was coming to understand the process of the blast furnace.

All the furnaces and the high line and dumping station were all incorporated, so from day to day their jobs could change. At the high line, large cranes as high or higher than the furnace themselves, would carry iron ore pellets, limestone and coke to shoots that were moved by trains shuttling back and forth. The trains were usually half as high as the furnace and the trains would drop their loads into other shoots that lead to ground level. On the ground below, there was another train, and continuing a line of sequence, this train would dump its load below the ground. In the final step the buckets would bring the materials all the way up to the top of the furnace. It was a round about way to get materials from one location to another, but this was the way it was done.

Number 7 Blast Furnace had its own dumping station away from the general area where foremen and the other top brass milled around. Here, four or five men would dump train cars of ore and coke into pits below the ground. Then from the pits below, a conveyor belt would carry the material to the top of the furnace.

The boys would certainly get their share of working in these areas. Most of the time they would be all working together, thanks to the secretary at the employment office. Well actually, thanks belonged to Ziggy, if he spent a lot of time with her. It seemed that it would be a while before the boys got used to their surroundings, and got into the swing of things in the Blast Furnace. But once they got rolling, there would be nothing stopping them from doing their job well.

It took about a week of bribing and trading before the four were finally able to find four lockers that were close together. The welfare room was for the use of all Blast Furnace employees. The lockers, showers, meeting rooms were all in one building and at shift change, the building came alive, a meeting place.

"Ziggy, there's Porky." Salami pointed to a row of lockers down the room. "I'm sure it's him."

"He looks different." Ziggy pulled his boots on, then headed toward Porky. "Hey Porky, what's up?" Their eyes caught, but that was about it. Porky did not reply. "Hey, when did . . .?"

"Lay off. Stay clear of me and I'll stay clear of you guys."

Ziggy was surprised by Porky's outburst of anger.

"What's with you? We're different but not down right enemies."

Porky gripped tight onto Ziggy's shirt and pulled him close to his face. "What's the difference? Even friends aren't friends. They just hang around for awhile, then leave. Now don't come on like a friend. Beat it!"

Ziggy fell away from Porky's shove with an understanding of what he was going through. The others gathered around Ziggy and waited to assess the situation. "What the hell's wrong with him?" Salami asked.

"Well I guess he's bitter. Maybe no-one should get in his way until he kind of snaps out, especially us."

"Hey, he was after Penelope and me. We did not ask him to have an accident." Said Frog.

"I know, but I think it's because he lost the only real friend he ever had," Ziggy stated.

Everyone was gathered in the control room to find out what jobs they were going to get on the up coming three to eleven shift. It was quite evident that all the good jobs had already been given out by the time Reese got to Ziggy and friends.

"Well that girl is gone and that leaves only you four." He paused for a moment to bite into the cigar and chew on it for a little while. "You guys are going to get every dirty job I can find until the last one of you is gone." Reese stared at the boys with a sinister smile.

Salami was the first to speak out in a rather angry voice, "We can take anything you can dish out."

Reese seemed to stare right through them, his attention focussed elsewhere. He did not seem to hear what Salami was saying. He turned to Frog, giving him the dirtiest look he could possibly mustered. "Don't you ever get dirty Miss. Frog?" he yelled.

Boo immediately stepped beside Frog and glanced down at Reese's balding head. In a voice that was as cool as a cucumber, and with just a slight smile on his face, Boo faced Reese. "We'll see how long we last, or should I say how long you'll last."

"Well in that case," yelled Reese, "it'll be the high line for the four of you, cleaning track, how's that sound girls?" Reese chomped hard into the cigar. Giving them one last stern glance, he turned around and headed back to the cast house floor.

Actually, it was not too bad working on the high line. You did a little cleaning and then for the rest of the shift you just screwed the old proverbial dog. It was not often that a foreman even came to check on how you were doing, and if one did, you would just say that you had just finished cleaning.

On the high line, the trains usually arrived about two or three times a shift. The buildings around the high line were quite dilapidated, and nothing seemed to work the way it was supposed to. When the trains arrived to dump their load of ore down the shoot, more often than not, there was always spillage onto the track. This was what the boys were supposed to clean. Not a particularly exciting job, but it was a dirty job that Reese had condemned them to.

The boys leaned on their shovels staring at the piles of pellets that had spilled onto the track. If nothing else, they were waiting for some kind of inspiration to move them to take their first shovel load of pellets.

"Take your time boys," Ziggy said in a slow growling voice, reminiscent of someone from the far southern United States. "We've got eight hours to go."

Usually when the train was about to arrive, it was supposed to sound its horn. On this occasion, it did not. The buildings on the high line were enclosed in a tunnel-like structure. With all the noise from the high line, it was difficult to hear anything, especially an oncoming train. Surely the locomotive engineer would not purposely ignore blowing the horn.

It was Frog, who first spotted the faded red cab of the train coming around the curve. "Look out," he yelled as he leapt out of the way. Petrified with fear, all four boys pressed themselves hard against the wall behind them. Only inches separated them from the oncoming passing train. The four shovels that were dropped when the boys leaped out of way, splintered beneath the steel wheels of the train as it rolled past them.

"Who's the jerk?" Salami yelled as he scrambled over the pile of pellets, only to be stopped by Ziggy.

"That jerk could have splintered us, just like those shovels." Boo, who was following on Salami's heels was grabbed suddenly by Ziggy.

"That was Porky."

"So," Boo replied.

"Give him a chance to get his mind straight."

"I'll straighten out his mind," Salami yelled as he lunged forward. Ziggy tried hard to hold on to him, to cool him down. "Okay, Okay but he would better not do it too many times."

"He's just trying to scare us, to get back at us for whatever reason." Ziggy grabbed the shovel and began shovelling the pellets. "Let's get rid of this pile and then take off to the other end."

Boo approached Frog leaning against the wall and attempted to peel him away from the wall, at the same time placing a shovel in his hand. "You too Frog."

Frog began to shovel the pile of pellets away from the track. But with every shovel full of pellets that he lifted, he glanced up and down the track. There was something about the trains on this high-line that he did not quite trust anymore.

Throughout the day, the boys worked and worked and worked. With each passing second of each passing minute of each passing hour, the boys thought and thought about their present situation. Although they had been in the plant for only a week or so, basically, they were doing the same jobs over and over again. They had stayed together and had always worked together. Was this the reason that advancement was passing them by, or was it really Reese's doing?

Porky had not been in the plant any longer than they had, and yet at this point it seemed that he had been able to land a better job. As to how he had been able to land this good job, neither of the boys really knew. Perhaps Porky did know someone that allowed him to pull strings in order to get such a good job. After all, in this kind of system, favours were usually given for future considerations. It was not as if this was company policy, though no matter how they played it, it always seemed to go down the same way.

'Who did Porky know,' the boys were asking themselves. Was it that Porky had gotten on the good side of Reese? Porky and Reese, actually, seemed to be two of a kind. Each of them out for themselves. They would play buddy-buddy until they got what they needed, then leave their victims lying in the dust.

Back in high school, everyone knew the way Porky had treated Pudden. Even at the accident and afterwards, although it seemed that Porky showed affection for Pudden, was it really affection or was it just a con job? Porky had the knack of convincing everybody that he was an affectionate kind of guy. But it seemed that both Porky and Reese were the kind of people who seemed to have bagged their share of victims.

Inside the steel mill, was a world created to serve itself, although all the workers in the steel mill played the same kind of game in one way or another. There were no neutrals. There were people like Reese, making the rules and people like Porky, carrying them out. For example, that girl that had started with them that first night, had she been transferred to another mill or was she just let go by the process of favours.

There were guys like Ziggy, Boo, Salami and even Frog that eventually would learn the game. It was a matter of fighting the norm until the victor stood alone. The boys and all those like them were a minority, who were fighting against the world, the world within the steel mill. In this world, the boys were at the bottom alone. Above them the system, the foreman and their followers. The general foreman and the hierarchy were present in name only.

To say that everyone in the plant had a part, was wrong. Many of the workers were good and honest men, yet they were caught up in the system of the steel mill. They only turned their backs and denied that the system existed. It is hard to say that Porky did not play his part in the system, he did have a job running the train. A job that was not back breaking, not even time consuming. Of the eight hours, four were worked, the remainder spent with whomever was part of the system.

During the course of the day, the pile of pellets disappeared, but not fast enough for Frog's sake. He kept eyes focussed, looking up and down the tunnel, and giving others warnings whenever he thought the train was coming. This time he stood on the safe side of the tracks.

Boo watched the train clanking down the tunnel. From where they were standing the wall was a good six feet from the track. This safe zone tapered to about two feet on either side of the tracks. No more than fifty feet on either side of where they stood. The tunnel had a dark and eerie look about it, with only inches from the top of the train to the ceiling of the tunnel.

Whenever the train arrived down the tunnel, the tunnel seemed to swallow up the train like Jonah being swallowed up by the whale. At one time the tunnel had been brightly lit, but over time dirt that had filtered into the light globes, eventually diminishing ability to illuminate. Small windows in the brick wall along the tunnel were the only indication that there was a life outside of the tunnel. Air flowed into the tunnel only briefly. Looking out the windows of the tunnel, the scenery outside was obscured by endless piles of pellets.

About two hours later, the piles of pellets were still there, thanks to more spillage from the train. Slowly the piles of pellets diminished but not fast enough. Dropping the shovel, Boo motioned to the others, "Rest time." The shovels clanked against the cement floor as they fell.

Heading out through the tunnel door and into the darkening night, the four boys headed towards number seven blast furnace. Currently, workers were rebuilding the number seven blast furnace from the ground up. A job that would take about a year. At this point workers were just starting to move equipment and trailers around as a continuous commotion of men and machinery centred around the furnace. The boys felt that they could investigate what was going on without being noticed. Knowing this, the four boys headed into the commotion.

CHAPTER FIVE
Own Up

The boys ambled around the area of the number seven blast furnace. No one seemed to notice that they were just roaming around. Most of the crew rebuilding the number seven blast furnace were from an outside company. They were more noticeable in their own brown hard hats which were of a different colour than All Steel's hard hats. The rest of the workers and labourers from All Steel wore the traditional red hats, so it was easy to walk around unnoticed. Occasionally one of the top brass would visit the site with their clean white hats, but basically that was during the day shift. The only threat on the site was the plant foreman and general foreman. If the familiar green colour of their hats were seen, all the men under their supervision would vanish or act as if they were busy working.

During this time of day, the last glimmer of sunshine had disappeared and the evening shadows mooned over the blast furnace site. Huge overhead lights attempted to cast as much light on the area as the previous sunshine had. Man's ingenuity was not able to do the job that mother nature's own could. The site resembled a carnival at night. There were lights, excitement and people on the move. There were not only men working the site but women as well. With the new equality laws that had now come into effect, every company including All Steel was required to hire a percentage of women. Ziggy could certainly go for that. He followed two girls heading towards the canteen trailer.

Like a set of dominos, the rows and rows of trailers numbered about 100. Behind the trailers there were two canteen trailers. The one on the left catered to the men who wanted meals. The one on the right was for those who wanted coffee and snacks. This was the one towards which Ziggy was heading.

Following Ziggy, like a little child in tow, Frog had made it as far as the landing before realizing what Ziggy was up to. Sighing, Frog plopped onto the rough-cut landing. As Ziggy found out the names and addresses of the two girls he was following, Frog thought about the predicament he found himself in. He had not even gotten the nerve to call Penelope since the accident. Maybe she would not want to see him again? It could have been circumstances of the night that threw them together, and that was as far as it was going to go.

The other guys could get girls any time they wanted, but he was not like them. Most girls seemed to look down at him. Most of the time they ended up laughing at him. That night, with Penelope, had been the best chance he had to get laid. Now he thought, he would never get another chance. How could he prove himself a man, especially here, working with the guys laughing at him, making fun of him as . . ., 'the last virgin in town!'.

"What's that Frog?" Boo and Salami had suddenly stopped in front of him. "What did you say?"

"Nothing, nothing."

Boo stepped onto the platform to gaze down the boardwalk separating the two rows of trailers. "Frog, keep your eyes peeled for any nosy green hats, will you? If one gets too close, give a whistle."

Frog, half understanding, watched Salami and Boo head down the boardwalk. 'What are they up to now?" he thought. Glancing up at Ziggy, he knew what he was up to. As for himself it was back to dreaming of the impossible. He could not ask the guys to help him out. Penelope, and the first step to ecstasy vanished after that night of the accident. Frog shook his head, almost shaking the glasses from his head. "I'm going to grow up to be an old virgin!" he lamented. Peering from the corner of the eyes, he hoped no one had heard him.

In the darkness of the night, Salami and Boo seemed to be hidden in the darkness. Lights had not yet been installed along the trailers. Unnoticed, the two searched the inside of the trailers. With dim light filtering in through the windows, the interior revealed little or nothing of interest. On the trailers doors, the name and number of the crew were stencilled and inside were long tables, benches and coat racks.

Standing at the end of the boardwalk looking down its length, Boo suddenly started to speak. "Over one hundred trailers for the use for just plain eating in, what a shame!"

"You're right," Salami agreed. "You would think they could find some other uses, good uses."

"They have quite a few of them . . .,"

"And a few other extra ones." Both turned to the end of the boardwalk where several other trailers stood as if cast aside.

"Well Salami, it would be a shame to let those extra trailers sit there idle."

Glancing into each other's eyes, the same devilishness of the graduation commencement could clearly be seen.

"You're right, you're right, a shame."

They headed back down the boardwalk. There was a certain lightness in their walk. Boo grabbed Frog while he was striding down the boardwalk and Salami whistled to Ziggy who followed reluctantly. There was still another couple of hours to work and still a pile of pellets to shovel. What Boo and Salami had in mind would have to wait until later, at least until they had a chance to talk about it.

In the night's light, the metallic paint of the Baby Blue sparkled, giving the feeling that all other vehicles were from a junk yard. Ziggy turned the key and the Baby Blue purred to a start. The others settled in while Ziggy pulled up to the gate. Everyone waited in silence knowing too well why Ziggy was stopped in such a place. Coming through the gate, heading towards them, two well developed girls strolled teasingly. Like gentlemen of leisure, Boo and Salami jumped out and escorted the girls into the car without uttering a word.

There was no comparing the girls as workers to the women out on the town. Pulling out of the parking lot, the Baby Blue headed out of town towards a country bar. Passing the area where Porky's accident occurred, Ziggy slowed down. In everyone's mind the scene was re-enacted. Life had to go on, and the past was left in the past.

The music of the country rock band echoed throughout the length of the bar. Mounted on a canopy over the bandstand, a stuffed moose stood glancing towards the patrons. In addition to the moose, other oddities hung from the ceilings and walls, things such as wagons, boots, saddles and various women's garments. Like any other night, the mechanical bull bucked its mount helplessly to the ground.

Not very far from the bull's right, Rita sat waiting for Salami and the others. Tonight, she had thought of not showing up. She felt that her relationship with Salami was headed towards nowhere, and fast. Salami had shown more feelings towards the other guys than he ever did to her. Oh sure, every once in-a-while they spent a whole evening together, but that was just because he was over to her house for supper. They would sit on the couch for a while and then he would say that he had to meet the guys somewhere and off he would go, only to come back when invited for supper again.

But there was one time that Rita remembered when Salami paid attention to her and only her. The night of Rita's cousins wedding. In her light blue dress and all dolled up, she waited for Salami to pick her up. They had to be at the church within a half hour. Standing, facing the front door, she stared as if she could see right through it.

"If he dares to show up just one second late, I'll lay him out cold on the front steps," she mumbled to herself. Inside, she was fuming and outside there was not a sign of him. Her dark hair flowed down, cascading over bare shoulders. She had soft features and a glow that was enough to turn any man's head. Certainly, enough to get Salami excited. But only if he showed up without the other boys escorting him.

On the other side of the door, standing there hesitating to knock, Salami tugged at a bow-tie and dusted invisible lint from the suit. His hair was combed and he had shaved. The car had gas and he even had a corsage that his mother had forced him to get.

Thinking he was ready, he raised a hand to knock. The Tap, tap, tap seemed to echo forever. He glanced from side to side, and wondered if the whole neighbourhood was watching. The loud knocking seemed to cause the building to vibrate. Rita stepped back thinking it could not be Salami. It was too early. Well, to find out she would have to open the door. She did. For a moment, they stared at each other. He was better looking than she had expected, and she certainly was enough to excite him. There had to be something wrong. Rita peered around Salami, and saw that there was no Boo, no Ziggy or Frog. Not even the Baby Blue.

"Where's our transportation?"

"Right there." he pointed, "My brother's Monte Carlo," Salami answered, unable to take eyes off Rita for fear if looking away, she would disappear. He could not believe how gorgeous she was.

'No guys, no Baby Blue?' She smiled at Salami, thinking that this is the night. It is going to be perfect. She took Salami's arm and they walked towards the waiting car. A perfect couple, Rita was beautiful, Salami handsome. Salami had done everything right, except for the untied sneakers that flopped as he walked. Salami stopped at the car's door and remembered the corsage. He glanced at her low-cut dress and wanted to, but something stopped him. He handed the corsage to Rita and opened the door for her. Reluctantly Rita pinned on the corsage. She wondered why, at any other time a sweater and a blouse would have been no obstacle. She recalled the times she had restrained his advances.

"We should be going before we're late," she mumbled.

Hurrying to the driver's side, he drove away as fast as possible, ton allow excitable thoughts to fade.

They were on time for the wedding. On time for the supper and the reception. Everything seemed to be going all right. All of Rita's relatives complimented her and Salami, saying they made a nice couple. To top that, Rita caught the bouquet, thanks to her cousin, the bride. The garter, well Salami did not want to go that far by catching it. He was not ready to settle down. By catching it, it would be like adding gasoline onto a fire. Other then that, Rita thought it was an almost perfect night, but the night was not over yet.

The evening seemed to pass too quickly for Rita. With her arm wrapped around Salami, they welcomed the coolness of the night. As usual, Salami had too much to drink and seemed to teeter a little bit as Rita reached into his coat pocket to retrieve the car keys. Sliding across the car seat, Salami rested his head against the headrest. He felt quite lightheaded, and as the car pulled away, he quickly fell asleep. Rita headed down Bay Street and then up Queen Street East, away from the direction in which they lived. She was heading toward the east end of town. "Salami! Salami!" she yelled, trying to wake him up.

"Where, where are we?" Salami responded sheepishly. He shook an induced head to try to wake himself, and at the same time listen to what Rita was saying. He grabbed his head with both hands and held it, trying to stop the motion of the sea swelling within. He felt as if he was going to be sick. "Where are we?" He asked again. She leaned over and kissed him lightly on the lips with continuing passion. She tried to explain in as few words as possible.

"We're here, my cousin's place. She asked me to look after it." In the condition that Salami found himself, all this was too much to take in all at once. The best that he could do was follow Rita up to the apartment. The light breeze blowing on this cool April night seemed to revitalize. He finally felt himself coming around and was beginning to sense awareness. He focussed blurred eyes to limited ability, and with his mind now less confused, he was starting to understand what was going on.

Rita hung onto Salami's coat sleeve with one hand, and with the other fumbled for keys in a coat pocket. Finding the right key, she unlocked the door and pushed it open. Salami was behind teetering back and forth, unable to stand on his feet he fell towards her. Rita tried to twist the key out of the lock but was unable to. 'To hell with it,' she thought and closed the door leaving the key in the lock. She found no need to open the lights, to get accustomed to the inside of the house.

Following her, Salami bumped along the hall and through the door opening. He stumbled and fell onto something cushiony, something watery. He was paying attention to the roaring sea in his head, but they were not sinking. It was a water bed that he had fallen onto and next to him was Rita. There was no need for any words of explanation, no words at all. Salami's mind was still groggy and thoughts were still very confused.

Salami felt Rita's hands caressing him, pulling him closer. He felt the warmth of her body through her low-cut dress. They rolled around as they kissed, fumbling with each other. At this point, Salami's tie seemed too tight and he found that he was sweating profusely beneath a coat and vest. Like a ritual, one then the other unfastened a button, a belt, a clip. It seemed awkward, even comical, yet required. The silkiness of her slip seemed to be a reward. He slowly slid it off. A moment, a second, warm blood rushed from toes to head. Closer they pressed, naked body against naked body, the passion of the night lingering until the morning sun filtered through the partly opened curtains. Laying together, arms wrapped around each other, both lingered in the ecstasy of the previous evening. Both wished that the moments would never end, this first time.

'That was three months ago,' Rita thought as attention was drawn back to the music playing all around. The commotion at the bar had now become louder. Salami and the other boys should be here anytime now. 'The guys,' she thought. 'always the guys.' That's all that Salami seemed to think about. Would she and Salami ever have that night again? Oh sure, there were other nights of necking in the car, in the front seat or the back seat, with the other guys and which ever dates they had. She had always been there, sticking by Salami. She had thought of getting involved with other guys, yet it only seemed right, that for now it should only be her and Salami.

Rita glanced at the clock again and it showed 11:10. Another five minutes she thought, and they would be coming through the door. Despite the commotion of the music, she gathered deep thoughts. She felt that she had to talk to Salami, she had to get her feelings across to him, and make him understand how she felt.

"Hi Rita."

Rita looked up, turning her head she saw Salami coming up from behind.

Salami and Boo each took a seat on either side of Rita. Ziggy hurriedly introduced the two girls, that tagged along, to Rita before heading onto the dance floor.

"This is Sammy and Lynn," he said, as he started to walk toward the dance floor. He grabbed Sammy's hand and walked away.

Lynn was tugging at Boo's jacket as he talked to Salami. "Uh, take Frog and dance Okay?"

Reluctantly she gave a little frown. "Oh, what the hell," she pulled on Frog's arm and lead him away like a little puppy. Frog followed holding glasses in place so they would not fall off his nose.

Salami ordered a round of drinks and Rita held his hand softly under the table, gently caressing his fingers. Before Rita could start to talk to Salami, he and Boo began chattering about work and the trailers. The two had a plan to share, they had to work out all the details before they made their next move. Rita squeezed Salami's hand even tighter, while she fixed eyes on him, thoughts drifted in and out of her head as she listened to the two boys talking.

"We could jack it up on a flatbed from the yard gang," Boo began, "There's a couple of trucks sitting there, we could use one of them."

"Where are we gonna put it? It has to be close to where we work and away from intruders." Salami disengaged his hand from Rita's under the table and wiped perspiration that had built up on his hand, onto a sleeve. "Away from any nosey foreman."

Rita leaned back in her chair, obviously disappointed that this was not going to be the evening that she would be able to talk to Salami.

"Down at the end of the high line," Boo said surely when raising his head and looking towards the bar. "near the women's trailers and those other storage trailers."

Salami nodded with agreement as Boo stood and headed towards the bar. Salami's eyes caught Rita staring at him. "Something the matter with you?" Salami asked, a little curious, "You look a little grumpy tonight."

"I've got to talk to you." She looked deep into his bewildered eyes. "We've got to talk.

"Well, go ahead." He listened to the music playing for a moment and then turned towards the dance floor where Frog seemed to be bumping people from side to side.

"How can we talk in here with all those . . .," the words were drowned out by the music.

Boo gave a chair beside him a shove with a leg and leaned back in the chair. He sat back with a bottle of beer in a hand with fingers gripped around the bottle. Rita leaned back in her chair. Boo looked toward the dance floor where Frog now seemed to be the centre of attention.

The music playing seemed to be carrying a boogie beat, with couples attempting to do a jive type dance. Most of the dance partners seemed successful, usually with the guys leading and the girls twirling. Unlike most, Frog was the one being twirled and not too successfully. While attempting to keep glasses on his nose and feet on the ground, Frog had managed to send several couples to the sidelines. Some of the dancers had been virtually put out of commission for the evening. People at the bar had been laughing and clapping to encourage his efforts, but they clapped even more when the music stopped and the band started playing a slow song. Falling exhausted into Lynn's arms, Frog gasped for air. "Another dance?"

"Ah, what the hell."

At the far side of the dance floor, another group was watching the commotion. They were the prim and proper class from high school, out slumming for the evening, and amongst them sat the prim and proper Penelope Snidermost, her eyes seemed glued to Frog's every move. She stared at him with what seemed a particularly hidden jealousy. It was not until almost the end of the song that Frog felt as if someone was staring at him. He turned around and noticed some familiar faces at one of the tables. To unbelieving eyes, he noticed Penelope Snidermost. He quickly pulled away from Lynn and let her hand drop out of his. He made a beeline for the home table towing Lynn behind him.

"Ziggy." Frog tugged at his arm. "Did you see her?"

"Who?"

"Penelope, she's right over there." Frog glanced back over a shoulder. "She's gone, she was there a few seconds ago."

"Well, better luck next time." Ziggy wrapped an arm around Sammy, and they headed back to their table.

Frog searched every table in the bar as if being a lost little child. He looked here and looked there but could not find Penelope. For a moment, he thought that he might have been seeing things, but he was not sure.

"We'll have to lift a green hat and maybe a couple of brown ones, and a truck that no-one will miss for a while." Moving the drinks and change on the table, Boo laid out a makeshift scene of the plant, moving his beer as if it were a truck.

Salami showed the route that they would take around the other trailers. "This way then down by the water front and up through the far end of the high line, His body swayed in mirrored action.

"Great! There's not too many guys working down by the water front." Ziggy's ears perked up and he was obviously excited about the way the plan was shaping up. Ziggy's motivation was also focussed on Sammy.

Rita was still sitting back in her chair, seemingly lost in thoughts. She had thought of how she could make Salami understand what she was feeling, but it was obvious that in this place and with these guys it would seem almost impossible to be able to talk to Salami. What was it that she saw in him in the first place anyway, was it his blond hair, his blue eyes or the fact that her mother liked him. Her mother just seemed to love to feed him when he came over, he would eat and eat and eat and she liked that, maybe Rita liked that too. If it was true that the way to a man's heart was through his stomach, then Rita obviously had him hooked. But the fact was, that she might have had him hooked sooner then he might want.

Frog, in the meanwhile, continued to search the bar hoping that what he had seen earlier was not imagination. He had hoped to see Penelope out there somewhere waving to him. But if she does wave at him, what should he do. He would have to ask Ziggy about this. As the night lingered, his hopes of seeing Penelope faded.

Ziggy left with the two girls, and Penelope had never shown up again. He obviously would have to hitch a ride with Salami and Rita as soon as Rita could pull him away from Boo and their scheming plans.

"Hurry up and drink up, I want to get home," the bartender hollered into the emptying bar.

Rita pulled a little harder on Salami's arm, trying to drag him away.

"See you tomorrow Boo," Salami called back as Rita dragged him across the bar floor, with Frog following just behind them, all heading out the door.

The lights were closed one by one and Boo just leaned back in the chair sipping slowly on the beer which had now become quite warm and stale. The waitress was cleaning several tables around him before arriving at Boo's. She looked rather young, but something revealed her age.

"No place to hang out?" she asked softly, just above a whisper.

Boo had clearly heard and acknowledged with a sideways motion of his head.

. . . .

It had been a warm afternoon and by the looks of it, it looked as if the evening would probably be the same. Boo leaned his head back against the fence and soaked up the sun. The shift change had started, and the other guys should be showing up any minute now. Down near the first entrance from the parking lot, Boo could see the Baby Blue. He watched Ziggy and two girls strolling up to the gate.

"See you inside Boo." Ziggy waved, just a little smile on his face.

Boo nodded and acknowledged that he had seen Ziggy. Boo watched Rita coming around in her father's car. Frog climbed out of the back seat, his red lunch box in hand while Salami climbing through the window calling out to Boo.

"Hey! I've got a great idea, you're gonna love it." The three headed for the gate discussing their plans. Rita called for Salami's attention.

"Salami! Just a minute," he did not turn to answer. She yelled louder, starting to lose patience. "Salami, wait a minute, Salami, I'm pregnant!"

Every single head turned as silence fell amongst all the workers within hearing range. There was a hushed laughter as Boo caught the look of despair on Rita's face. Salami had not heard. He had been talking about their scheming plans, or he had and did not want to acknowledge.

"What did she say? Those trailers are set on dollies," Salami continued talking.

The guys took their time walking to the change room. They knew that if they were late reporting to Reese, they would get the high line again, and that's what they wanted, a night of shovelling and sweeping pellets around. Through the course of the shift, they would do a little of that but mostly their minds would be on the trailers.

Having changed into work clothes, Ziggy led the pack while Frog, as usual, followed up the rear. They entered the foreman shack just in time to hear Reese yelling at them. They could see Reese's angry expression.

"Late, late, late again, what's the matter with you guys? You guys are on clean up on the high line."

As the boys left the office, the only thing that could be heard was Frog's red lunch box clanking through the closed door. The four arrived on the high line and for the next hour they checked out their plan. They checked out the area, and to be on the safe side, happened to do a little bit of work.

"Okay, you guys take off," echoed Boo's voice through the dark tunnel. "Get what we need. I'll stay here for another hour. Porky won't stop to ask any questions, if he sees me here for awhile he'll think we're working."

Ziggy hid a shovel behind a beam. "We'll meet at the west end of the tunnel, when we have what we need."

The sky over the plant was covered by a grey haze that seemed to give the boys the feeling that it was already dusk, even though the summer sun was perched high in the sky. It already felt as if it was going to be another clear cool night.

Frog brushed dust off clothes and pushed glasses back against a reddened nose. He pressed his face against the window and looked inside the storage trailer. Suddenly the hairs on the back of the neck seemed to stand up as eyes focussed on the objects inside. A smile came to his face and then faded as quickly as it arrived. He turned the door handle without opening the door. Grabbing and pulling the handle with both hands the whole wooden shack seemed to creak. He knew he could not let the guys down, he just had to get those jacks.

Suddenly the door seemed to give. Falling backwards onto his butt, Frog stared at the door handle gripped in his hand. A nervous look prevailed on his face. Quickly he began to stuff the handle into a jacket pocket, but with a change of mind, he sent it sailing over his head. Without a sound the spinning knob plopped silently to the bottom of an oil drum a few feet behind.

Quickly standing, trying not to look guilty, Frog rubbed his aching backside. The door creaked open and Frog entered the silent building. He inched forward about four feet to where the screw jacks stood, in a way the jacks seemed to laugh at Frog's bravery. Frog did not particularly enjoy the eerie silence. Grabbing the jacks, he made a quick dash out the door and did not bother to look back. Like all getaways, there is always a slight set back. Half carrying, half dragging the jacks, Frog suddenly heard a voice yelling at him.

"Hey, hey, hey you. Hang on a minute." A seemingly large man shuffling feet, walked up behind Frog. "Hang on Joe,"

Frog glanced down at the huge set of feet and looking up felt someone grabbing his collar. The man's huge hand grabbed the jacks, while Frog put up very little resistance.

"Hey, these are too heavy for a little fellow like you to lug around." The big guy gave him a big smile. "Use this wheelbarrow here and save your back for the women." He disappeared as quickly as appearing. He was almost out of sight when Frog called out to him.

"Hey thanks, thanks a lot."

The big guy gave a wave without turning and walked away out of sight.

Ziggy had no problems collecting the hard hats they needed. In the first trailer entered, he picked up a green foreman's hat. He put the green hat on and stuck his hat into a bag. Wearing a green hat, no one would ask any questions. Checking out two other trailers, Ziggy picked up two white construction hats and one brown hat, one that belonged to the company which owned the trailers. Having done his part, Ziggy stopped at the canteen to see the girl that he had met there. Sammy obviously noticed the colour of his hat.

"You've been promoted already, and only in two weeks?"

"It did not take them long to notice a good man when I came along." Ziggy felt perspiration building upon his forehead. He felt able to con Sammy, but if others came around, it might be hard to explain why he was wearing a green hat. "Well, there's no time to dawdle, I won't get any work done if you distract me," he said. Waving good-bye, Ziggy promised that they would get together at another time on safer ground. Picking up his stride, he headed to the meeting place, a safer place. With girls, he had no problems, but when it came to other things, that frightened him, he had to put up a pressured front. He had to be the leader, and he had to be the strongest.

Salami leaned against the yard shack and waited for just the right truck to come along. Just about now, the yard crew would be coming in for coffee, and he felt he would have the pick of the litter. Within seconds, the trucks pulled up and their operators headed to the shack for coffee. Salami waited patiently for the operators to seat themselves down and to start drinking their coffee before he did anything. Then he picked out the truck required, a three-quarter ton dual wheel flatbed with the blue paint covered with the coke dust from the steel plant. This was the one. It had no radio and no company number. Without hesitating any longer, Salami jumped in and started the vehicle and headed towards the high line. Salami had guts. He would do just about anything, but some things he had to be told, or guided by someone else. Now if Rita could just get him to listen to her, she would have no problems. As far as Salami was concerned, what the guys said, went.

Boo stood just outside the high line watching two guys unload a dolly. The flatbed dolly would be just the right size for the trailer, Boo assumed. It would be just a matter of relieving the workers of their dolly.

"Hurry up, yelled one worker, let's unload this stuff." The worker glanced at his watch and noticed that it was already getting to be quite late, and that it was almost time for their coffee break.

Salami slowed down the truck and coasted to a stop behind Boo.

"Hang around here until I wave at you to come," instructed Boo.

Boo walked toward the dolly just as the two guys were finishing. Stepping between the truck and the dolly, Boo pulled the pin just as the truck jerked ahead.

The coffee break must have been more important than the dolly. The guys never even stopped to look to see if the load was in tow. With a wave of a hand, Boo called Salami. Quickly, Salami backed the truck into place while Boo dropped the Pin. Having done so, the two headed away to pick up the other guys. So far, the plan was working beautifully, everything was falling into place.

Most of the time, Boo rarely said anything. The entire plan had been his, and he had carried them out, but rather than being in the limelight, he would rather Ziggy accepted all the glory, and he remain in the shadows.

Salami had stopped the truck long enough for Frog to load the jacks. Once Ziggy had jumped into the truck, the hats were passed around. It was an exhilarating ride to the trailer, and they could hardly wait. As Salami pulled in front of the trailer and stopped the truck, a hush fell over the four. They were waiting for Ziggy to give the signal, to say go.

"We're ready Zig," Boo said, in a rather blasé kind of voice.

"She's just waiting for us, so let's go." Ziggy took one deep breath and straightened out his green hat.

It only took a few minutes to set up the jacks underneath the trailer, just enough to raise it high enough for the dollies to be backed underneath. Salami, very-carefully, backed the dollies underneath the trailer while Ziggy held up oncoming traffic, even a security truck! Perspiration rolled down Ziggy's temples. He felt a certain nervousness, a sort of tension while all this was going on. It was an exciting kind of tension, he was really enjoying. It seemed that Salami had backed up far enough, so Ziggy signalled the security truck to move on. The drivers in the security truck waved back, and Ziggy sighed with relief.

Having lowered the jacks, the trailer now rested perfectly on the dollies. They threw the jacks onto the back of the flatbed and climbed into the truck. Having done so, they drove off, with no questions being asked. It had worked beautifully.

"Frog, you take the next watch at the high line," Boo said, his mind reeling as he talked. "At shift change, we'll sign out with Reese, and then head back to our trailer."

"Why?" Salami asked, "When our shift is over, we head home." Salami did not seem to be following Boo's particular line of thought.

"We'll stay for the eleven to seven shift and do a little scrounging around without having to worry about doing work."

"Great idea!" Ziggy said enthusiastically.

Reese's eyes were glaring with anger. An evil grin crossed his lips. "See ya tomorrow girls!" The guys walked by bumping into his desk and chair while he was trying to set up the day's log.

"Don't make a mistake now," Boo said to Reese, as he pinched the foreman's walkie talkie from the desk. In no time at all the scrounging had begun.

Now located in its new place, the trailer waited to be filled with essentials to make life in the plant bearable for the guys. All night long goodies were brought into the trailer. Some were small; such as plates, cups, pots and pans. Others were a bit bigger; a fridge that Salami and Boo had moved out of one of the mills. Workers watched and some even helped and no-one suspected anything unusual was happening. The two boys sat drinking pop from the confiscated fridge, taking a breather before their next effort moving their cherished prize.

"Hey Boo," Salami said, "What was Rita shouting about, when we were coming to work today?

"I think it was about someone that was not careful and did something that put somebody into a fix. Now the proper thing should be done, or something to fix the fix before somebody brings out the shotgun, would you agree? Because the one that was not careful might end up with hundreds of little-little holes all over his body."

"What the hell are you talking about?"

"She's pregnant, you fool."

"Who?"

"Rita, who in the hell else are we talking about?"

Salami's eyes bulged with surprise.

"Yea, Rita, and it's you that's gonna have little holes all over."

"Me? We only did it a couple of times, I'm too young to get . . .,"

"Married. Own up man, you're the one, and it only takes once, and you've got to do the right thing." Boo squeezed the pop can in his hand then tossed it over a shoulder. "If you love her, you'll marry her, and if not, put up some cash and end your worries."

Salami dropped the pop can as thoughts raced through his head. Picking up his end of the fridge, Salami whispered to himself, "I do like her a lot, yes, I really like her."

The fridge slowly made its way through the mill to its new destination. By now the trailer was filled with odds and ends, and the guys toasted to themselves while easing into confiscated, comfortable chairs. The boys sat there each contemplating his own life, their thoughts contemplating about the past, present and the future.

CHAPTER SIX
Free Show

Reese was the first to greet the boys when arriving for the day's shift. "Good afternoon girls," Reese said in a usual depraved kind of way. "Are you girls ready for new jobs? I guarantee you, they'll be dirty, as dirty as I can find them."

"You're all heart, Reese," Ziggy said. "Without you giving us all these dirty jobs, we'd have no reason to dislike you."

"You, and this new girl, whatever her name is, get to clean the belts at the dumping station today." Reese stared at the new girl. "She won't be working here for long unless she can prove that she deserves to be here. Frog, you're at number four cast house slag runners. Salami and Boo, grease pit, below number four charging buckets." Nobody moved a muscle as they talked amongst themselves. "That's it girls, get going."

Boo stepped on Reese's foot as he pushed past on his way out the door. Ziggy, of course, introduced himself to the blonde while giving her the once over, his eyes caressing her body up and down to examine every inch. She certainly was well shaped, and tight jeans showed her muscularly hard body. Her makeup though, seemed out of place, or she seemed to be made up for other reasons. Ziggy would certainly have to find out why. He watched her hips sway from side to side as she walked out the door. Ziggy thought to himself, that it would be really difficult getting any work done today, because working with this girl he would have other thoughts on his mind.

As Frog walked into number four cast house, a chill travelled up and down his spine. There seemed to be something familiar about this building. A feeling of Deja vu, as if he had been here before. Frog shivered as he listened to the roar of the furnace and sensed the heat from the cooling runner of the furnace. He felt perspiration building up underneath the hard hat. With shovel in hand, he walked along the slag runner, slowly making his way to the spout. He lifted a cooled piece of slag and then watched it tumble into the slag pot. With grey sloping sides, the pot, sixteen-feet down to its bottom seemed like a huge monstrous crater that was ready to swallow anything put into its mouth. Frog worked slowly, his thoughts were not on the furnace or on the mill, but were of the safety of his home. As Frog loosened each piece of slag and slid it into the pot, the pot swallowed greedily, waiting for yet another piece.

Salami and Boo made their way towards their new home, their minds racing in thought as well. For them, life was a matter of how many tricks and schemes they could come up with, either for fun or for profit. It seemed that at any moment a new scheme was about to be born.

At the end of the high line, their trailer was clustered in amongst the other seldom used trailers. A few were already occupied by the new female work force. At one time the blast furnace was made up of only males, eventually equal rights in the hiring of women was shoved down the throat of All Steel. Over time, the composition of All Steel's employees was changed from just men to those shapely curves of females. The company had thought, that this was only a current fad, so they were housed in less permanent buildings such as trailers, believing that eventually all the women would end up leaving All Steel. But it seemed that the women were not leaving, and for this, Salami and Boo were very, very thankful.

Ideas seemed to flash through their minds, and all that they could think of was what kind of schemes they could pull off. The two boys stood around and watched the girls leaving the trailer and heading for the gate. With hawk-like eyes, they devoured the many different types of women. There were small women, tall women, slim women, and some women that were a little too wide for the boys to appreciate. As usual, they thought that there had to be something to be gained here, having all these women around. Maybe some fun, or maybe some profit.

"Usually, with this many woman in one place," Boo said, scratching a shadowed chin, "Perhaps there should be a madam."

"No, it's too risky," replied Salami, his eyes following the swaying of their hips as they walked out the gate. "We'd never be able to convince that many girls, not even Ziggy."

Crossing the tracks, the two walked toward the girls trailer and stared as the women faded out of sight. Stopping at the corner of the landing, the two thought, as if this new scheme was the only thing, at this moment of importance.

"There is money to be made here. We've just got to figure out how," said Boo, his eyes surveying the trailer.

Salami laughed as he recalled the previous scheme.

"Pictures, like what we took of Penelope Snidermost. There would be money in that."

"If these women ever found out we'd be up shit creek, and I ain't willing to be left to the mercy of a bunch of angry women."

"I get the drift."

With that, they put the idea to rest and headed to their own trailer to do some more thinking. Salami switched on the walkie talkie, to keep in touch with what was going on. Boo popped the cork on a bottle of wine, and sitting back comfortably, Boo and Salami thought about the women and their trailer.

Striding along quite quickly, Ziggy managed to stay a few steps ahead of the new girl, Linda. As he walked slower, she walked slower as well, and seemed to be swaying her hips in a rather beckoning kind of way. Ziggy concluded that she seemed to be doing more advertising than walking. She did not seem to be in any particular hurry to get to the job.

"What's a girl like you doing in a place like this?" Ziggy asked. No sooner had the question popped out of his mouth when realizing that he had stuck the old proverbial foot into his mouth.

"Hey, we women got rights. Why shouldn't I be able to work here?" Linda's eyes flashed red with anger. "I've got a right to make as much money as you guys, doing the same kind of work," she responded angrily.

All of sudden, Ziggy realized that he and this girl were not thinking on the same wave length. She was a devil in disguise, thought Ziggy. "The same work," he laughed, "You won't last the shift. Reese will have you hightailing your ass back to unemployment."

"We'll see about that," Linda retorted as she brushed past Ziggy, her hips swaying faster than before. "Well, are you coming, or will I have to do all the work myself?" She yelled without looking back at Ziggy. He followed like a little lost puppy, shaking his head, knowing that they certainly had not hit it off on the right foot.

Salami and Boo had downed about half the bottle of wine when a sinister smile crossed Boo's lips. Taking his hard hat off, he sent it sailing across the room, where it came to rest at the foot of a Playboy pin-up. "Salami, my man, what's on everybody's mind?"

"Ah, that's an easy question, sex."

"And what goes with sex?"

"Well, you can't get it without women."

"Right again."

The two suddenly sat up as the handle of the door twisted. It was Frog. He had a devastating look of dreariness. Seeing that it was only Frog, Boo relaxed.

"I'll prove my point, Salami, using Frog as a typical male specimen."

"Frog?" blurted Salami.

"We'll pretend." Boo turned to Frog. "Frog, what do you think of most?"

"Girls and getting laid before I get too old."

"Do you like seeing naked girls?"

"Yea," Frog's face was beginning to brighten. The thoughts of the furnace were quickly fading.

"Would you pay to see all the naked girls you wanted?"

"Damn right I would."

"Well, Salami, that's the key to our money-making scheme."

Salami downed the wine, then tapped his temple with a finger repeatedly as if deep in thought.

"We know where the women are and there are plenty of average typical guys in this place."

"Right," Salami's finger stopped tapping his temple.

Frog stood bewildered as Boo and Salami quickly rushed past him. They had no time to fill Frog in on the details right now, for every moment of hesitation would be a moment wasted.

"Salami, check the trailers and their layout," Suggested Boo.

"I'll scrounge around for some material."

With visions of naked women running amuck in his mind, Salami rubbed hands together. He descended sinisterly upon the trailers. Back in the very dark recesses of his mind, that thought of Rita being pregnant had started to worry him. He would never show his weaknesses or bother anyone with his personal worries, not even Rita. Since that day at the gate, Salami had not found the courage to see Rita or even to phone her. A kid, it did not seem possible. He could not picture himself being married. Maybe it was a mistake. Maybe Rita was confused, or maybe it was just indigestion. Maybe she was out to screw him. Salami pushed these thoughts further back into his mind as he bent over and peered beneath one of the trailers. A cool sweat seemed to have formed around the band of his hard-hat. Was it excitement of this new adventure, or worries of domestic life?

Boo stopped walking, suddenly and his body seemed to freeze in mid motion. Ideas were forming and fading. Without moving or looking right, his mind focussed on a rack of plastic tubing about three inches in diameter, white with the necessary elbows, there seemed to be plenty of material that no one would miss. Boo continued searching around, looking for all the necessary material to be able to fulfil his plan. Ascending a flight of stairs two at a time, Boo headed for the number 5 welfare room. He entered through one of the doors and then before opening the second steel door to the main room, he stopped and stared at a wall mirror. The image of himself reflected from the cracked mirror streaked with coke dust. With a flick of a finger, Boo straightened out his hard hat and grinned at smug reflection in the mirror. Before glancing away, he pointed a pistol shaped hand to the mirror and pretended to pull the trigger of a pistol.

"Come on girl, pull your own weight," Ziggy said, coughing from the dust. "Hey, this work too much for the equal women?" Ziggy's voice did not reflect his usual hazy smooth sultry voice, the voice the girls loved to listen to. Through the dust, he made out a silhouette of a figure. A smug shake of her head was the only reply Ziggy received.

At the dumping station, train-car after train-car after train-car, full of coke and iron pellets, were dumped into the hoppers. Below the vibrating hoppers, the conveyer belt carried the material to other hoppers and distributed the coke and pellets to a furnace. Every once-in-a-while some of the workers on the night shift, in an attempt, to get a bit of sleep, caused the belts to overload with coke and iron pellets.

By the time, Ziggy had arrived for this shift, the belt was overloaded with pellets and dumped in excess onto the floor. For Ziggy and Linda, the job of cleaning up the spill seemed endless. A virtual nightmare of shovelling and shovelling and shovelling the pellets and the coke that had spilled. To make matters worse, Ziggy could not take his eyes off Linda. She had the most incredible body he had ever seen. 'Women were made to be women,' Ziggy cursed under his breath. When they tread on male turf, Ziggy felt that was too much! His usual good manners seemed to fade to a point where he felt like Reese, and that scared him. At this point, he wanted to get rid of her, and before the end of the shift for that matter.

Wiping black coke dust from his eyes, Ziggy walked down the incline toward Linda. Without giving any explanation or showing any emotion or giving her any reason, Ziggy said, "I'm going' for supper. I'll be back later, keep working, or do whatever the hell you want."

"What's the matter?" Linda yelled back angrily. "You can't handle the work?" Linda said. She seemed to be in a real fighting mood.

Without turning to face her, he felt a rage building up inside. He headed out into the cool freshness of the night. It was good to get away from the coke dust. The walk back to the guys' trailer, which did not seem to cool the anger built up inside. Maybe a couple glasses of wine and a bit of supper would take his mind off her.

Frog was just removing some cold chicken from the fridge when Ziggy walked in. "Hey Frog, what's up, where are the others?"

"They are up to something, and it must be good because they did not have time to tell me about it. They never tell me about anything." Frog placed the chicken down as Ziggy sat across from him. He offered Ziggy some chicken, but he declined and instead poured himself a glass of wine.

"I'm glad your mother, that sweet lady, made ya such a big lunch, she must really love ya. Well Frog," Ziggy began to say between mouthfuls of wine. "How are you and Penelope Snidermost getting along?"

Frog threw a chicken leg onto a plate. "Shit, I never got up enough nerve to call her, and every time I think about calling her, I sweat all over. Then my mom tells me to go and take a cold shower."

"A cold shower is good."

"Hell no, I get more excited than anything, then I want to call her before it's too late, ya, ya, ya . . . know what they say?"

"About what?"

"If a guy doesn't get laid before he's twenty, he loses the urge, then he starts to hang around all those gay bars. Shit, Ziggy, you gotta help me out."

"If your mother keeps sending you to work with food like this, the least I can do is help out mommy's little Frog," joked Ziggy.

"Thanks, Ziggy, this chicken is only the beginning." Frog leaned back pushing glasses against his nose and wiped chicken fat from a clean hairless chin.

A stillness filled the trailer. Ziggy and Frog sat quietly, each deeply engrossed in their own thoughts. Looking up, Ziggy attempted to speak. "Frog, what do you plan to do after the summer's over, I mean are you going to continue your education, college, university or something?"

"Hell, no, what am I going to do in university, I barely made it out of high school." Frog continued to munch on mother's chicken.

"What do you think of guys like us, that go to college or university?" Ziggy made the motion of eating, but tentatively he watched and waited for Frog to answer.

"Who's going to one of those places?"

Ziggy was caught off guard. He leaned back and shrugged shoulders.

"I thought we were all going to hang around together, who is it?"

As Frog munched on the chicken, he watched Ziggy put a piece of chicken down on his plate. Ziggy's face seemed etched in thought. Ziggy knew he would be breaking away from the gang. It was his parents that wanted him to continue with education.

"It's my parents. It's them that want me to be a doctor, or lawyer, or some part of the establishment."

Frog listened carefully as Ziggy talked, and at the same time continued to devour the chicken. He knew that he should be saying something intelligent, but the right words seemed to escape him. It was usually Ziggy that had all the right things to say.

"I don't know if that's what I want to do, I don't know if I want to spend the rest of my life working in this hole." Ziggy looked up and found Frog staring. It was a blank stare as if he had not heard or understood anything said. He pushed himself away from the table and told Frog that he would catch him later.

A tin pop can, clanked along the ground from the constant kicking Ziggy was giving it. It was a pretty fair walk back to the dumping station, and the tin can, seemed to be the best way to relieve tension. Everyone seemed to look up to him, and so did the girls that he had no problem getting to like him. Up until now everything was easy, a breeze, but now his parents wanted him to make a decision that would affect the rest of his life. Inside, he did not want change, he just wanted daily life to be like it had always been. But he knew that nothing stays the same forever. That new girl, he was working with now, he never had trouble with girls like this one. She seemed to cause a build up of tension within. What was she trying to prove with that crap about equal rights, equal pay, equal work? And she comes in looking like she's ready to party, her clothes so tight and revealing, and that makeup! At any other time and place, Ziggy knew that he certainly would come on to her. Tonight though, there would be no come on, that was for sure. Maybe a raging battle between them, but certainly not a come on. It seemed that Linda was one of those girls that was out to put her stamp on All Steel. How and when she was going to be crushed was certainly something Ziggy was going to work on.

Ziggy gave the can one final kick which sent it sorely against the steel door ahead. Ziggy's treacherous abuse with the can finally came to an end. As Ziggy walked through the door, he once again faced the dust filled dungeon. He stood before the conveyor belt, just gazing down as it rolled along, piled high with ore pellets. All he heard was the clattering sound of the belt as it disappeared further down, only to come around again the other way.

The sound of the belt and the black dust seemed to swallow him up. Ziggy glanced up and down the length of the conveyor belt, and found that the girl was nowhere to be seen. Stooping down, he picked up a shovel and went through the motions of working. Along with other kinds of sounds, his current thoughts were also drowned out by the clattering of the belt as it rolled over the conveyor rollers.

Time seemed to pass, how much time was hard to imagine, but it was passing. He thought about the fact that he seemed to have shovelled a lot of pellets that had spilled on the ground off the conveyor belt. The door opened and there stood Linda, fanning the dust that had settled on her face. In the dusty corridor, Ziggy watched Linda's silhouette in the doorway. She was a beckoning sight as she swayed in those tight jeans.

"The work is in here if you don't mind," Ziggy hollered above the roaring clanking of the belt. "The shovel is waiting for your soft tender hands." Ziggy was finding it difficult to understand why he was getting on her case the way he was, but it was just the way he felt at this moment, hating the fact that he knew she could cause quite a bit of trouble.

Linda gave a sneer as she wiped hands down the sides of her body. Ziggy continued to stare, obviously attracted to what she was doing. Ziggy had no difficulty staring at Linda, though she was very attractive and certainly not hard to look at. Yet there was work to be done, and there were other girls he would rather be with. Turning his back to Linda, he emptied another shovelful of pellets.

"Hey, what's with you?" Linda shouted.

"You think you're gonna work your way to the top?"

"Do you know a better way?"

"There are ways."

"Well for now, this is the way." Ziggy grabbed the steel shovel from the ground and holding it, he dangled it in front of her. "This is your equality, shovel, these are equality pellets for equality pay, so do equality work," Ziggy spoke sarcastically as he shoved the shovel into her hand.

Linda stood firm, her eyes burning a stare into Ziggy's eyes. She shoved the shovel back into his hands. "I'll make my way to the top, my way. I'll get a good job with good pay and there will be no bums like you in my way."

Ziggy watched Linda walk away. Those tight jeans disappeared in the darkness of the coke dust as she exited out the door. He sent the shovel sailing through the air, only to land on the bus that would deliver it into the fiery mouth of the furnace along with the rest of the pellets. "Where the hell do you think, you're going?" There was no reply, just the clanking of the belts. 'Dumb broad,' Ziggy said to himself as he started to shovel the pellets with a new-found energy. As he shovelled furiously, other thoughts preoccupied his mind. School, as mom and dad wanted, or to stay here with the guys. But what kind of life would this be? Some good times, sure, but nothing ever lasts forever.

"What'cha lookin' for?"

Clank! Salami's hat clipped the edge of the trailer. He was startled by a soft voice. He knew it was not Boo's. 'Where had Boo gone,' Salami thought to himself, 'he was right here a second ago, while I was checking beneath the trailer'.

"Did you lose something?" a soft voice asked.

Salami stood up and turned around to face who was speaking to him. His mouth dropped open, the voice did not match the person. She could, and just might crush him if he said the wrong thing.

"Uh . . ., someone . . ., someone called for a plumber." Salami eyed her carefully just in case he had to make a run for it. He did not see any resemblance of a girl, just the voice. Salami noticed the unbelievable rolls and rolls of fat, he could have mistaken her for a Sumo wrestler. A smile vanished before it could get to his lips.

"There's a leak . . ., uh . . ., water leaking from one of these trailers, someone called, I'm supposed to look for it."

"Well go ahead and look, and fix it, I'll be looking for you if there's no hot water when I come to wash up."

The Sumo wrestler-like girl brushed by Salami while he turned away pretending to pay attention to something underneath the trailer. 'She must work out in a gym,' Salami thought. He wiped his nose with the back of a hand and grabbing his hat from beneath the trailer, quickly headed away from the trailer in search of Boo.

Salami made his way up the steel steps to the welfare room to peer out over the dock area. It was a peaceful looking view, the calm lake, reflecting the moon's glow and the big Lakers that were sitting motionless at their moorings. This view somehow made him feel good, like he belonged here. As if he were a part of the happenings that were going on here. In life, there had not been much that he wanted. He had been happy with having a little loose change, some beers, and good times that he had with the guys.

"Hey Boo," Salami called out as he entered the smoky welfare room. Boo was sitting in the corner with his feet up on the bench, others were either sleeping, playing cards, or chattering about unimportant things. For Salami and Boo, every day seemed to be different and every day brought something new; a new venture or new scheme, something that always kept life exciting.

"If we could sign this big fat broad that I just saw, we could make big money in the wrestling ring, man she's big!" Salami's arms spread open to try and show how big she was . . . , whack! Salami knocked the hat off some guy that was sleeping against the wall. Jumping up, the little ole' guy said something in Italian, but Salami just ignored him until he gave up and left. "Man! Big! She even smelled worse than some guys we know!"

"How far from the trailers is the repair shack?" Boo asked. He had an idea and Salami seemed to sense it. Never a dull moment.

"A . . ., about ten feet . . ., y . . . you . . . got a good idea?" A devilish grin covered Boo's lips, and Salami knew that they were in for a good time.

"Hey, we gotta be careful, you know that big broad, if she catches us, she'll be breaking all our bones one at a time."

Sitting up and pulling a knife from his pocket, Boo began scratching something on the green coloured bench. "This is what we're going to do." A plan was being set in motion. By the next shift, they would be raking in the money.

The main walkway doors swung open, clanking against the slime green brick wall behind it. It was Reese who appeared, a cigar travelling from one side of his mouth to the other. As the door opened and Reese stood there looking around, Boo and Salami were hidden behind the door. Puffing on his cigar, Reese created a virtual cloud of smoke in front of his face. A little man peering out from behind Reese pointed a finger to where Boo and Salami had been. Reese swung around suddenly puffing smoke into the old man's face, and slammed the door against the slimy green wall of the welfare room.

Boo and Salami had escaped Reese's sight, stopping on the landing to peer out over the lake as Salami had earlier; each thinking their own thoughts, they felt inspired by the view.

Salami mumbled something first. Then the words he wanted to say came out. "Do . . ., Do . . ., Do you think Rita is pregnant, really pregnant?"

"She said she was."

"I know she said it, you told me." Salami leaned back against the wall with the hard hat banging several times against the bricks. His face revealed some very deep thoughts that he was bothered by and needed some questions answered, truly answered. Was it a good idea to ask Boo, who always seemed mysterious? He never gave responsible answers, maybe it was his background. None of the guys knew if he had any parents, brothers, sisters or in fact where he lived. Salami thought maybe he should wait and ask Ziggy. He would have a responsible answer. "Boo, do you think I should get some money and get rid of it?"

Boo turned quickly, his eyes were black as if something had cut deeply into them, as if striking a personal nerve. His hand gripped the rusted railing, white appearing on Boo's knuckles and he answered slowly. "Hey, give the kid a break, the kid hasn't done anything wrong yet, Rita's a good gal, marry her, you ain't got nothing to lose, and you have everything to gain."

What Boo had said, surprised Salami. It sounded unusual coming from someone like Boo. Though it was exactly what he wanted someone to tell him. Salami had come from a big Italian family, and he liked it. He would not mind having a big family of his own.

Boo glanced one last time at the lake and then turned and headed down the stairs with Salami following quickly behind, calling out. "Thanks Boo, I . . ., I . . ., I'm going to marry her." A huge smile covered Salami's face from ear-to-ear. He did a little dance, letting Boo in on all his plans, for the future. Salami noticed that there was a slight gleam in Boo's eyes, but one would have to look very deep to see it.

Reese puffed feverishly on the cigar as he pushed his way through the control room doors. He was still very angry after missing an opportunity to catch Salami and Boo being somewhere they were not supposed to be. Reese eyed the girl with her tight jeans showing the outline of the seams of panties beneath. Taking in an eyeful, Reese waited for a moment before verbally coming down on her. "What are you doing here? Aren't you supposed to be at the dumping station with Ziggy?"

Taking a deep breath, she turned to face Reese, her full breasts caught Reese by surprise as he chomped on the cigar. "I came here to see you about my job and working with Ziggy."

"You can't handle your job? Well, that's easily remedied, I'll just send you back to employment."

Linda looked around and noticed that the room was empty, it was just her and Reese. She leaned back against the desk and slowly began to spread her legs. Reese felt a sudden surge in his loins as he eyed the seams of her panties showing on the front of the jeans. "I like my job . . .," she spoke in a sultry voice, reminiscent of Marilyn Monroe, "but that guy Ziggy keeps making advances. I would not mind if it were someone strong and handsome and more authoritative. You're very authoritative," she added. While Linda spoke in a sultry voice, she caressed thighs with a hand rubbing particularly hard on the seams of her panties.

Reese removed the cigar from his mouth and wiped the slobber from parted lips. His eyes were glued to her legs. He did not particularly like girls working in his mill, and he also did not like Ziggy and his chums. "Well, I don't give good jobs to just anybody, unless they earn them. Are you willing to earn it?"

"Yes," Linda replied enthusiastically, "I'll do anything for you, I'll earn a good job." She eyed Reese up and down and pretended to lick her lips as she played with the button on her blouse. Linda knew what she was doing and she knew that Reese was going to play.

Looking around the control room, Reese wished that this had been a more secluded place, behind the control board. Reese knew that was secure, and that no one would bother them. He reached for the handle of the door of the control room, and opening the door, he examined the inside surroundings. The room was dark and rather small, but Linda edged Reese into a corner and started caressing his hips with her hands. Reese dropped the chewed-up cigar, his hands reaching to caress her firm breasts. Reese learned the game quickly. Every movement that was made in the dark room somehow seemed louder than the humming of the controls. The clicking as their zippers went down, the moaning as each fondled each other, and pressed their bodies closer and closer. They were pressed back into the corner as far as they possibly could have gotten in the hidden space behind the furnace controls.

Frog stuck his head inside the office door of the control room and searched for Reese. It was almost time to cast and everything was ready to go. The furnace would surely burst its seams if they did not tap it soon. He walked into the control room and called out Reese's name in sort of a whisper, knowing full well that Reese would probably bark back at him. Shrugging shoulders, he sat down on the bench to wait for Reese.

Out of sheer boredom, Frog watched the meters and the needles fluctuate, they seemed to go on endlessly. Each day that Frog had come into this room the hum had been the same, never changing until now. Frog straightened himself up and pushed glasses against the back of his nose while listening to the strange sound. It did not sound like the humming of the meters.

'Thud . . ., thud . . ., thud.' With each thud the meter at the end of the control board seemed to swing erratically. 'Thud . . . thud . . . thud.' 'There's something wrong,' thought Frog to himself, 'I better get someone.' 'Thud . . . thud . . . thud.' Getting close to the meter, Frog tapped the meter. That did not seem to work, it did not stop. 'Thud . . ., thud . . ., thud.'

There was one thing for certain, Frog had plenty of curiosity. He reached for the handle leading to the control room and pushed the door slightly ajar. He peered through the crack until his eyes became accustomed to the dim light. 'Thud . . . thud . . . thud.' Frog could see. What he saw was Linda heaving as Reese pushed against her, then the sound again. 'Thud . . . thud . . . thud.'

Frog opened the door a little further and felt an urge building up inside which necessitated pushing his legs together. This was unbelievable, more than Frog could handle at this moment. He had to know who it was. 'Thud, thud.' Suddenly two faces turned towards the opened door as the light blinded them temporarily. Reese pushed hard against Linda and at the same time grabbed pants as Linda moaned. Had it been satisfaction or despair? Frog had sure gotten an eyeful before retreating to the cast house. He could not wait to tell the guys.

"It's about time you came," called out one of the men when Reese showed up on the cast house floor. Reese wiped sweat from his forehead and eyed one man after another. Were they all guilty, all of them? Which one had it been that had seen him? 'Was it him,' he thought.

Frog pretended to be staring in space, wondering what the other guys were gonna think of this and what they were gonna do. It was hard to believe that Reese, and that new girl were making out in the control room, but Frog had seen it for himself, it had been as plain as day. Crossing his legs, Frog relived those brief moments of ecstasy between Reese and Linda, and he fantasized that he had been in the control room with Linda, not Reese. 'If only wishing made it so,' he thought as his mind drifted, afterthoughts of Penelope.

"I kept hearing this thud . . ., thud . . ., thud," said Frog to the guys in the trailer. The scene was being described with every gesture that Frog could make to simulate what he had seen in the control room. Laughter filled the room as Salami rolled around the beat-up sofa, holding the sides of his stomach because the laughter was making his stomach ache.

"The needle was going like this," Frog explained waving an arm back and forth, and the rest of the boys yelled in unison, "Thud . . ., thud . . ., thud."

"Now we know how she's going to work her way to the top job."

There was a sting to that statement, especially with the present conflict between Ziggy and Linda.

"Boo, too bad we could not have gotten some pictures of Linda working her way to the top," Salami joked.

With Boo's ever scheming grin, he just nodded and pressed a length of pipe together.

"But, first," with a finger pointing skyward and a beer in the other hand, Salami balanced himself on the edge of the sofa. "we'll set up a pre-showing and charge a small admission fee."

Frog leaned closer to Boo as he watched the pipe being moulded into a twisting shape. "But, well, will this thing work?"

"Will it work, has anything we've ever done, not worked?" Salami asked. "It will work, Boo, won't it?"

Without even looking, Boo shrugged shoulders, "It might."

"It will," Salami boasted confidently as he swigged away on a beer. Salami kept a watchful eye on all the aspects of the construction.

Ziggy did not seem to be participating in the assembly of this apparatus. His thoughts were on Linda, and her way of doing things, and what his destination in life was going to be. When should he decide about whether he was going to stay with the gang or change his direction in life? Did he really want to spend four years or more getting a degree? And then working another fifty-years before being able to do all the things he always wanted to do. Taking advantage of the good years now, and get the best out of life now that he was young. He would worry about life later. That was the way he wanted things to go. Right now, it was just too confusing, so he stared at Boo, who never seemed to worry about things. Boo just took things as they came. 'Why am I not more like Boo,' he thought to himself as he emptied the last gulp of beer. Ziggy tossed the bottle into the garbage can. Smiling to himself, he thought that at least he had gotten something right tonight.

"Salami," Boo called out, "we need a mirror up in the locker room and some kind of magnifier, a level or a transit."

"No problem," Salami boasted proudly, tossing a beer bottle past Ziggy towards the garbage can. The outcome was not quite the same, "Shit, almost," Salami cursed. Salami headed out the door, and Boo continued to construct the whatever it was. Frog slid in behind the table across from Ziggy.

"Ziggy," Frog whispered several times, "Ziggy, I gotta talk to you."

"About what?"

"Well, that night and Penelope."

"Go on."

"After seeing what I've seen, you know, Linda and Reese, I got to . . ., thinking." Frog's horn-rimmed glasses rested low on his nose. He leaned closer to the table, and Ziggy leaned closer to Frog, anticipating being told something intriguing.

"You know what it's like, Boo and even Salami knows . . ., so . . .,"

Ziggy tried to figure out what Frog was talking about. "We know what what's like," he asked, perplexed.

"He wants to get laid!" yelled Boo.

Frog rested a blushing head on the table, his face hidden behind a beer bottle, "And I think he wants to get laid, with Penelope Snidermost."

"Well, I want to know what its like before it's too late," Frog said quietly, a sound of despair in his voice.

'More things to do and worry about,' thought Ziggy, he had an image to uphold and Frog was a friend. "Just for you, Frog, I'll see what I can do about getting you and Miss. Snidermost together."

CHAPTER SEVEN
Play the Game

Finally, placing the last section of pipe down the side of the wall, Boo peered out through the cracks in the wall. The three to eleven shift and the eleven to seven shift were over, and Boo had remained in the plant past his regular shift to set up the apparatus of pipe and haywire. Golden rays of sunlight sparkled through specks of graphite falling from the sky. This might seem like pollution to some, but for a moment, Boo was caught up in the splendour of the dancing rays of the early morning sun that had washed away the night.

This had not been the first time that Boo had stayed in the plant beyond his regular shift. At times, it seemed as if Boo had spent days in the plant without leaving. In the trailer, there was a bed and food, television and girls, so, often there was no need to leave. Many times, the guys had wondered if there was anything or anyone waiting for him, but as before, they never pursued the subject further.

Hidden within an old oil barrel with a small hole on the side, an elevation level sat with its lenses focussed on a mirror. After adjusting the focus, Boo pressedan eye to the hole in the barrel. A blurred image first appeared and then more came in focus, the image came in from the level through a pipe, up the wall, across a pipe bridge, down a trailer vent, which caused the light to reflect on the mirrors. A figure appeared on the periscope lens. This brought a pleased grin on Boo's face.

. . . .

Ziggy and Salami continued to chat as they lounged across Reese's desk. The other guys slowly drifted in to get their orders from Reese. Salami took a bite from a salami sausage without stopping his conversation. Ziggy tried not to watch, but could not help but listen to what he was saying.

"She's a good cook," he said. "and her mother is even better so . . .,"

"So, so, what's that got to do with Rita?"

"Well, if she can't cook, her mother will, they like me. Whenever I'm there, they feed me until it's time to leave."

"That's love? You're not marrying her mother."

"No, but if I ever ask Rita to get married, I know I'll never starve. Now here's a very important question." Salami bit off another chunk of salami sausage and Ziggy turned away. "I'm supposed to go to her house tonight, and I'm going to ask her, but I don't know how."

Ziggy was not listening. He elbowed Salami as he took another bite of salami, it seemed that he had a bottomless pit, no matter how much he ate, he never seemed to be full.

"Salami, look over there." Ziggy had noticed Reese coming up the stairs to the cat walk and then watched him stop to talk to someone.

"Hey, that's your friend Linda, and they're sneaking into the power room."

"Maybe Frog did see something after all. Let's go Salami."

Swallowing the rest of the salami sandwich, the two headed across the cast house to the cat walk, to the other side of the power room. Creeping very slowly along the cast house wall to the power room, they listened to the voices. Ziggy raised a hand to stop Salami, as the two pushed their ears to a rotting corrugate wall.

"I did not figure out who opened the door, but I don't think anyone is onto us," Ziggy and Salami heard Reese's voice say.

Linda pressed closer, pushing Reese against the wall. "That's not important, what's important is that we understand each other".

"Scratch my back and I'll scratch yours,"

"Something like that." Now let's talk favours. I want a better job, something cleaner and not too strenuous. I want that guy, Ziggy as far away from me as possible." She caressed Reese's lips gently with the tip of a finger. "Now, what can I do for you?"

Reese's heart was beating and pounding feverishly, he felt a surge building up in his groin. "Hey, I'm like you, I want a cleaner job and I want to move up in this organization but there's a general foreman that needs his back scratched."

"Ooo . . ., when do I meet your boss?"

Ziggy motioned Salami to move. Hurriedly they headed to the control room.

"Ziggy, what are we gonna do about this?" Salami swallowed hard. "They're going to try to get rid of you or make it so tough you won't want to work here."

"We'll do something all right," Ziggy turned away.

Linda and Reese walked in, as if the pair were the worst of enemies.

Sitting down, Reese took a pencil in hand and with a swift stroke on the work sheet ended what Salami and Ziggy knew to be their jobs. The office was empty during the time they waited for their assignment. Without looking into their scorning faces, Reese said, "You two, the pit, and I'll be down there later on to make sure that the coke is cleaned out."

Salami brushed close to Reese's chair, banging it, letting him know that he was ticked off about this assignment. Once outside the door, Ziggy motioned to Salami while he waited and watched Reese's moves. While Reese picked up the phone, Ziggy slipped the brim of his hard hat between the door and the jam.

"Hello, Wendle, I'm calling about that day job on NO. 4 furnace."

'Shit,' thought Ziggy to himself, 'he sure isn't wasting much time.'

"Yea, I want that day job, I, I, want that day job, I know I'm not in line for it, but I've got something you could use in exchange for the promotion. We'll be in the old welfare room at No. 3 furnace, let's say . . ., about ten o'clock?"

Easing the hat from the door, Ziggy contemplated the situation and started to plan an attack on Reese. 'Boo and his camera,' thought Ziggy as he and Salami headed down to the trailer.

"Frog, get away from there." With his eye, as close to the barrel as possible, Frog adjusted the level. "There won't be any girls in there till shift change, so you just better rest those excited hormones of yours, Okay." Boo said.

"We'll make a killing with this thing."

"Just be careful who you tell." Boo placed the last of the steel bars against the walls to camouflage the periscope.

"Hey, Boo, do you have any film left in that camera? What the hell is Frog doing?" asked Ziggy.

"That's our periscope into the girls change room."

"Does it work?"

"It must, Frog hasn't taken his eyes away from it for the past hour."

Ziggy leaned closer to Frog to get an idea of the set-up. "What do you see Frog?"

"Just a bunch of showers."

"No girls?" asked Ziggy, to Frog's shaking head. "That film, Boo, do you have any?"

"Yea, what do you want to take pictures of?"

"Not me, you, I want you to take pictures of Linda and the general foreman, I think it's him, they are going to meet in the old welfare room at number 3 furnace at ten o'clock."

"And you want me there before they get there to catch them in the act?"

"Right, and make sure you are hidden."

"No problem, Zig." Boo slammed the lid of the barrel down, making Frog jump away in surprise. "That's enough now. Start spreading the word. First showing at two o'clock and make sure you tell them it's a buck for a half minute." Frog scurried away as Boo concealed the eye hole.

. . . .

Climbing down into the pit, Ziggy told Salami what the situation was, and at the same time he eyed the amount of coke that needed to be removed. "We'll get some pictures of Linda and the General foreman together.

"That bitch is sure trying to make waves. What are you gonna do with the pictures?"

"That will be our insurance that our jobs will still be here."

Picking up a shovelful of coke, Ziggy flung it with a furious speed.

A little while later, Salami brought up the subject of Rita. It was not that Ziggy would not help Salami, it was just that Ziggy was never put into this kind of situation before. He loved girls and then left them. He was never tied down, and if Salami asked for help, Ziggy would try.

"How do I ask her? Do I bring her flowers and candy, and then get down on one knee and propose?"

"Hell no, you've been watching too many old movies." Ziggy, paused for a moment and eyed Salami, his hair was a mess and his boots were untied. The buttons on his shirt were in the wrong holes. "What the hell do you want to get married for? What's to say she wants you?"

"She's knocked up! If she was not, we'd probably get hitched in a couple of years anyway."

"Hell! Okay, first you show her you're the dominant one. Passionately take her in your arms and look deep into her eyes with no expression on your face, and you ask her. Before she has time to think about it, you kiss her."

Salami stood with the shovel in his arms, his eyes glaring at the handle. "How do I know if she will or won't, if I don't wait for her answer."

Ziggy shoved his shovel deep into the coke and leaned on it, shaking his head. "Salami, that's the idea. Keep them off step. Always be one step ahead of them." Looking at Salami's clothes, he said, "And make sure you get dressed for the occasion. Now take your shovel and try it again and don't wait for an answer."

Taking the shovel, Salami pulled it close to him, kissing it as he mumbled, "Wi . . ., wil, will you marry me?"

Shaking his head, Ziggy turned away, knowing too well that Salami would go about it in his own backward kind of way.

. . . .

Walking along the cat walk, Boo kept a cautious eye open, to make sure that he was not seen going into number 3 furnace. Under the shirt, he concealed the camera that he was going to use to take the pictures that Ziggy requested. Boo had other ideas as to what to do with the pictures, and what he wanted to do to Linda, as if he was the victim. Then again, Boo did not need a reason to justify his actions.

The old number 3 furnace had not been in operation for the past fifteen years, but instead of tearing it down, they just let it stand to collect dust, and use it for a tax write off for having the furnace on the property. It was in no way operational, and most of the important parts had already been removed. The only thing that remained of the structure was the shell of the furnace itself. Cobwebs hung endlessly and everywhere from the corroded pipes.

One would imagine huge spiders to come scampering to claim their prey. At night, the emptiness of the silent steel furnace would be enough to send shivers up the spine of any feeble person. Boo grinned at the thought of Frog walking alone in this maze of steel.

Back in the corner of the cast house was the welfare room, which pretty-well remained intact. Sometimes workers who were seeking somewhere to hide from their work would seek out the seclusion of this welfare room. In one corner of the welfare room was a table and along the wall, the now dilapidated benches. A lone solitary light bulb shone dimly in the centre of the room. Except for the once white suspended ceiling, the only other noticeable decoration in the room were the pin-up pictures that lined the walls. Boo glanced at the pictures, noticing the dates. The playboy pin-ups had been around for a long time, because the playboy girls had clothes on. Boo shook the table to test how strong it was before climbing on. Sensing that it was strong enough, he climbed on the table and lifted the ceiling panel. It was hard to see into the ceiling, but he judged that it would probably hold his weight. Placing the camera on one of the ceiling panels, he pulled himself up into the dark recesses of the suspended ceiling. He balanced himself on the beams and placed the panel back into place. With a small pocket knife, he cut several holes in the ceiling panel. It would be just a matter of waiting for the prey, so to speak. Boo checked out the holes to make sure that he could focus through them with the camera. He focussed the camera to make sure that he was able to photograph the different corners of the room.

Brushing cobwebs and dust from her shoulders and hair, Linda cautiously peeked into the room, she was relieved to find it empty. Being satisfied that there was no one else around, she boldly walked in. Boo watched her brush lose braided hair and roll lip gloss across puckered lips. She unfastened top shirt buttons just enough to reveal a tantalizing view of firm breasts. Linda had a good deal to show, and Boo hoped to be able to get some great shots.

Having given the room, the once over, she tried sitting down and then tried kneeling against the bench, but decided to lean against the table with legs slightly parted.

'If she stayed there,' Boo thought, 'I will get some good shots.'

It was past ten, a good twenty minutes past ten, and Linda seemed to be getting a little edgy. Boo was also getting to be a little edgy, especially in the cramped quarters of this suspended ceiling. The sound of shuffling feet startled Linda and Boo. What appeared was a thin goggle-eyed man with a green hat. Linda's first reaction was to escape this situation. She thought that getting involved with Reese, to get what she wanted was bad enough, but this guy was obviously worse. If he had been a woman, he would probably would have been an unwanted spinster. 'But a job was a job,' Linda thought as she smiled weakly, pressing shoulders back. Linda's abundant breasts was the first thing that caught the general foreman's eye.

Removing his hat, Wendle, slouching from the hips up, peered through thick glasses. He now appreciated what he was going to be getting himself into, and this excited him even more. There was no need for either of them to speak, both knew what they had to do. As Wendle approached Linda, she undid one button and then the next, and then the next, until firm young breasts were bare and totally exposed to Wendle's view. Boo was not waiting around for the perfect pose, he just kept clicking shot after shot, after shot.

With a loud bang that startled Boo, he seemed to be very-much on edge up here on the suspended ceiling. Wendle dropped his hat and gloves and reached for Linda. Wendle was not sure what to do, but he did stop caressing Linda long enough to unzip pant zippers. Throughout all happening down below, the camera continued clicking, picture after picture, after picture. There was no time to wonder how many shots were left. When he ran out, he ran out, Boo was not worried, he already knew he had a lot of wonderful pictures. Wendle lifted Linda onto the table. This was becoming too much for Boo. He continued to carefully balance himself on the beams. The sounds of the creaking table rang in Boo's ear, as he watched Wendle rocking back and forth with Linda egging him on.

Boo focussed the camera for a better shot. He slipped slightly from the perch and a foot struck the panel sending flakes of dust downward onto Wendle and Linda.

"The ceiling is falling," Linda exclaimed nervously.

"No, it won't, not yet," added Wendle. But it did not matter how close to ecstasy Wendle was, Boo could no-longer balance on the beam.

"It's falling!" The panel above them cracked and the anticipated danger that Linda had felt, was now too close for comfort. Boo tried to grab the next beam but his motion was not fast enough for the dropping of his body. His weight split the panel and chunks fell onto the table. Linda pushed herself away from Wendle just as Wendle exploded from sexual ecstasy. Each clutched their clothes and scrambled for the door as the panel above them fell crashing to the floor. Kicking frantically, Boo sent another panel crashing downward. Wendle and Linda ran out the door without even bothering to look up.

"Another time," Linda said as she headed for the cat walk. Wendle brushed at wet pants in an attempt to dry them before emerging into the open cat walk.

Dangling from the beam, Boo held in an explosive laughter that was dying to come bellowing out. The scene had been, absolutely, too much, and he wondered if he had caught those last ecstatic moments on film. He waited for the longest time dangling from the perch in the ceiling.

. . . .

Down in the pit, Ziggy continued to shovel the sloppy coke. He was fighting another battle in his mind, struggling with thoughts that he could not seem to shake. "So, who cares if Linda gets ahead. Who cares if I get shoved around, who cares?" Everyone cares, that is the problem. The guys cared if he stayed around working with them. His parents cared if he went to University. Ziggy cared about other people, and not about himself. It seemed as if he had no will of his own, no chance to decide what he wanted to do! With every thought that entered his head, he managed to shovel faster and faster, flinging the coke from the shovel. Like the thoughts that were swirling around in his head, the coke in the pit never seemed to end either. It would have been much simpler if he was not told that it was up to him to do what he wanted to do.

Salami watched from above, waiting for a chance to descend the ladder, but as long as Ziggy kept throwing the coke viciously against the wall, he knew he was not about to go down with Ziggy out of control. Anyway, it was just about quitting time.

"Hey, Ziggy, Ziggy, it's time to quit, come on, let's get out of here," yelled Salami. Their eyes met as another shovelful of coke smashed against the wall. Salami knew that Ziggy had something on his mind, but he was not about to get him any more upset then the man already was. "See you at the periscope."

Ziggy flung several more shovelfuls of coke against the wall. Ziggy felt that the shovelling and smashing of coke up against the wall seemed to help relieve the anger inside. It had been a good way to get all this anger out of his system just before quitting time. No sooner had the thought of leaving the pit crossed his mind when the scale-car was heard rumbling overhead. It seemed that spillage was always prevalent when Porky was running the scale-car. With a furious force, Ziggy flung the shovel against the wall. The faces of the enemy were foremost in his mind, Linda, Reese and Porky. It seemed that being with the other guys was his only way of escaping problems, of escaping reality.

. . . .

The money felt good in Salami's hands. There had been plenty of exchanges of money for an opportunity to peek into the periscope. Customer after customer entered the building, and when they walked out, their eyes bulged from what they had seen.

"End of the line," said Salami, pointing to the growing line of men waiting to get a peek at the female workers. Many of the workers had worked with the women every day, and perhaps sometimes fantasized about them. Now, they could view them in the flesh, naked as a jaybird, and for only a buck. Of course, Frog took a turn in line several times. Even though every time he peeked his glasses kept fogging up.

"Okay, Frog clean your glasses and get back in line." Boo clicked the stop watch. "Next."

It was the shift change and there would be plenty of female bodies strutting around, coming and going. There were plenty of female workers. The top brass thought that they would not be able to hack the work, so this trailer had been set up temporarily, instead of a regular building, thinking that many of them would not last very long. As it turns out, the trailer was extremely over-crowded. They were promised a new building, perhaps sometime in the future but for now, Frog hoped that the future was a long way away.

Frog listened to the men at the end of the line, as he eagerly wiped eye glasses clean.

"I'm in love, she's beautiful, she's got cannons like this."

Frog gawked at the exaggeration.

"She's a millwright's helper. I'm going to ask the foreman to get her on my crew."

"Which one is she?" Frog asked.

"The one with the big cans, you can't miss her."

"No way," butted in another worker. "Lise has bigger cans than her."

"Which one is she?" asked Frog, again hoping to get a better description.

"Next," Boo called out. As another eye focused at the eye hole. The watch clicked.

"Hey, I see nothing," roared an older guy in broken dialect.

"What? Let me take a look." Boo pressed an eye to the level and adjusted the focus. "It's perfect, a great view and your getting your money's worth."

"A big lady, she's blocking my view."

"She's all woman, that's Big Bula. She's got too much for a little guy like you to handle, you just take another look, on the house."

Inside the trailer, a 250-pound woman walked around making room for herself. She was known to everyone as Big Bula. The big bear from Bruce Mines. A good man, correction, a woman to have around, Bula could outwork half the men in the plant and most were scared shitless of her. As she paraded around in the flesh, you could not help but wonder where the shape of a woman had gone, or was it just lost under all that muscle? She had stopped in the centre of the room and looked about. Bula eyed the other girls, then she eyed the door and eyed the wall. Then in her big husky voice she bellowed, unravelling the nerves of all the other girls. "Who the hell is watching me? I think someone is spying on me behind my back." The rest of the girls glanced at her then quickly looked away. "I don't like anyone looking at me funny behind my back. I'll break your damn necks if I catch you spying on me behind my back." Bula sneered at everyone then pushed her way into the showers.

"Good, she's gone." The old guy smiled up at Boo.

"Have a good look, but not too much, the excitement might kill you."

"Hey, your money. No money, no peek." Salami did not look up, the money in his hands was most important. "Hey, pay the buck."

Ziggy waited until Salami had finished counting the money. "I don't need to pay to see the girls."

"Oh, it's you Ziggy, come on in," Salami ushered him in, and then collected a buck from the next guy.

Ziggy noticed Boo, and yelled out, "Hey Boo, how'd it go?"

"No problem, it's all on film." Boo's sinister grin seemed to ease Ziggy's mind.

CHAPTER EIGHT
Just Once

While the other guys were preoccupied with sending the male population of the plant into a sexual frenzy, Ziggy eased back and enjoyed the comfort of the trailer. He was toying with the receiver of the telephone that Salami had lifted, and contemplated the thought of Frog and Penelope together. An unlikely pair at best, but there was some kind of a physical attraction that seemed to have drawn these two together the night of their graduation dance and the party afterwards. 'Was there still something there,' Ziggy thought, at least for Frog's sake, he would attempt to get them back together again.

Ziggy listened to the ring within the receiver. While he listened to it ring several times, Ziggy knew what he was going to say. It could take a bit of pleading, but no girl had ever turned him down, and this one would be no different.

"Hello," the voice at the other end answered.

Ziggy hesitated for a moment and then spoke, "Hello, would Miss. Snidermost be home?" Ziggy asked in a rather seductive voice.

"May I ask who's calling?"

"This is Ziggy."

"One moment please. There's a call for you Miss. Penelope, from a Mr. Ziggy," he heard the lady at the other end of the phone call out. Ziggy balked at the thought of being referred to as Mr. Ziggy.

Penelope scurried down the hall to her pink bedroom and grabbed the telephone on the bedside table. She hesitated for a moment knowing that it was usually proper for ladies to be a little slow in responding. While nibbling on finger nails, she wondered why Ziggy would be calling her. "Hello, Penelope speaking." The thumbnail was too short, so she picked at a baby fingernail instead, nibbling on it as she felt a rousing ache build within at the sound of Ziggy's voice.

"Penelope, I was wondering, if by chance, tonight if you . . ., would consider an invitation to take in the town. We could kind of make it a double date, I would be so pleased if you would consider showing your date the finer aspects of life. Frog would be so pleased to escort you tonight." Gasping for breath, he waited for the slamming of the phone or the screeching cry of a half mad girl.

"I'd be honoured to double date with you, I think Frog would be an excellent escort."

"Uh . . ., yeah!"

"What time should I be ready."

"Oh, say, about eight?"

"Thank you, good bye."

Staring at the receiver, as if it had all been a dream, Ziggy wondered if Frog needed any assistance at all.

"Hey, Ziggy, you done with the phone?" Salami asked, hurrying to pick up the receiver. "Tonight's going to be the night."

"Yea, you said it," Ziggy thought of Penelope and Frog, not of what Salami was saying.

"Thanks to your coaching, tonight me and Rita will get almost hitched." Salami noticed the bewildered look on Ziggy's face. "Something wrong?"

"No, just that Penelope Snidermost, just said she would go out with Frog."

"You're kidding."

"Now, I'm going to tell Frog."

Watching Ziggy leave the trailer, Salami dialled Rita's number. "Hello, is Rita there?" Rita's mother answered in her usual warm Italian accent.

"Rita, not here, Salami, she be back for supper. Ah, you nice boy, you come too, I make plenty good food for you."

"Thank you, I'll be there, good bye." Salami rubbed his stomach with both hands, and a big smile covered his face knowing how great her cooking was!

. . . .

"Watch where the hell you're going." A big husky voice called out, but it was too late. Boo was sent flying through the air, while at the same time trying to clutch onto the level in his hand. The notorious big Bula lumbered past. Boo, nestled against the garbage cans, protected the level from harm. He stared, watching big Bula waddling away down the road. Under a breath, he muttered, "Yuk!"

Frog, was dancing around as if he was on cloud nine, noticed Boo. "I'm in heaven, I'm going to get laid." Frog rambled on, leaving Boo struggling to get back on his feet. Boo extended a hand to Ziggy who he had hoped would give him a hand, but he too walked by leaving him amongst the garbage. Ziggy was mumbling something, something about a double date with Penelope Snidermost. Dumbfounded, Boo managed to get to his feet and followed them, brushing discarded salad from filthy clothes.

96

. . . .

"You invited who?" Rita pounded the kitchen cupboard. Her sweet mother looked at her quite heartbroken. "He hasn't called me in almost a week, and the first time he calls you asked him for supper?"

"Ah, he's a nice boy, don't you like him?" She reached out and patted Rita's head like a little puppy. A tear rolled down the corner of Rita's eye and with a soft touch her mother wiped it away. "He's a nice boy, the whole family likes him."

"I like him too, but he just doesn't know how I feel, he doesn't feel the same way I do about things."

"What kind of things?"

"Oh, just things," Rita fell into her mom's open arms, feeling the warmth of motherly love.

"Well, just before supper, you take him into the living room, just the two of you and talk. I keep everybody else away, okay?" Rita nodded.

Keeping everybody away was a task in itself. Besides Rita's Mom and Dad, there were eight kids all under the age of thirteen. Grandpa could not be forgotten, although he never paid much attention to anyone or butted in. As long as he could eat, he was usually satisfied. Like any close Italian family, a family meal without the rest of the family was certainly frowned upon. So tonight, there would also be Aunt Anna, and her husband, and their six children, all joining in the family meal.

Knowing that tonight was supposed to be a very special night, Salami thought that he should do it up right. He was dressed in his very-best black dress pants, very-best white shirt and black vest, and of course customary sloppy running shoes for good luck. Chocolates seemed appropriate, well actually a couple of chocolate bars would do, and the flowers that he had, were swiped from next, actually, Aunt Anna's to be exact. Salami stood quietly facing Rita's door. He hesitated to knock, knowing that maybe Rita would want nothing to do with him. He did not have long to wait before the door was opened and he came face to face with about ten eager faces. Of course, all the kids standing there at the door spotted the chocolate bars and flowers; flowers for Rita and chocolate bars for them. Once the kids had been hurried away and the dust cleared, Rita stood there facing Salami. She wanted to hug and hold him, but had promised herself to wait and see what Salami's motives would be tonight.

"These are for you," Salami blurted out, holding out the chocolate bars and flowers. Then he stood his ground, not knowing what to expect. Rita accepted the peace offering, and at the same time leaned out and glanced at the house next door. As she had thought, the tulips of course, came from her Aunt's house. She gave Salami a little smile and walked back into the house. "Come in Salami, we can sit in the living room until supper."

Salami had expected to see a herd of kids at every turn. Looking around, he did not see any of them, so he followed Rita to the couch in the living room. To his surprise, there did not seem to be a single soul in sight. This was certainly a very different situation from others he had encountered in this house. Everything seemed to be going smoothly. Now, if he could only get lips moving and get the worst over with. "Rita."

"Yes," she responded. She seemed to answer too quickly for Salami's liking. For a moment, they looked at each other and did not know what to expect.

"I know I haven't called lately, and we haven't talked about things much, but I do like you. I like you a-lot, I think." He attempted to kneel then changed his mind. Instead he reached for her hand and ended up holding the tulips. "We've been together for a long time, me and you, and I don't want to be without you," he said. Balancing on the edge of the couch with one knee almost on the floor, Salami felt that this was the moment. He eased closer to Rita and felt a cool touch of her hand.

"Supper's ready." Unwanted little brats barged into the room with their voices echoing, seeming to drown out anything Salami might have said. "Come and get it, supper's ready."

Jumping up with tulips in hand, Salami was tempted to beat each one. To beat the living daylights out of them. Rita grabbed the flowers back before any further damage could be done. It seemed that the opportunity was gone now, and he would have to work up his nerve again and wait until later, when maybe they could be alone again.

When Rita and Salami walked into the kitchen, all eyes were on them, all but Grandpa who just sat there waiting for his food. Taking Salami's arm, Rita's Mom sat him to the right of her husband and across from Grandpa, whose eyes stared at him as if he were the main course. Rita sat herself down beside Salami and felt her hands shaking just a little bit. There was so much to talk about. She would not be able to pretend that she was not pregnant, at least not for the next nine months, sooner or later everyone would know who the father was. After all, she had only gone out with Salami, so it was natural that everyone would know.

When everyone was seated, and the kids were seated at little tables of their own, Rita's Dad said grace. Rita's Dad was a rather big man. A little quiet at times, but he and Salami seemed to get along great, most of the time. Like Salami, he did not let things really bother him too much. He said it was the woman's job to do the worrying. He had also told Salami that after the woman does the worrying, it was up to the man to get things straightened out.

It was that last thought that bothered Salami. Glancing up, Salami saw a gentle man with a face that was solid and stern. No sooner had the Amen faded, when arms reached and grabbed for the food being passed around. Grandpa was as quick as anyone as he made sure his plate was filled to the brim. Salami had been over for supper enough times to be able to fit in. And usually, his plate was filled as fast as anyone else. The main-focus of attention now, was the meal. No longer was anyone looking at him or Rita. Everyone was talking while the kids were playing with their food. In a very short time the mounds of food on the table were dwindling. Heaping the spaghetti sauce onto his plate, Salami smacked hungry lips, his way of showing praise for what he considered a great meal.

"Salami, you're a nice boy," said Rita's Mom with outstretched arms. She loved to praise him in front of her sister and husband. "Rita has a nice young man. A good Italian young man." Turning to Salami, she covered her heart with work-worn hands. "Salami, your Rita made this nice spaghetti sauce."

Smacking his lips, with sauce trickling down his chin, he stood and turned to Rita. "Rita, let's . . ., would you like to marry me?"

The room was filled with a deadly silence, except for Grandpa slurping up spaghetti. All eyes focussed on Rita, their mouths hung open in utter amazement and wonderment. Each waited in anticipation for Rita's answer.

Rita's trembling hands covered her mouth. She did not know if it was embarrassment or the shock of the question that she had just been asked. She quickly pushed her chair back away from the table and rushed up the stairs to the safety of her room. All eyes followed until she disappeared out of sight. The room remained totally silent.

No-one knew what to say, if anything at all. It was the voice of Rita's father that cut through the silence.

"Well, Rita," he shouted. "What is your answer to this young fella?" Rita appeared at the top of the stairs, her head bent down, not facing anyone, she blurted out half crying, and half laughing, "Yes! Yes!"

Rita turned around abruptly and rushed back into the bedroom only to be followed by her Mother crying an ocean of tears of happiness and sadness. At the supper table shouts of joy rang out and toasts were made to the future groom. Everyone patted Salami on the back and expressed their joy and happiness in welcoming him to the family. All of them were shouting words of congratulations, except Grandpa who continued to slurp spaghetti.

Rita was sprawled across the bed. Her mother sat softly on the edge and for a moment neither of them spoke. Rita's Mom, unbeknown to Rita, had pieced together all the pieces from all the questions that Rita had been asking over the past few weeks. With a smile and a nod of her head she hugged Rita, and rocked her baby back and forth in a way that only a Mother could understand.

. . . .

The Baby Blue rolled along down the tree lined street. The wind felt warm rushing through the open windows, sending tufts of Frog's hair into his eyes. In the front seat sat Ziggy and his date, Annette, another pretty girl from a long string of girls. She sat there in the front seat with Ziggy, as quiet as a church mouse. Only Frog spoke as he asked every question in the book of etiquette, then tried to answer them himself.

Ziggy stopped the car and put it into park. He turned to Frog who was completely engrossed in his own conversation. Realizing that the car was not moving, Frog turned to Ziggy. "Why have we stopped?" he questioned.

"We're here, Frog, at Penelope's front door, where your date is waiting for ya."

"Oh . . ., Oh . . ., yea." Combing back wild hair with extended fingers, Frog got out of the Baby Blue with all the spirit and vigour of a new born colt.

"This is going to be some night!" Leaning closer to Annette, Ziggy whispered as if no one else should hear, "As soon as dinner is over, let's get rid of these two, whatever the cost."

Annette nodded without understanding any of this situation. Just to be with Ziggy was enough to contemplate without worrying about someone else.

Standing in front of massive white doors, Frog tugged at the suit coat, and then pushed up the ever-slipping glasses back onto his nose. He felt that he was ready, so he lifted a hand ready to knock. Resembling a scene from a haunted movie, the door opened before Frog had a chance to knock on it. Frog came face to face with the housekeeper.

"May I ask who is calling and for whom?"

"Frog, for Penelope."

"Mr. Frog wait here, please." Turning around with a rather bewildered look on her face, the maid left Frog standing outside the door. Although it was only minutes, it seemed like hours before Penelope appeared in a low-cut dress that threw Frog for an absolute loop. He could not take eyes off her. Frog had one thing in mind, and only one accomplishment to fulfil, and Penelope was sure of getting the ball rolling with a dress like this. Extending an arm to Penelope, Frog led her to the car and introduced her to Annette. Penelope gave a big smile and a Hi to Ziggy. For some odd reason, Ziggy had the feeling that Penelope said yes to the double date because of the fact of being close to him. If she was using Frog to get to him, she was bound to be in for a big let down.

No sooner had Frog closed the door of the Baby Blue, when it squealed out of the driveway sending Frog leaping into the lap of Penelope. Frog felt exhilarated excitement being so close, so quickly. But Penelope had other ideas of when getting close would be appropriate. Miss. prim and proper, Penelope Snidermost shoved Frog to the opposite side of the seat and flattened out the ruffled dress.

Throughout the long ride to the dinner club, Frog attempted to make small talk, but most of it ended up being answered with a simple yes or no. Frog felt totally inadequate as if all efforts to prepare for this date were going down the old proverbial tube. He could not go asking Ziggy for help in front of the girls, so he felt really stuck. Once in the dining room club, and after they were all seated at their table, the girls excused themselves to go and find the powder room.

This opportune moment gave Frog a chance to ask Ziggy for help. "Ziggy, help!" leaning across the table, Frog begged him.

"She's ignoring me. I'll be ninety and still a virgin at the rate I'm going."

"Look Frog, it's hard to get things going when there's a crowd."

Frog glanced around the room.

"No Frog, I mean the four of us. You'll have a better chance with just the two of you."

"I won't know what to do."

"It'll come to you, just let it happen naturally. Look, I'll tell you what, after the dinner and the show you take the Baby Blue and Penelope and do whatever you want. Keep the car all night, and tomorrow. As long as you need it." Ziggy handed the keys over to Frog, who smiled with a somewhat childish glee.

"You mean it Ziggy?"

"Yea, it's all right."

Clutching the keys in a hand, Frog put them into a pocket. In a little while the girls returned to the table, and being a gentleman, Frog stood to pull the chair back for Penelope. Frog had not noticed that in pulling the chair back, he had bumped into the man sitting at the next table. Although it seemed like only a small bump, it had resulted in the man's toupee falling over his eyebrows. As far as the rest of the dinner and the show were concerned, everything seemed to roll along smoothly. At least everyone was relaxing, except the waiter. Although he was working an overtime shift, he did not know why he had to serve this particular table. He knew that the steak sauce on his vest would never come out, and that the wine sloshing around in a shoe was cold. The tossed salad that was supposed to be in bowls was tossed into a pocket. On the way back to the kitchen, he glanced and noticed a sign posted by the management. Tonight, he felt that the words on the sign were quite appropriate, and he was almost tempted to enforce them, especially for the little guy with the suit and glasses. He glanced at the sign once more. It read; 'The management has the right to refuse service to any undesirable person.'

The waiter, standing close to the table with the bill on a platter, waited to be acknowledged. He knew he should not be standing so close to Frog, something could go wrong, and it did. Thinking he was waiting to clean up Frog wiped his face and tossed the unwanted napkin onto the platter. Enraged, the waiter slapped the bill in front of Frog, and then stormed off.

Ziggy signalled Frog, indicating that it was time to leave. So, arm in arm he and Penelope walked past the cloak room where he heard a voice coming from the darkness. "Don't come back here you little runt, or I'll fry you in steak sauce!" It was enough to send Frog and Penelope packing. Frog and Penelope, arm and arm scampered away until finding themselves safely inside the Baby Blue.

"Something wrong, Frog?"

"No . . .," panted Frog, I just wanted to spend as much time as I could with you."

"How sweet of you. Where are we going now?" Her voice was soft and somewhat passionate.

"And where would you like to go?" Frog's voice cracked.

"Surprise me." Gears grinded, tires squealed as Frog hurriedly attempted to get to a secluded place. It was not long before the Baby Blue was heading out of town. Down the same highway where Porky's accident had happened. Passing the exact spot, each of them recalled the grim moments of that evening. Frog slowed down as if in remembrance, but only for a brief moment. After that it was back to the present and off to find the solitude of a bush road where they had been that fateful night. Penelope slid closer to Frog, a shy smile covered her face while her hand caressed the stick shift.

Frog was feeling the tension building up inside, anticipating the moment when he and Penelope would be together. This caused his foot to press further down on the accelerator, making the Baby Blue go faster and faster. This time they were alone, no one was following, and Penelope seemed as eager as Frog. Screeching tires left the pavement as dust kicked up in the red glow of the baby Blue's tail lights.

Pulling off into a clearing overlooking the river, Frog gripped the steering wheel tightly, almost afraid to let it go. Penelope turned off the key as she caressed Frog's hand. Being cool was not one of Frog's better endeavours. This became evident when he attempted to reach around Penelope's neck. "Ouch!" screamed Penelope, rubbing her forehead where Frog's elbow had landed.

"Sorry, I never do things right. I don't even know why you even came out with me." Frog pounded his head against the steering wheel. "I know I'm not like Ziggy and Boo, or even Salami, but I do like you."

"I like you too. You're different than those guys, even smarter."

"You're just saying that." Briefly he glanced at Penelope, to see if she was just saying it or meaning it. Her deep blue-green eyes reflected from the lights of the dashboard. Frog stared deep into them with a feeling that she had meant what she said. 'What do I do now,' he thought. He had to get his thoughts off Penelope. Blood was starting to rush through his head, and was making him feel dizzy. 'A drink will help,' he thought further. "Would you care for a drink?" asked Frog.

"A drink? Where are you going to get a drink out here?"

"Ziggy always stashes something special under the seat." Bending down, he reached under the seat and searched, reaching back as far as possible. "Always a special bottle for a special girl," said Frog. He found that he was unable to locate the bottle. Now reaching with both hands he mumbled to himself, "Now where is that blasted thing."

Penelope bent close to Frog, wanting to help. "Do you need help?"

"No . . ., No . . ., I've got everything under control. Ah! Here it is!" he said with a sudden joy of having found the special bottle.

"Oooo . . ., champagne, Ziggy, has class."

"Oh, I told him what to get," Frog lied as he pulled and twisted the wrapped plastic cork.

"I guess I should say that you have good taste, Frog," Penelope corrected herself.

Frog was about to take a swig from the bottle when he stopped himself and handed the bottle to Penelope. Penelope did not just take a lady-like sip, she guzzled it down to Frog's astonishment. He did not particularly like wine or champagne that much, but he certainly could not let her show him up. So, with a deep breath, he tilted the bottle back and drank from the champagne bottle, tears of champagne trickling down the sides of his lips and mouth. He had not downed as much as Penelope, but he made it look as if he had. He placed the bottle between his legs and gasped for air. The bubbles of the champagne seemed to have taken his breath away.

From that moment on, everything suddenly seemed blurred, or perhaps it was that his glasses were fogged up again. Penelope eased herself closer to Frog and started licking the champagne on Frog's lips and chin. Carefully, her tongue lightly traced the outline of his lips and then slowly Frog's lips parted as their tongues touched. It seemed to go on forever. Frog had never known such ecstasy. His arousal soared to new heights, his hand still clasping the bottle between his legs. It seemed that the awkwardness of the moment was behind him. Frog let the champagne bottle fall freely to the floor while a hand caressed Penelope's previously forbidden body. The both of them, once very shy, embraced as if they had never been strangers.

This was by far the most romantic situation Frog had ever, ever found himself in. With their legs wrapped around each other, in the most awkward position possible, Penelope and Frog made the best of the little space available inside the Baby Blue. Frog thought to himself that he was almost there, almost where he had dreamed of being for the longest time. What he had dreamed of and anticipated for such a long time, he believed was about to happen.

Suddenly out of nowhere, there was a hissing sound, and Penelope and Frog's ears perked, and they both seemed to freeze in mid-motion. Both turned their heads searching for the source of the hissing sound.

"The car is sinking!" yelled Penelope.

"It can't," retorted Frog, "We're on land."

Frog untangled legs from Penelope, and she managed to pull her dress down. Grabbing a flashlight from the dashboard, Frog jumped outside, flashing the light on the tires. "Someone let the air out of the tires!" he yelled to Penelope.

From a nearby bush Frog and Penelope heard the taunting cat calls and giggles from somebody laughing hysterically. "Okay, who's out there," asked Frog in the bravest voice he could possible muster. The only response was more giggles and laughter. Checking the tires, he noticed that someone had stuck some twigs in the tire's valve stems. "Shoot," he cursed while removing his coat that was already half off. Frog found that he needed to apply all his energy for finding out how to pump up the tires.

"Don't turn your back, or the air will seep out again," a voice yelled out of the darkness startling Frog and making him jump up.

Penelope came to Frog's rescue, only verbally.

"Show your faces you little snot-ass kids!" yelled Penelope, her hands clenched in a boxer-like stance.

It was not people that emerged from the bushes but rather, mud pies. Wet sloppy mud pies splattering the Baby Blue as Frog found safety ducking behind one of its fenders.

"You want a fight?" Penelope rushed forward, gathering mud in her hands and aimed at the shadows in the bushes. It turned out to be an all out and out fight, with Penelope emerging as the victor and Frog as her reward.

"Frog," ooed Penelope when it was all over, "Let's go to my house, there's no one there and we could clean up a bit. We're such a mess, splattered with all this mud," laughed Penelope, "And look at you."

Frog looked around and saw that whoever had been in the bushes were now gone. Having gotten back into the Baby Blue, Penelope and Frog slammed the doors shut, and only dust was left behind as the Baby Blue sped off down the dirt road, hoping that the dust would choke the villains hiding in the bush.

Frog felt quite awkward in Penelope's big house. For the most part, he was not used to such niceties. He did not quite know how to act, or what to say. For the most part, he really felt like a fish out of water, rather a Frog out of water for that matter. For the moment, it did not seem to matter. Penelope took the initiative by taking him by the hand and leading him through the main room to the swimming pool out back. Music filled the air and the stars above glittered ever so softly. Frog thought that this was perhaps the most romantic moment he had ever experienced in his life. Sitting herself down on an air mattress, Penelope pulled Frog towards her while in the background a Dan Hill song echoed in the night. "Sometimes when we touch, the honesty's too much," said the words of the song. The disruptions of the past little while did not seem to matter anymore. Those hooligans in the bushes, and the mud fights were all behind them. Even Frog's blur had disappeared, his glasses rested on the patio.

What happened next between he and Penelope seem to happen too quickly. 'Is this what it was like for Ziggy and Boo?' Frog thought. Being the first time, would Penelope ever share another moment like this with him. Penelope and Frog lay wrapped in each other's arms, both body and soul. Each caught up in their own thoughts. After years of wanting someone, it became apparent within hours of passion that it was all over in a matter of minutes. The sex was over too quickly, and Frog felt a little disappointed. He did not know quite what to expect, this having been his first time, but somehow it just seemed to be over too fast.

"Penelope," Frog was slightly surprised at the sound of his own voice. "Do you think that maybe we . . ., if it's all right with you, I mean could, we go out again . . ., sometime?" he asked in a somewhat clumsy way. Penelope nodded in agreement. Penelope seemed to glow in a rather loving way as she brushed the hair away from Frog's eyes. Suddenly the music had stopped and only silence enveloped Frog and Penelope.

"Penelope dear, we're home, Penelope!"

"My parents!" she whispered sending Frog into a panic.

"My father is not a very understanding man, you better go quickly."

"Go where?" asked Frog gathering shoes, oat and other paraphernalia that had been removed in the heat of passion. Frog scurried around the patio. "How do I get out of here?"

Penelope pointed with her finger, "Go over the fence." Frog gathered whatever he could grab a hold of and started to run.

"Be careful of the d . . ., OH . . ., Hello, Mother, such a beautiful night, isn't it? How was your evening?" Penelope asked quite innocently.

Frog managed to get over the fence just in time. He picked himself off the ground and hobbled along in the darkness as he searched pockets for glasses. 'Arf! Arf! Arf!' The bark of a dog could be heard as if it was pursuing some kind of prey, only this time the prey seemed to be Frog. The dog closed in ready to pounce on its prey. A yappy no-good-for-nothing French Poodle grabbed at Frog's pant leg. Frog made it through the yard, over the hedge, across the flower bed with the mangy little mutt still clinging to a pant leg. He was a persistent little guy that was not willing to give up Frog's pant leg any more then a good juicy bone. No matter how much Frog would plea and shake the dog, he could not seem to get loose from the dog. It was not until Frog climbed into the Baby Blue that the dog finally let go with one last yap. Giving Frog one last look of disgust, the dog left the intruder who had invaded its property. Giving Frog one last grunt it walked away as proud as a peacock.

. . . .

Big Bula was a mean old girl and was as foul mouthed as they come. Her use of the English language, or the lack of, was second only to the multitude of four letter words and phrases of degradation that she used. At times, even the bravest of men would back away, ashamed to even be seen in her presence. The girls, as well, kept away from her as much as possible, but in the locker room there was just no escaping Big Bula and her sewer-mouth. She was as big as a mountain and with a flimsy towel draped over a shoulder, she strutted around naked as a jaybird. standing big and tall in the middle of the shower room, rolls and rolls of fat stretch to the limit. Turning around slowly, her eyes carefully examined every single girl there.

"I get the feeling that someone is spying on me, watching every move I make, I don't like it." Her voice grew louder and louder. "I know one of you has a perversion, and I don't go for that kind of thing," she said.

"Maybe some," a soft voice barely audible made its way through the steam of the shower room.

"Speak up girl. You got something to say to me, say it." Bula clenched a fist tightly and shook it in the girl's face. "Speak up or I'll put you into tomorrow."

"It's only, that I once saw a movie where this guy kept peeking into a girl's room from behind a painting on a wall. Maybe someone is doing that." Big Bula heaved her chest. A grin fit to kill covered her face. Boldly, she strutted around, causing the other girls to scurry out of the way. Bula checked the door, and then she checked the window. Having done this, she checked the vents.

"Hey, all I see is that Big Bula," said the little man returning from yesterday's visit. Again, all he saw was a big blob of a woman.

Boo shoved him aside and peeked into the periscope, and sure enough the big butt of Bula was mooning him.

"Okay, take another look," Boo said, "after looking at that you deserve to see something better."

CHAPTER NINE
Revenge

The shift was over and Boo had closed-down the periscope for the day. Handling it carefully, he placed the level on top of the fridge in the trailer. Ziggy was sitting at the table flipping through the pictures that Boo had taken of Linda and the general foreman. "Hey, these pictures are pretty damn good. We can sure create a lot of heat with these pictures," Ziggy laughed.

Boo nodded in agreement, and laughed at the thought that he could possibly use them as blackmail. Ziggy did not want things to go too far or get out of hand. Not just for Linda's sake or Reese's, but for the guys as well. "I think you better stop what your thinking, Boo. Just show the pictures to Linda and get her off our back."

"But, we could be on easy street."

"No, Boo, just her."

"Okay, Ziggy," Boo conceded. "Girls like that find other ways to get ahead, and they don't worry who they step on in the meanwhile." Ziggy took one last look at the pictures and then handed them back to Boo.

"Okay, we'll do it your way." Boo said as he headed out the door.

By about mid-afternoon, Boo caught up with Linda. He followed her along the cat walk towards the number 3 blast furnace. Approaching, he grabbed an arm and pulled her inside the blast furnace cast floor. The dirty glow of the furnace stood in a monolithic stance. Before she could utter a single word, Boo took out the pictures and started flipping through them one by one showing her each one as he watched the ever-changing expression on her face.

"So, what's the deal," she asked angrily. "You want some pussy?"

"No, nothing as drastic as that," Boo responded.

"So, what then?" Linda reached for the pictures, but Boo pulled them away and slid them into a pocket. "Just leave Ziggy and us out of your scheming with Reese. Use someone else to step on."

"Then do I get the pictures?"

"Maybe," Boo smiled mischievously, and with that said, he headed back out onto the cat walk.

As Boo had anticipated, Linda headed directly to Reese and spilled her guts. "He's got pictures of Wendle and me, very explicit."

Reese shook his head in horror. "Are you sure?"

"I've seen them, that guy, Ziggy's chum, he showed them to me."

"If this ever gets to Wendle, you can kiss your job and mine goodbye." Getting up from the seat, he paced back and forth. "We've got to get rid of those guys for good."

Linda questioned the possibility of this happening. "Then whose gonna get the pictures?"

"If someone does me a favour, I'll do them a favour. I've got someone in mind." Reese picked up the phone and dialled an in-plant number. "Yea. Give me the scale-car operator." A few moments later, Reese gave Linda a reassuring wink.

"Yea."

"Reese here. I've got a job. A job in exchange for a favour. You know a guy named Ziggy and his chum, Boo?"

"Yea, I know them," the voice was harsh, as if condemning the names 'Ziggy and Boo, good ole boys.'

"Well, fine, all you have to do is get some pictures they are carrying around with them and bring them to me."

"No problem."

The phone plunked at the other end, and with the hum still in Reese's ear, he hung up the phone. He stroked Linda gently under the chin. "It's done," he said, a smirk of satisfaction covering a twisted face.

. . . .

For the rest of the shift, Ziggy and Boo waited for some-kind of reaction from Reese. They had anticipated either a job change or some-kind of confrontation, but for the entire rest of the shift nothing happened. They had finished all their work and no one seemed to be breathing down their necks. It seemed that for the rest of the shift, they had it easy, but in the back of their minds, they were constantly looking over shoulders, waiting for the proverbial knife to be stuck in their backs.

Before the next shift change, the guys had gathered in the trailer and were chatting about everything and nothing. It was Salami and Frog's turn to take care of the periscope, but before they left, Salami announced to the guys that he was going to be getting married, and elaborated on the details of the past evening. Frog, in particular beamed with excitement and was expecting someone to ask him about his previous night with Penelope.

None of the guys were particularly shocked to learn that Salami was going to be getting married as soon as possible. As Salami had put it, it was so his future father-in-law would not know the reason why they were getting married. Rita's father was a millwright and worked in the furnace. He knew most of the guys around the furnace. So before anything could accidentally slip out about his daughter, it was felt that it was better to hurry up and get married and this way stay on his good side.

"Let's get going, Frog." Salami ushered Frog to the door, pushing him along before Frog could tell the guys anything about the fact that he had finally gotten laid. "You can't let those peepers out there wait, after-all, time is money, so let's go."

Suddenly on the count of 1, 2, 3, Ziggy and Boo yelled as the door closed. "Congratulations, Frog!"

Outside, Frog beamed with pride and joy. "They know," Frog said surprisingly.

"Sure, do Frog, you're a man now, and you don't have to worry about going blind or anything like that, you know." Salami gave Frog a little pat on the back as they headed for the shack.

Among other things, Boo and Ziggy had been making plans to hold a stag for Salami. In their minds, Boo and Ziggy were thinking of the names of all the people that would not be sold stag tickets. There were certain people that they did not want to attend Salami's stag.

Knowing that it was still a bit early to punch off their shift, they decided to take the round about way to the gate and use the time to discuss the stag. Ziggy and Boo headed under the high line and walked along the dock towards the number four gate. Still being too early, the two back-tracked to the tunnel where they could wait without being seen, until it was time to punch out. It seemed, that no matter what time of the day it was, the tunnel was always dark and filled with graphite and coke dust. Along with everything else, each and every light bulb was covered with the fine particles of dust that had gathered on them one minute after having been cleaned, it was a useless task to try and keep the lights clean.

Amid the laughing, at a joke that Ziggy had just given the punch line for, there was a sudden swishing sound to Ziggy and Boo's ears. Boo grabbed his sides and doubled over while gasping for breath, and then another swishing sound and Ziggy felt a pain, an excruciating pain in the side ribs. The swishing sound came several times, and they felt the butt end of a steel pipe land brutishly against their aching bodies. Dazed beyond belief, there was no time to react to the sudden vicious attack. Boo clutched the wall as he slid to the ground, expecting more blows from the steel pipe. The swishing sound, and the beating had stopped. Both felt hands ripping through their pockets. Nothing was found, and the assailants, pipes in hand threatened them both. Ziggy and Boo were too dazed to understand anything that was being said. In their half-opened eyes, they noticed the long pipes hovering over their heads, ready to strike.

Ziggy managed to raise himself, and pressed his back against the wall attempting to face the attackers. Boo managed to reach for a leg, and clutching onto the attacker's pant leg with the tips of fingers, but he was not able to maintain a grip. Within the dust filled air caused by the commotion, Ziggy and Boo's eyes became red with irritation, and they strained to see the two figures retreating quickly down the tunnel.

"Hey, stay and fight, Hey!" Ziggy choked on his words. Having made it out of the tunnel, the two gasped for the fresh air outside of the tunnel.

"Did you see his face?" Boo asked rubbing the pain in his belly.

"I'm not sure. I don't understand why, but I think it was Porky."

"Porky! What the Hell does he have against us?"

"He does brown-nose up to Reese, you know."

"Reese and Linda, I get the idea." Boo's face turned cold.

. . . .

"I don't want to pay you money if I got to look at Big Bula," said the little guy, back again for another viewing. He held fast to his dollar bill. "If I wanted to see something big I can look at my wife."

"Okay, Okay, Frog answered. You don't have to look at her." Frog stood only slightly taller than the old guy, and looking down on him, Frog noticed the old guy waving the dollar bill in his face. Frog promised that he would not have to look at Big Bula, and if Big Bula came into sight while he was peering into the periscope, he would not have to pay.

Business was certainly bliss, as the word about what was happening spread. For only a buck a peek, it was a great opportunity for the men to enjoy themselves. Many of the men from the other side of the plant, that usually headed out number one gate, were making their way all the way over to number four gate, just for the peek-for-a-buck show. The guys had cornered their own little market in the sex business. It was an absolute sure thing. If there were girls to be seen, there were certainly guys willing to pay for it. It seemed that the guys were not the first to run this scam, and they certainly were not going to be the last. The boys were concerned about whether or not it was actually wrong to be doing this. At times their consciences got the best of them. They questioned if someone would get hurt in this kind of a situation. It seems that when you are young, and just getting started in life, sex, no-matter how you get it, is all part of the game. As Ziggy often said, 'girls usually have the same thoughts and urges as the boys, and that they want the same things that the guys want as well.'

Frog certainly did not feel guilty when taking a buck from each guy as they came into the shack. There were young guys, and old guys, and married guys, and single guys, and perhaps some that were even a little perverted. I want five bucks' worth said one big fella. Frog gave a little weak smile, and grinned when accepting the five-dollar bill.

Walking around with a towel flung over a shoulder, her loose boots clubbing on the floor, Big Bula eyed all the other girls again. Again, her face was covered with an accusing frown as she paced back and forth in the crowed locker room. She was certain now, that someone was spying on her, watching her from behind her back. She believed that each girl she looked at was the culprit. None of the girls had the courage to look her in the eye, for fear of being clobbered on the spot. Big Bula's voice echoed throughout the room, freezing the girls in place.

"I know someone is watching me, and when I find out who it is, I'll . . .," Her fist slammed into an open palm.

Grabbing a helmet, one girl placed a helmet on her head and entered the shower while the others hurried to their destinations in various degrees of dress. Big Bula continued to pace back and forth, always turning her head this way or that way, or looking behind. Her eyes looked out the window, under the stalls and into the lockers. She knew that someone was watching her.

"Next," Salami clicked the stop watch and waited for another man to pay a dollar.

"I don't want to look at Big Bula, the old man shook a finger at Salami.

"I checked," Salami answered. "she's not there." Salami kept an eye on the stop watch, hoping that the time would run out before Big Bula stepped in front of the periscope.

"Fifteen seconds, ten seconds," Salami counted the seconds off.

"There she is again!" The old man stomped a foot and shook a finger angrily at Salami. A roar of laughter filled the shack. "How come every time I look, I gotta see her?"

"Okay, let me see," said Salami, pushing him aside. Salami placed an eye to the opening, and sure enough, there was Big Bula, blocking the view.

"I know someone is watching me, and today I'm gonna find out."

She rested a muscular hand on huge hips and tapped an elephant boot into water, splashing it all around. "No one has anything to say?" The girls just went about their own business, doing whatever it was that they were doing, but always being careful and watchful that Big Bula's hand did not come crashing down on them. Bula eyed each girl with such scorn, and shook her head with such discontent, that each girl knew that someday they would probably be the ones to incur Bula's wrath. In the meanwhile, Bula raised eyes upward and thought about what might be going on, and who was in fact watching her.

Salami peeked into the periscope, and then raising his head, ran hands through tangled hair. His eyes were wide with disbelief.

"What the hell is taking so long? I want my five bucks worth." The big fella towered over Salami, demanding satisfaction for his money. "What's holding up the show?"

Reaching into a pocket, Salami retrieved a five-dollar bill and crumpled it into the big guy's hand. "If you and the other guys are smart, you'll start hightailing it."

"Big Bula is on her way!" Salami yelled. Salami eyed the dumbfounded men who were staring at him. "RUN!" Men scampered in all directions. The exit crowded with men all trying to get out at the same time.

Leading the pack was the big fella, yelling as he ran. "Big Bula's mean, she'll tear apart the first guy she gets her hands on!"

A hateful look covered Big Bula's face when reaching for the air duct. With one powerful tug the entire air duct came crashing to the floor. Girls screamed at the sudden burst of noise filling the trailer. With her powerful hands, Big Bula pulled up a nearby bench and reached deep into the air duct. She pulled the periscope with a massive hand, and the entire apparatus crumbled in her grip. All the girls attempted, as best they could, to cover their naked bodies while girlish screams echoed throughout the trailer. Everyone raced to find a safe hiding place where their naked bodies could not be seen, but there was no safe place.

Bula smashed the pipe endlessly against the floor until the mirrors hiding inside splattered across the floor in shattered pieces. Having wrapped a towel around herself, she headed out the door. Her clomping boots could be heard banging against the trailer floor, above the screams and crackling voices of all the girls.

Bula's monstrous body seemed to fill the entire doorway, as she faced the roadway. She stood there in front listening to the multiple sounds of the slamming doors. The road in front was usually busy with people, was now totally deserted. Clad only in a towel, she stepped onto the roadway while the girls in the trailer peeked out through the trailer windows and the doorway.

Not one single solitary guy turned or waited to see if Big Bula was really after them. All they did was run without glancing back, even for a moment. As well, Salami and Frog also wasted no time escaping. Frog managed to scurry down into a pit, and Salami managed to jump into a barrel and pull the lid over him.

Bula's eyes scanned the grey pipe leading from the trailer to an overhead piping and then to the repair shack at the end of the high-line. Totally unconcerned about her appearance, Big Bula entered the shack with fists clenched, ready to beat in a few brains. Bula followed the pipes running down the side of the shack to a barrel. Lifting the lid of the barrel she noticed the level focussed on the girls' shower room. With massive strength, she ripped it out, as if it were a rotten tooth, and held it high above as if it had been a victorious trophy.

"Girls!" Big Bula yelled out as they all gathered about inside the trailer. "I told you someone was watching. No doubt it was them so-called-men in this plant. Not just one guy but all of them." She extended arms to display the level for all to see. Bula shook a fist at the level. "This is what they used to spy on us. This is what they used to violate our privacy."

The girls examined the level, and then glanced around, expressing a feeling that there were still someone watching. Among the girls, the only one that was not clothed, was Bula. She stood in the middle of the trailer semi-covered by a flimsy towel wrapped around her waist. All she was thinking about was a way to get even. For how sweet revenge would be if they could get even with the men in this plant.

"Are we going to stand for this kind of intrusion on our privacy?" she asked angrily.

"NO!" was the answer each girl yelled back in unison. For the most part, the girls were not particularly close to Bula, and if nothing more, most certainly feared her. If anyone were to be a leader in this situation, it certainly would need to be Bula. There was no doubt that most men would certainly back down when she approached them.

"Are we going to fight back?" she asked. There were a few weak, 'Ya's' that sounded from the group, not particularly a strong response. Bula looked at each girl and found a few ya's suddenly becoming a chorus of ya's. The girls felt united in their cause against the men in this plant. Holding the level high above her head in outstretched arms, Bula egged the girls on into a kind of frenzy, as cheers filled the trailer and obscenities of all kinds were cast at the level that represented all the men who were behind the peep show.

Salami held a breath for a moment and tried to make as little noise as possible as he lifted the top of the barrel ever so carefully. Peeking through a crack, a blue eye scanned the interior of the shack and found that there was no one in sight, not even Frog. He seemed nowhere to be found. Feeling confident that the coast was clear, Salami crawled out from the hiding place, and taking a quick breath of relief, hoped that no one had heard.

With his back against the pit wall, Frog edged along searching for a way out. Finally, he reached the edge of the pit and managed to pull himself up to safety, hoping not to come face to face with Big Bula.

"Hi, Frog!" Salami yelled from above when they encountered each other. "What are you doing down there, digging a grave?" Salami laughed.

At the sight of Salami, Frog managed to fall back into the pit. "You trying to scare me to death or something?" Frog asked somewhat angrily. After all, it had not been Salami that Frog had anticipated, but perhaps Big Bula.

"Hell no, Frog, I'm just glad to see that Big Bula did not get her hands on ya." Salami reached for Frog's arm and helped pull him from the pit. Cautiously, they headed out, occasionally turning from side to side as if expecting an onslaught of half-crazed women.

Reaching from the door to the outside, he hesitated for a moment. Salami reached for the door handle and then stopped. "Hey, Frog let's go out the back way." They trotted their way along the dark scale-car line to the furthest door away from the shack. Opening the metal door, a creak sounded from the lack of use, as the daylight flickered and entered the vast darkness. "No one in sight, Frog," Salami said with some confidence. "Let's hightail it out of here."

With hands snugly tucked in pockets, Salami walked along as coolly as hip-cat, with Frog beside him taking quick short steps. As soon as they turned the final corner where the gate could be seen, they became entangled in a crowd. Girls, a group of girls closed in, surrounding Salami and Frog. They were chatting amongst themselves, and at times a few of them seemed to eye Salami and Frog, giving them the once over. For a moment, the encirclement made it impossible for them to move away. The last couple of hundred yards to the gate seemed like the final steps to the slaughter house.

As they approached the gate, it seemed that the girls would not dispersing. The crowd of girls gathering at the gate seemingly grew larger and larger as the men approached the gate. The slowed down their pace, especially those that had used the periscope. Standing at the gate, the girls eyed the men as they chatted in low voices amongst themselves, so that the men could not hear what they were saying. With their eyes staring down at the ground below, the men breathed a sigh of relief when they realized that the girls behind were not following them. Leaving the gate Salami and Frog quickened their pace and headed for the Baby Blue.

"Let us in!" they shouted, slamming the car doors behind them after piling into the back seat.

"What's with the girls?" Ziggy asked.

"They found out about the periscope. We just made it out with our hides still intact." No sooner had those words left Salami's lips, Ziggy squealed the Baby Blue out of the plant parking lot.

"Do they suspect us?" questioned Boo, as he sipped on a resting between his legs.

"I don't think so," said Frog, as he adjusted slipping glasses once more onto the bridge of the nose. "They did not see us in the shack or leaving the shack."

"Then there's nothing to worry about." Boo gestured with the beer bottle.

"What if some guy snitches to one of the girls, that it was us?"

"Hell, no, Frog. If a guy snitches, the girls are going to have his balls as trophies." Boo waited for the others to agree before taking another swig of beer.

With the windows of the Baby Blue open, and the warm summer air blowing carefree through their hair, the guys headed out for yet another evening of fun at a local bar. Music blared from the car speakers, and this was a welcome change from the constant clanking of the mills. They felt a sense of freedom, a sense that they were now free from their daily burdens of work at the plant.

. . . .

Ziggy was dancing with a new girl while Salami and Rita sat close to each other whispering amongst themselves. Across the table, Frog sat twiddling thumbs in hoping that Penelope would come tonight. Though he had phoned early enough, Penelope's voice sounded hesitant, but hopeful that she would be able to attend. Down the hallway, Boo was making a telephone call to the plant. He placed a finger in one ear to drown out the sounds of the band as he waited for a voice to answer at the other end of the line.

"Number four blast furnace scheduling foreman."

"Yea, I'd like to know what B Crew is working next week. And, what shift Linda is working?" Pressing the receiver back onto its hook, Boo mumbled, "Thanks."

Working the night shift was usually a pretty good shift. Things usually were not as hectic as the day shift and the general foreman and superintendents and the rest of them were usually sitting comfortably at home leaving it up to the few foremen and workers to keep the plant running. This evening was warm, and the air was a little sticky from the heat of the day. The wind had died down a bit, and for some reason, the night seemed darker than usual and would stay this way until after midnight when the moon would finally make its way into the sky.

Boo sat in the corner of the locker room while some men huddled close to him. Some were young, and some were wild, some were high, and some were out to lunch all together. A lot of the men considered outcasts in society seemed to hang onto every word that Boo said. Shuffling the pictures of Wendle and Linda back into a pack, Boo placed the package back into a pocket. The looks on some of the faces of these men resembled hounds that were slobbering just before being thrown a meal. They seemed like a pack of cave men, Boo said as he stood up to leave, "You guys got it straight?" Heads nodded in a show of acknowledgement.

Grinning, Boo headed downstairs from the locker room and out into the shadows of the plant. This was not his regular shift, so basically, he could move around without anyone asking questions. Boo had a destination in mind, so headed directly for it. The furnaces loomed majestically overhead, unaware and uncaring of what happened below its floors or within its wall. The workers seemed to exist in a world within a world. Many of the men were so enveloped within this world that they could not seem to cope in any other environment except that of the steel plant.

Like many of the other men, Boo also seemed to be caught up in the world of the steel plant. As days passed, he seemed to be spending more and more time in the plant. He did not seem to have any real reason to leave. The trailer had everything he needed, including two or three girls that seemed to spend a lot of time there, and tonight would be just another night.

Stepping onto the dust covered cat walk, Boo made his way along the number three furnace to number four. The lights from the control room reflected on the bodies of workers coming and going. Boo stopped as if to search for a person of interest. It was Linda who was leaning against Reese's desk in a stance that was no doubt meant to excite Reese.

Disappearing into the darkness, Boo waited for the control room to clear out. Once everyone had their job assignments, the control room was cleared of bodies, leaving only Reese, Linda and Porky chatting amongst themselves.

"Look ass hole," Reese spoke angrily to Porky, "If you don't hold up your end of the bargain, we can all kiss our jobs goodbye."

Porky's body stiffened, but he did not back down from Reese. "I'll do my job. I've got just as much at stake, maybe more."

"Just see that you do it."

"I will," replied Porky, grabbing gloves and pushing past Linda, he stormed out the door.

"Linda, you better get to your job before someone starts getting ideas."

"Are you gonna take care of things?"

"I will." Reese stuffed a cigar into his mouth while Linda slowly walked away swinging hips enough so that Reese understood what his reward would be if he could get things all cleared up.

Standing on the cat walk, Linda glanced down over the railing. Below were the tracks carrying the torpedoes full of molten iron ore. Walking carefully and clinging to the wall, Linda continued towards number three furnace. Her eyes caught glimpses of shadows from the reflected light that danced around the cat walk. The shadows created images which were amplified only by one's own imagination. 'Sometimes,' she thought, 'things really do go bump in the night.'

"Ah . . .!" Linda clutched the railing as her heart started to beat uncontrollably. There was a shadow looming larger than life before her. A shadow that seemed to suddenly want to force her body over the railing. She backed suddenly against the wall, in search of something to hold onto. From behind a column, a shadow suddenly emerged into the light and Linda came face to face with someone staring at her in the most gruesome way she could imagine.

"Goooood Evening," spoke Boo in a bad imitation of Bella Lugosi. "A lovely evening for a walk." Boo emerged from behind the column showing only his head, just in case Reese happened to glance out from the control room, because the view from the control room to the cat walk was excellent.

"What the hell are you trying to pull!" Linda yelled at Boo, and at the same time trying to hold her ground. She was ready to run if she had to. "You get a kick out of jumping out of shadows and scaring people?" she asked angrily.

"No," Boo responded, "But it's not a bad idea. It gets the adrenalin going, doesn't it?"

Linda did not find this funny at all. Boo glanced back at the control room and found that it was empty. "I believe you're interested in some pictures that I might have."

Linda stepped forward eagerly, and then suddenly stopped in her tracks. "I might be, I take it you want something in exchange."

"We could reach an agreement." Boo checked the control room again, then motioned Linda to follow him. Boo made passage across the floor of the dead furnace with Linda following reluctantly behind. This particular route was very familiar. It was the same forgotten welfare room where Linda and Wendle had met. In this scenario, nothing seemed to have changed, rather then Wendle and Linda, it was Boo and Linda. Linda thought that if it was only a matter of giving Boo a piece of tail, to get the pictures back, then it was no big deal.

In the dust-filled light at the entrance of the welfare room, Boo held out the pictures. Linda reached out but was not quick enough to grab the pictures. "I take it you guessed at a way to gain these delightful pictures back."

"Guys like you all want the same thing, so let's just get it over with, Ok?" An uncontrollable rage filled Linda's eyes, there was nothing she could do but be angry at this point. There was no other way to get the pictures back, but do what she knew she had to do. Reese and Porky had failed, so Linda would have to get the pictures back her way. Pulling off a work jacket, she barged past Boo and shoved open the door to the welfare room.

"I've got twenty pictures, here," said Boo, with a snicker on his face, anticipating what was about to happen. "One favour per picture?" he asked.

"What about the negatives?" retorted Linda.

"Well, if you do really well, I might even give them to you at the end. And that is only if you don't complain too much." Boo grinned happily. Linda on the other hand did not seem to share the joy of the present situation. "Go in," commanded Boo, "a picture will follow shortly."

What followed was the most hideous time that Linda could have imagined, and even in her worst imagination it was not hideous enough. What she considered creatures of the night seemed to emerge out of the woodwork.

The creatures that Boo had talked to earlier now seemed to crawl out of the oozing darkness. Emerging from what seemed the very pits of hell, and where they would return to when their lives were finished. Deep down in his very toes, Boo was sweating profusely. He knew that these guys, these creatures of the night were the very bottom of the barrel of the men working at the plant, and if anything, ever went wrong, Boo surely did not want to tangle with any of them.

These creatures, the scum of the earth gathered around. Boo felt most intimidated and surely out of place. It seemed that it should have been someone like Al Capone rather then himself that was giving out the orders to this kind of men. They looked every bit mobster gangsters, reminiscent of many early movies.

"All you guys have to do," said Boo, "is to give the girl a picture and then just go ahead and enjoy yourself."

"I'm first, yelled a big bearded man stepping in close. He was monstrous in size and towered over everybody. He extended a huge hand, and no-one complained. Not one man uttered a single word.

"Fine with me," said Boo, gulping as he handed him the most explicit picture that there was, just in case he complained.

As his huge frame disappeared through the door, the rest of the rats, these creatures, lunged at the pictures. "I'm first." "No, I'm first. Hell, you guys are after me." "I'm second." "I'm third." This was all that Boo heard as the men scrambled to grab one of the pictures in his hand.

One by one these mean-faced men disappeared through the door, and when they emerged there was a glow in their eyes. The look of joy and ecstasy covered their face as they glanced at Boo and walked away. Boo held onto the last two pictures. They were the first two shots that he had taken. These pictures did not reveal much, and were not worth anything. As it turned out they would be the last twist of the knife in Linda's back, a last twist of the knife that would count more than any other.

"What the hell are you guys standing around here for?" Reese called out in an authoritative voice when seeing the men standing around Boo. "This is no party, you guys got jobs? I suggest you get to them." It is amazing what a green hat could do to some men, even the toughest looking men back down when a green hat comes into view. Towering over Reese's pudgy frame, the men sneered as they filed by and walked away. "What the hell are you grinning at?" he yelled at one man. "What's in there?" Reese spoke in anger to the last visitor leaving the welfare room. The smirk on the guy's face disappeared quickly as he followed the rest of his buddies out the door, without answering Reese. "What the hell is with these guys?" Boo suddenly stepped out from the shadows, enough to startle Reese. "Hey, you're not on this shift!" he yelled, biting off the end of his cigar and spitting it to the ground. The slimy spit smeared over the floor and disappeared into the constantly shifting dust.

"One question at a time. Reese. Your lips are flapping too fast, and your brain can't seem to keep up." Slowly he pulled two pictures from a shirt pocket.

"Get to the point, ass hole."

"Ooohhh . . .," Boo pretended to be frightened of Reese. "These good ole' boys were just having a good ole' time with a good ole' friend. I think she's a friend of yours, and Wendle's, and who knows who else." Boo waved the pictures in front of Reese's face. "Here, Reese, take these into that room, and I think the situation will certainly explain itself."

Reese grabbed the pictures and crumbling them in a fat little hand, at the same time he tried to focus on the pictures in the darkness. A look of satisfaction covered Boo's face. Wiggling fingers good-bye, Boo walked away, leaving Reese standing there alone.

Reese glanced at the pictures, and then at the door. His curiosity had the best of him now, and wondered what was waiting for him in the welfare room. Pushing open the door a glimmer of bright light hit his eyes, then focussed on someone or something in the room. There was someone leaning against the table in the welfare room and that was all that he could see.

"Come on in and get it over with."

He heard Linda's voice speaking through the darkness in a rather nonchalant kind of tone. She was leaning against the table with legs spread apart, breast exposed, and with pants lying at her feet, trampled by the many visitors of the night. She did not bother to look towards the door and she was unconcerned as to who it was. Reese tightened a grip on the pictures as he approached Linda. The only thing that Linda was concerned about was whether-or-not Boo was going to turn over the negatives or had he just forgotten.

. . . .

"Thanks, man."

"Ok." Boo gripped the man's hand as he passed and gave it a good hard shake. Just outside the room where the safety meeting had just finished, the four friends gathered and were leaning against a railing. Another group of men headed for a room on the same floor as the locker room. The old guy thanked Boo and gripped his hand fervently.

"What's going on with these goons?" Ziggy asked in a low enough voice that only the four could hear.

"They're just some of the good ole' boys that I just helped out a bit, and they returned the favour."

Three o'clock each day the main locker room was busier then usual. The men on day shift were leaving, and the men on the afternoon shift were coming in. Groups of men gathered to converse as did Salami, Boo, Frog, and Ziggy. All gathered for different reasons. Little clusters of men; the Italians, the French, the Polish, the young and the old all gathered amongst themselves.

Usually the girls would gather in their own little groups, but today Big Bula had gathered them all together in one group; outside the main doorway that led to the men's main locker room. Big Bula waved arms frantically, signalling everyone to come in closer. All the women from the blast furnace area had gathered, including all other locations in the plant when the word spread that the women should gather. The woman showed up in large numbers. Taking a deep breath made Big Bula's chest protrude, like that of a muscle builder rather then a normal woman. Big Bula nodded in appreciation, noting that so many of the women had shown up.

"Girls," she said. "you all know what happened, and you know what we're going to do about it." Her voice was loud enough that all the girls could hear what was said, yet low enough so that the men in the locker room would not be able to hear. "Just follow me, and when we get there everybody spread out, Ok?"

With a heave, Bula pushed both doors open and a flood of bodies rushed up the stairs. Frog, who was leaning over the railing was the first to catch a glimpse of the onslaught of women.

"They're coming! Hey, guys hide!" The words had hardly left Frog's lips when the first wave of women landed at the top of the stairs. Screams for scalps and balls as trophies to hang from car mirrors could be heard as the onslaught of women came towards the boys. Covering his face with arms to protect himself, Frog backed himself into a corner as Salami raised fists ready for a fight. Boo and Ziggy tried the direct approach while the girls filed by one by one. "Hi, girls, anything we can do for you?"

Bula pushed past, knocking Ziggy and Boo hard against the lockers. The men found whatever they could, towels or otherwise to cover themselves. Even those that were fully clothed wrapped towels around themselves for extra protection. Others tried to get into their lockers, or on top of them, or any place but at the hands of these sex starved women. All exits were immediately blockaded by the meanest mothers in the plant. The attack on the men was vicious. No man was left out as hands caressed their bodies. Screams that echoed throughout the locker room were those of men who had lost their dignity. At the end of a row of benches, an old Italian man just weeks from retirement, lay half stripped with hands covering his chest. His old heart pumped age old blood through tired veins.

"This way girls. We've hit the jackpot," Big Bula yelled as she led the way. Sixty girls followed; howling, ravaging wolves.

Unaware of what was going on, men were relaxing in the cool flow of water in the shower room as they washed away the dust and heat of the day from their bodies. Men; old, young, tall, and short were all languishing in the coolness of the shower's waters. With a vicious suddenness, the women stormed into the showers.

"Look at what we have here!" Big Bula's voice echoed off the walls of the tiled shower room.

"What a catch!" Yelled another girl as the others followed suit.

"I want that one."

"Look at the puny one."

The men had no exits. Hands dropped to cover their private parts, but the girls ran freely throughout the showers enticing the men anyway possible. Big Bula grabbed two men and forced their heads into her large voluptuous breasts. One after another all the women took their rewards as cameras flashed picture after picture of this vicious attack on the men.

Who were these brave men; the ones that had boasted and bragged that they had done and seen everything? Surely there were none of those present today? Over the following weeks, without a doubt, many would start bragging and telling stories, more exaggerated then ever about what they thought really had taken place in the men's welfare building. These stories would take on a life of their own, larger then life itself.

The women took their sweet time in having a field day, leaving all the men cringing like young adolescents. The women took their souvenir pictures, and underwear, and artifacts, and whatever they could get their hands on; and having done so, left as excitedly as they had arrived, vowing that they should do it again at another locker room. They would invade every locker room in the plant. No man or locker room would ever be safe again.

Frog had remained in the corner as Salami had stood out front ready to put up a fight if any woman came too close. Boo and Ziggy had backed into the lockers before Big Bula could stuff them in.

"That's one for you, Bula," Boo said giving her a pat on the back grin.

"That's only the start, cutie." Her massive hands squeezed Boo's face, lifting him onto tip toes. "We'll be back and that's a promise."

Quickly, the shower room emptied, as lather dripped from half-cleaned bodies. Hurriedly, all men dressed, and a conversation quickly started. What were they gonna do about this? What about the pictures? Were the girls going to spread them around? Were the girls going to do this again, or something worse?

The men did not know what the hell to make of this whole situation. Fifteen minutes had passed without having come to any kind of conclusion as to what the men should do. The guys waited by the railing, immersed in concerned conversation. A discussion about what the women were up to.

"Do you think the guys are gonna come after us for starting this whole thing with the periscope?" Frog asked. Dangling one leg over the railing in case of a needed fast getaway, Frog rocked on the railing with an unsteady balance.

"Hell, they got their jollies from using the periscope," Ziggy had no sooner finished the sentence when a voice sent a shiver up his spine. The others froze in their tracks, and sought an escape route with panicked eyes.

"What the hell happened?" yelled the husky voice of the security guard. It was his voice that broke the silence. "Who's the guy you called about?"

Salami and Ziggy stepped up, backing Boo and Frog into a corner. From the shower room, a head peeking around the door jam spoke up. The security guard headed to talk to the man.

"He's in her,." the man said in a very saddened voice.

Boo sighed. Ziggy and Salami questioningly looked at each other.

"He's in the corner of the shower."

Other men followed the guard into the shower, each stretching necks to try and get a peek at what was going on. The security guard removed his hat and plugged his nose with the back of a hand. There was a look of disgust covering the guards face as he and the man that had called stared into the far corner of the shower room. Whispers spread from one to another, and bodies moved away to make room for the plant medical attendants to pass.

"What the hell happened to the little bastard?" the security guard asked the eldering man.   "I don't know," said the man moistening lips as he spoke. "One minute he was talking to me, and then . . ., then, then . . ., things happened, and the next thing I know, the young fella is crouched in the corner just like he is now."

Everyone knew what had happened in the melee of attaching women though no-one knew if anything physical had happened to the young man. In the meanwhile, water flowed from the overhead shower, running over his head and shoulders and down arms that were grasped tightly around spindly legs. A stream of water flowed from the floor to the shower drain carrying excrement from the boy's bowels. His face, ghost white, hung low between legs.

CHAPTER TEN
Stag

For a while everything seemed normal, at least there were no serious confrontations between the boys and Reese. Linda, on the other hand, was now on another shift, as was Porky. That left the boys working with Reese, but they certainly stayed as far away from him as they possibly could. At the start of each shift, Reese would put in a sarcastic remark to one or all of them, and hint that he was going to get back at them one way or another. Boo usually grinned at Reese, trying to get his goat, in a way. Whereas the others just ignored him totally.

Salami was starting to get nervous about his upcoming marriage. Not that he wanted to particularly get out of it, but it was just that he did not know what he was supposed to do. Rita and her mother, on the other hand, were arranging everything. Franco, Rita's father, was even trying to find a place for them to live. They kept telling Salami not to worry, 'Just eat your supper.'. Franco, kept saying in a joking manner, or was it? 'Just show up for the wedding.'.

Franco was well known in the blast furnace, and he made the rounds each shift, selling as many stag tickets as possible for his soon to be son-in-law. Unlike Ziggy, Boo and Frog, who were inviting just those that were friends of Salami's. Franco invited anyone that would buy a ticket. Selling all the tickets did not take very long for Franco. At one stop in the scale-car area, one guy, who said he was a friend of Salami's, took twenty tickets. Porky gave him a mischievous frown when crumbling the tickets with dirty fingers and tucking them into a shirt pocket.

. . . .

Porky's truck was still parked in front of his house. It was still in the same demolished condition as it was the night of the accident. There was still dried blood on the metal, on the passenger side. Pudden's blood withstood the rain and the passing of time. Although many times, Porky had put Pudden down, and had certainly taken slurred shots at him, making fun of him anytime, Porky had lost a true friend. Porky considered Frog, Boo, Ziggy, and Salami the true cause of the accident. They were certainly totally to blame. With these stag tickets, maybe he could extract a little revenge out of the situation. He was sure that Reese would help, and so would all the others considered his friends.

Salami leaned over and kissed Rita good night. A thundering applause could be heard echoing from the Baby Blue, with the boys egging Salami on. Rita just shoved Salami away. Her face turned a pinkish red, as she blushed with embarrassment. Still attired in untied sneakers, Salami returned and joined the others. The light from street lights glittered on the Baby Blue as it pulled away from the curb. This particular night was the night. It would be the last bash for Salami as a single man. Within a week, Salami would be part of a newly married couple, Mr. and Mrs. Salami.

"Did you guys read that memo on the bulletin board today?" asked Frog. The Baby Blue turned sharply around a street corner while Frog waited for anyone to answer the question. The boys just stared at him, waiting for him to continue with what he was saying. "Well," he said. "It was this memo, that was a warning stating that from this day forth there would be no fraternizing between the sexes during company time."

"No fraternizing between the workers," responded Boo. "Yet the big shots get to screw around any time. That doesn't seem fair," Boo added as he rested an arm on the back on the front seat to face Salami and Frog. "I hear Linda is working these days as a janitor at the general foreman's office."

"Screwing her way up the ladder of success so to speak," laughed Salami. "At least she's out of our hair."

The boys all found Linda's situation quite appropriate. It was certainly what she had been working towards.

"For now, I still don't trust that broad," added Ziggy, stepping on the gas to speed faster down the road. In his mind, he still felt uncontrollable hatred toward Linda.

"And, as she's working her way to the top it becomes easier for her to get the big shots to come down hard on us," added Boo.

"Yea, but we still have our ace in the hole," added Boo.

"Yea," Frog agreed with a nodding head.

"We can still produce some revealing pictures."

"I thought you turned them all over to her?" asked Ziggy surprisingly.

The light from street lights filled the interior of the car, and the boys could see a happy grin on Boo's face. One could almost see the little devil horns sticking out of Boo's head.

"Yea," Boo added. "but I forgot to turn over the negatives."

"Shit, no, really?" asked Ziggy, a burst of laughter filling the car.

The stag for Salami was being held in an old hall down in the West end of the city. The West end was the older part of town, and the area was mostly inhabited by the Italian community. Through the years, the buildings had not changed much, except that they had grown a lot older. Many of the kids that had grown up in the West end had been a rough bunch, and many still lived there. The Bayview and Buckley area made up what was known as 'Little Italy' on one side of the street and on the other side there was All Steel. To many of the people living in the West end, anything outside of their community was very much foreign. It seemed that a man's job in the plant was often passed on to a son and then on to a grandson. Someone could live their whole life in this small community of the West end and never know what-else was occurring on the outside of the community.

Rita's father was one of these men, and although Salami hung around with outsiders, it seemed that he was trapped in the same mould as Franco. Although there were so many things in this great big world, taking a walk in the West end would make one feel as if there was nothing that anyone needed beyond what the eye could see. The families that live here were a very close knit group, and they were a happy-go-lucky kind of people. They were usually happy with what they had. Their only hope was that the coming years would be as rewarding. Their past in the old country was not prosperous.

Salami noticed the proud smile on Franco's face as he stepped into the hall and the man wrapped an arm around Salami's shoulder, hugging him with mustered profound affection. A resounding cheer could be heard throughout the hall from the gathered. Everyone clapped and whistled in wishing Salami well. Franco led Salami around, introducing him to friends at the various tables in the hall. With each introduction made, Salami was always offered another drink. Each table meant another drink.

It was Boo who led Ziggy and Frog to a table at the far end of the hall where a bunch of rough looking guys were sitting. Many of these guys had frolicked with Linda. Hesitatingly, Frog sat himself down beside the biker who was in the process of opening a beer with chipped front teeth. He popped the cap off a second bottle and offered it to Frog with a smile. Frog quickly accepted the beer as not to offend this huge mother.

As the evening progressed, all the empty chairs in the hall became filled and the chatter throughout the hall intensified. Last-minute arrivals from the afternoon shift stood around the tables reaching for hot food being served. Basics of a stag were ravioli, spaghetti, meatballs, hot bread and drinks for Salami as he continued to wander from table to table. Franco was about the same height as Salami, maybe five feet eight or five-nine, but a bit stockier and he was certainly able to hold a lot more liquor then the staggering soon to be son-in-law. Throughout the night, the party in the hall continued with plenty of food and plenty of drinks, and certainly plenty of stories about the plant.

The jovial atmosphere certainly did not change even when Porky walked in, followed by Reese. No one seemed to notice anything peculiar when Porky placed ten stag tickets on the table by the door. "There's names on the back of these tickets," he said to Rita's younger brother sitting behind the table. "They should be here shortly so when they get here, just let them in."

Reese proceeded to mingle with the crowd in the hall, the crowd that Porky had sold a portion tickets to. Reese continued to chomp on a wet cigar while giving out orders to his henchmen, "I want you guys to get a hold of that guy named Boo, and see if you can get him to give you the negatives, or at least to tell you where they are." Reese pointed Boo out with the tip of his cigar. "Now when the other guys get here, surround him then take him out the back way. Some of you hold back just in case his buddies try to get involved."

Wiping spaghetti sauce from his moustache, Boo looked up and down the long table. "Ziggy, where's Frog?"

"He turned purple and headed for the can. I think his glasses were seeing double."

Grabbing several bottles between fingers, Boo took an order from some of the guys.

Reese motioned with the cigar. Eyes followed Boo to the bar, and several guys quickly blocked the view of Boo's table and the bar.

"Hey, give me two Blue and four Canadian, one O.V., I'll pick them up on my way back." Taking a deep breath, Boo glanced down the hallway where the washrooms were and where he was sure to find Frog.

Raising an arm to push open the door, Boo felt four hands grip tightly under arm pits, and feet lifting from the floor. Other feet were carrying him down the hallway towards the back of the building. A blur of green flashed in Boo's eyes then a cracking sound echoed. A steel door swung open with his head bouncing from it. All he could see was the blackness of the night. The freshness of the air was not clearing his thoughts. He was at the mercy of his abductors.

"Hey!" Frog caught sight of the four goons manhandling Boo. Frog yelled again. "What's going on?" Before he could have the question answered, an extended hand punched hard into his stomach, knocking the breath out of lungs. Frog sprawled back into the bathroom gasping for air, and at the same time trying to hold down the remainder of a heaving stomach.

The back exit-door slammed closed while two guys stood between the bar and the hallway. Porky and several others had left by way of the front door, leaving Reese watching through cigar smoke.

Two guys forced Boo's arms back against the grit of a brick wall. Tiny stones in the wall pierced and scratched through the back of his shirt. Pinned against the wall, Boo had no leverage to strike back, and reaction time had been slowed by the consumption of beer.

"You have something we want," spoke one of the guys. Boo turned away from him as he spoke. "Hey, look at me when I'm talking." With a pair of vice grip hands, the guy clutched under Boo's chin and forced his head up to face the aggressor.

"What might I have of yours?" Boo asked questioningly. Porky immediately stepped in front of Boo. "Uhhhhaaa . . ., Porky!"

Porky's fist pounded into Boo's lower stomach sending Porky recoiling, ready to strike again. "You have some negatives that we want."

Boo's stomach tightened after the pain shot deep into his gut, stomach muscles slowly relaxed so did his bladder, letting the warmth of fluid flowing down his leg. Would anyone notice in this dark ally, unlikely thought Boo, his condition could only get worse. Porky was ready and willing to deliver another fatal blow.

"The negatives, Boo?"

Boo shook his head to indicate 'no', having no intentions of handing over the negatives to Porky. Anticipating another blow, Boo tightened stomach muscles. Porky's arm sailed through the air but the blow never materialized. Suddenly, Frog barged through the door landing on Porky. Frog and Porky wrestled to the ground while Frog attempted to throw aimless punches that never reached the intended target. The goons standing around pulled Frog away from Porky while throwing punch after punch mercilessly at Frog, finally sending him crumbling to the ground.

Boo struggled to free himself from the clutches of restrains. Regaining balance, Porky lunged at Boo, clenched and pounded Boo in the face, causing blood to spurt profusely from above Boo's eyebrow. The blood from his lips flowed and gelled under sweating skin.

Looking towards the bar, Ziggy expected to see Boo picking up another round of beer. "Shit, it doesn't take that long to take a piss," Ziggy said to himself. Noticing Reese flanked by two guys heading towards the washroom at the end of the hallway, Ziggy became suspicious. He got up quickly and headed towards the bar, and at the same time grabbing Salami's arm, motioning him to follow.

Salami, was holding his drink in his hand, tipping it to his lips ready to drink, found it splashing all over his face, most of it dripping down his chin. "Hey, it's hard to drink when someone's dragging you about," he yelled. "What's the idea?"

"Something's fishy," Ziggy answered quietly. "Reese to be exact."

The two boys followed Reese down the hall with Franco following behind. It was not that Franco did not trust Salami, it was just that he knew what often happens at stags. Usually the soon to be groom would end up leaving early and then head across the river to the United States. The trip across the bridge would usually result in lining the groom up with one of the ladies of the night. The favourite spot across the river was sneaky Pete's, a little whore house that was located under the bridge just on the other side of the border. But Franco was not about to let any other woman including one of the ladies of the evening get involved with Salami. Salami belonged to his Rita and only to his Rita.

Once outside, Salami and Ziggy wasted no time in their efforts to even the odds. They realized immediately what was happening. Reese backed off to one side, waiting to see the outcome of this fight, but Franco stepped in between Salami and Porky, and grabbed Porky's fist as it lunged in mid-air. He squeezed it in his palm and twisted until Porky fell onto pleading knees. In no way was this an even fight. There would be no way that the underdogs would come out on top in this fight.

With the pounding of fists, blood flowed from those who were losing the fight. Reese eased his way along the edge of the wall while

Porky and the others outnumbering Boo, Ziggy, Salami, Frog and Franco, now found themselves feeling the turn in the tide. Without Reese on hand, all became less enthralled with the fight and it did not take long for Porky to slither into the darkness of the night with the others following quickly.

Frog was the last to try and break up the fighting as he tried to wrestled Franco to the ground. Like a rock of Gibraltar, Franco stood and resisted being brought down by the glassless Frog.

"Hold it Frog," Salami yelled, attempting to pull Frog away from Franco. "Here, put your glasses on." Salami and the others pulled Frog away, and Franco placed the glasses back on Frog's face.

Frog apologized and brushed imaginary dirt from Franco's clothes and begged forgiveness for not being able to see who he was fighting. All Frog heard was laughter, a boisterous laughter from amused buddies.

"What did those guys want?" asked Franco, his voice calm but stern.

"Uh . . ., nothing." Boo wiped a trickle of blood from his temple. "They just have a small dislike towards me."

"You should be more careful, and not get into situations like this," Franco said as he slapped Boo's shoulder, giving him an assurance of friendship. "That's what buddies are for."

"Thanks guys." Boo gripped Frog's hand and interlocked their thumbs in the sign of friendship. "Thanks Frog."

"There's plenty more to drink and eat, so let's get back in." Everyone agreed with Franco and showed it by whooping it up in the dark alley.

Boo held the door open while the others filed back into the hall and joined the stag as if nothing had happened. Frog turned around, but before he could say anything Boo spoke up, "Hey, give me a minute." Boo nodded and Frog acknowledged the request.

Once everyone was back in the hall, Boo eased back out the door and into the shadows of the alleyway. Wiping at wet pant legs, he recalled the warmth felt earlier that evening. 'Did anyone notice?' he thought to himself. He could not take the chance so walked along the alley, his footsteps echoing in the darkness. He walked and left behind all those that cared about him. Boo walked down the back streets of the West end of town. He walked slowly while mulling over his existence up to this point. The blood that had once flowed freely down his face had now hardened around cold lips and eyes. The cool night air felt good against a puffed face. The side of his mouth still felt very tight from the beating and self-worth pride had been somewhat tarnished.

Boo walked through the quiet streets and the long walk seemed to have cooled a raging temper, but as far as where his life was headed, that was still up to further contemplation. Boo had always been a loner, and there was only so much he could talk about with others. For the most part, he kept almost everything to himself. Arriving at a one room apartment did not seem to cheer him up any, and he knew that there would be no-one to greet him. No mother, or father, or even a pet to count on to welcome you home, only the roosting pigeons noticed his arrival.

Boo stopped at the cedar covered home and then gave a quick glance behind, and then another ahead. The lawn was covered with weeds and the fence needed a coat of paint ten years ago. There was nothing that he could do about it. He once had tried to tidy things up, but was rudely told to mind his own business. The man who owned the house was a distant relative. How distant, Boo was not sure, but he had allowed Boo to rent a room in the attic. Boo had lived here as-long as he could remember, and that was over ten years previous. Before that his memory was unclear. The room was warm in the long cold winters, and he appreciated the generosity that this distant relative had extended.

Boo heard the creaking of the wooden steps as he looked up. No-matter how softly he stepped, each creaked as he walked up the side of the house to the attic. Unlocking the door, he pushed it open and flicked the light switch causing a dim light to come on. In the thinly furnished room there was only a hot plate, a bed, and some boxes used as a dresser. In the far corner, there was a sink, a john and a shower.

There was no smile and no sign of happiness on Boo's face as he looked around the sparsely furnished room. Boo's eyes seemed to glance into nothingness as he eased a tired body onto the bed. This night, as for many of the other nights, he would be alone. The morning would just be another day to add to a long and dreary existence. The trailer and the guys, that he spent so much time with in the plant, seemed to have become his entire world. As he fell asleep, his heart ached for this newly created world.

After the stag ended, Salami and Franco left the hall with their arms around each other's shoulder's trying to harmonize on an old

136

song entitled O'solo Mio, a favourite of Franco's. Ziggy, as usual, ended up with a girl. The girl that enticed the men and driven them into a feeding frenzy at the stag as she danced on the tables removing clothing one piece at a time. They had left together listening to the boos and hissing and sighs from those wishing they had been chosen instead of Ziggy.

Frog was one of the last to leave. Unlike many of the men, he had lasted the whole evening. He had managed to have become stinking drunk, and by the way in which he staggered out the door indicated just how drunk he was. He walked out the door in a round about way so no-one would see him getting into his mother's waiting car. His mother had waited patiently outside and had promised earlier that she would not pick him up at the front door.

"How was your evening dear?" she asked in a voice soft and sweet, the way a mother's usually is. "Did you have a good time?"

In a drunken stupor, Frog just nodded a whirling head as he listened to his mother soothing voice. She was the sweetest lady and always a mother. She always provided milk and cookies whenever the guys came over, and had never stopped Frog from doing whatever he wanted to. In the many times that Frog had stumbled in life, and there had been many times, she was always there to pick him up and send him on his way again.

Frog did not remember the ride home that evening, or any of the conversation that had occurred. Wrapping an arm around her shoulder, Frog and mother weaved up the path to the house to a soft bed waiting to comfort during a dreamless sleep.

As Frog lay on the bed, his mother draped a cowboy printed bedspread over him and removed shoes. With a smiling face, she planted a kiss on a rosy cheek and folded Frog's glasses on the nearby bedside table. In a voice, just above a whisper, she spoke, "Your lunch for work is ready and the alarm is set. And if you feel sick tonight, there's a pail by your bed." Frog sighed as the lights went out.

. . . .

"Ehh . . ., haaaaa . . .,"

The sound of the alarm clock ringing startled Frog. As eyes opened, a hand slammed against the shrill ringing. With a free hand, he rubbed an aching forehead and eyes. He felt run over by a transport truck, and his head pounded with pain. He realized what a morning hangover entailed, and he disliked it. "I'm too young to die," he commented to himself. Looked around, he noticed the objects floating around. Fumbling for glasses, he placed them on a twitching face, and suddenly everything became much clearer, but still he was unable to focus. The objects in the room still seemed to be floating around. He felt oozy, and a dizziness filled brain matter.

Stumbling around, he managed to get himself dressed, although he did not comb static hair, because the roots were so sore to the touch. Frog headed immediately for the kitchen. He needed something to drink. His mouth felt as dry as the sands of the Sahara Desert on a hot sunny and blistery afternoon.

"Good morning, dear," Frog heard his mother's voice softly speaking. She knew what kind of condition he was in, and knew to speak softly. "Here's a nice cool drink of juice," she said. "this will make you feel much better."

Frog grabbed the glass and gulped it down, hoping not to need to tilt the head too far back to down the juice. The way his head felt, he knew that even the slightest backwards motion would send excruciating pain bouncing off inner cranial plates.

"I did not make breakfast for you this morning dear," she said. "I knew you would not be able to hold it down." She handed him his lunch box with the Mickey Mouse characters on it and held the outside door open. "I'll have a nice supper for you tonight. You'll probably be feeling better by then, and will be able to keep it down." His mother gave him a small kiss on the forehead, and Frog walked out the door, a child in a man's body.

The morning air caught Frog off guard when a deep breath was taken. With every step forward, he seemed to take two steps back. Frog knew that if he continued walking this way, he would never make it to work this morning.

"Frog, you would better quicken up the pace or you'll never get ahead in life," He heard Ziggy calling from the Baby Blue. Pushing glasses against his nose, and closing one eye, it seemed to help him focus. He headed down the path to the Baby Blue, trying to give the impression that he was not in the kind of condition he was in.

. . . .

Reese was chomping on yet another cigar whenever nerves were frayed. Today, his nerves were particularly frayed, and he found himself on edge. Amongst other matters, he was upset that he and the boys had not been able to retrieve the negatives from Boo last night. Wendle was on his way down to see him, and if he did not watch his back, he knew that Ziggy, Salami, Boo, and Frog would certainly pull the rug out from under him. It was getting quite late, and maybe they would not show up for the shift. Reese hoped, as he glanced down at the paper work scattered across the desk. All he saw was the boys' faces instead of required paper work. At this point, his imagination seemed to be getting the best of him. Reese's body jerked when startled by a noise. He turned around and saw the four boys walking in. Cuts and bruises showed all over their faces. The cuts and bruises from the previous night's fight. They seemed to be wearing them proudly, as if the scars and bruises were tormented trophies.

Boo eyed the goons with trepidation, as did the others. Frog showed a certain amount of courage as he walked right up to Reese. Boo stared sternly into his eyes for a moment, a stare that felt and seemed to last an eternity. For Reese, the moments seemed to last an hour. A devilish grin covered Boo's face.

"Reese, do you need all these nose pickers to help you with your work?" Boo stepped a little closer, forcing Reese to back away.

Oblivious to all that was being said, Reese sat in office chair swivelling it from side to side, and barking out work assignments as if nothing was happening.

"Frog, number four cinder-snapper. Ziggy and Salami, number six cinder-snapper."

There was a moment's hesitation as Reese shuffled through work sheets as if trying to find the dirtiest job, or the easiest job, to get Boo off his back. Boo approached Reese and peered over a shoulder. "Boo, number six clay-man," he finally said.

Without speaking a single word, all four walked out of the control room as the goons stepped aside to allow a pathway out. Reese seemed to breathe a sigh of relief. He noticed the questioning eyes staring at him from his henchmen.

"You've got your jobs, get to them!" Yelled Reese to the men as he stuffed the wet cigar into his foul mouth.

Ziggy, Salami and Boo left Frog alone on the cast house floor before they headed for the number six blast furnace. Frog's job was mainly to take care of the slag runners, a one-man job on the number four floor, and a two-man job on the number six floor. When the furnace was casting, its molten iron filled the main troughs in front of the furnace, then flowed along the iron runners to the torpedo shaped vessels on the right side of the furnace. Once the torpedoes were nearly filled, then the slag from the furnace would start to flow down the runners on the left side. Frog's job was to make sure the slag flowed into the waiting pots. After the cast, he would have to clean the runners that had hardened with excess slag.

Walking carefully along the slag runners, Frog poked at the hot slag with a long steel bar. He found that the slag was still too hot to clean. The last slag cast had been late, so the shift ahead had left the mess for the day shift to clean. Standing at the end of the runners, Frog leaned carefully over the slag pots and found that they had been changed and that the empty ones now waited. The pots resting on the railroad car frames resembled upside down dunce caps. The cast iron pots had a smooth interior and were about three feet across at the bottom and twelve feet across at the top. Frog peered down the ten or twelve-foot depth of the pot and found that his head began to swim with a vertigo dizziness. He decided to sit down for a moment and think about what he had to do.

Several minutes later, Frog stood up and grabbing the long steel bar began to clean the runners by poking the bar with a vengeance into the hardened slag that had built up around the runners. Having loosened the slag, he reached for a shovel and dug deep into the cooled slag to be tossed into the pots waiting below. Every shovel-full of slag tossed into the waiting pots caused sweat to roll profusely from a heated forehead. Sweat oozed out of cheeks, sweat filled with the alcohol from the night before. If nothing more, Frog felt that this hard work would certainly get him into shape, and perhaps take his mind off the headache pounding fiercely in brain matter. A headache pounded harder than any drum beat ever imagined.

The number one runner ended at the building wall, and the number two runner extended beyond the building. The runner was supported on pillars so that the slag would pour directly into the centre of the slag pot. The number three runner also extended beyond the cast house, but this runner was seldom used. Over the years, the furnace did not produce sufficient iron, so this runner had remained mostly unused. It was basically kept maintained only if there was an overflow of slag.

Pausing for a moment, Frog leaned over the railing of the number two runner. The welded angle iron bar vibrated from Frog's swaying. Every time he stood up to straighten out, his head felt a little dizziness. In addition, heat from the runners did not help alleviate the dryness that was building up in a dry mouth. Frog had decided that before continuing to work on the remainder of the overhang, he had to have a drink of water. Frog leaned over the water fountain and felt the cold water splashing parted lips. It felt good and the coldness of the water brought a certain relief.

"Twenty minutes to cast," mumbled Reese as he chewed on the end of the cigar. His big fat belly spewed with cigar ashes clinging to the work shirt, pressed itself up against the metal water fountain basin. "Twenty minutes," he yelled "If you're ready or not."

Frog closed eyes to let his mind go blank, oblivious to Reese's orders. At this moment, it was the coolness of the water splashing against his face that he cared about. Reese walked away, disappointed that Frog had not responded to his orders. Reese was eager to reply back sarcastically, but instead just walked away, leaving Frog alone to battle the constant pounding of pain inside the head. With the constant ringing of the morning alarm still in his head, he wished that he was . . ..

Frog listened to the furnace blow pipes and noticed that the gases going into the furnace were not giving off their usual high pitched blowing sound. He knew that when the gas pressure became steady without climbing, that it was about time to cast. Spitting the water from his mouth, Frog wondered how long he had been standing at the fountain. He knew that it must have been too long. He had not finished clearing the runners and he had not packed the gates.

The main runners coming from the trough were packed with sand and cinder, which is a fine coke, and they formed a dam or a gate that separated them from the other iron runners. When one pot was filled, Frog knew that when he broke the gate the slag would flow down the next runner into the next empty pot.

In what resembled a half run and a half walk, Frog shovelled sand onto the gates. He shovelled a couple shovels of cinder on each gate making them ready for the cast. He would clean he slag at the end of the number two runner as soon as the cast started. He felt that he had plenty of time. The other workers had started to emerge out of the lunchroom, and had started to pack the iron gates and to test the drill and the clay gun. While they went about their work, Frog walked down the number two runner and started to clear the excess slag.

Standing on the walkway heading to the number six control room, Reese found that he had a very clear view of all slag pots. With a tick of his pencil he checked off the pot numbers on the cast tally sheet. While walking in the direction of the cast house floor, he stopped suddenly and laughed through the smoke of the cigar surrounding his face. He laughed at Salami and Ziggy standing by the slag runners of the number six furnace.

There had been a freeze during the cast. The slag was hot and thick and the two of them were dripping in black sweat pouring down their face. Puffing on the cigar, Reese walked down to the number four floor and peered out over the cast house. The iron runners were ready, the drill and even the slag runners were ready. A sour frown covered his face, and with a circular motion of a raised arm, he signalled the operator and the drill started sputtering.

An inch and a half bit on the end of a six-foot shaft edged its way slowly into the clay at the bottom of the main trough. Suddenly with the majestic beauty of fireworks the sputtering of iron shot furiously from the furnace. A spectacle that was a marvel to see, no matter how many times it is seen.

Standing on the slag runner, Frog rested a foot on a piece of slag clinging to the brick below the sand runner. Frog cursed with vengeance at the guys from the last shift for letting the spout wear down to the brick. Leaning a shoulder against the hand railing, Frog tried to loosen the slag with the chip-bar. The sound of shearing brick rang silently in muffled ear. He felt that one good pry, and the stubborn piece should fall free into the pot. With a ting the chip-bar gave way and it sprang against the hand railing. It was the only sound that Frog heard. The slag had loosened somewhat but not all of it, as Frog's grip on the chip-bar slipped. Like a lead balloon Frog felt his body spiralling down, down, down. Underneath his feet the firmness of the runner had given away to the smooth sides of the pot. Frog slid down to the bottom, like a spiralling penny, finally crashing against the curvature of the bottom of the pot, and then to a peaceful rest. Laying at the bottom, Frog stared directly upward. His eyes were partially opened but the rest of his body and mind were in a complete daze.

Reese pointed to the iron gate while someone poked it open causing the iron to flow down the runner to the torpedo. Through the smoke of the iron and of the cigar smoke, Reese kept a close eye on the trough, waiting for the slag to build up. With a sweeping motion of a hand the main slag dam should have been broken. Looking up, Reese waved a hand again, and again, and at the same time searched for Frog. Throwing down the cigar angrily, he watched the slag building up over the dam. Trickles of yellow hot molten slag flowed slowly making their own paths down the runners and across the main floor.

Walking down along the walkway of number six blast furnace, Big Bula pointed out several buildings to a new worker that she was showing around. If anyone could tell it like it was, with the language she used, the new employee would get the idea what work and life was like in a plant like this one. With blue eyes and no visible signs of any facial hair, the new worker gulped down everything Bula said.

The highlights of the plant were important, but Bula was giving the young guy highlights of the raid the girls made on the men's locker room. Blushing with embarrassment, the young boy turned his head away from Bula and glanced over the slag runners of the number four furnace.

"Some of those guys in the shower had terrible shapes, no balls at all. If they had been fish, I would have thrown them back." Bula's face twisted up as she chewed on a bottom lip.

Like a little lost child, the young boy patted on Bula's arm as he pointed towards the slag pots. Bula's eyes followed the direction of the pointed finger and watched the trickling of slag overflowing the runners. As if gasping for air, the boy seemed to be breathing quite hard. Bula gulped one hard swallow as her face quickly turned death white.

Blood flowed from Frog's nail-less fingers as hands clawed at the smooth sides of the pot within which he was trapped. There was no room to take a run at the sides. Only a foot and a half extra above a jump would have enabled him to reach the rim. A foot and a half, only a foot and a half. A soundless scream left Frog's lips. A horrifying scream imprinted into the minds of Bula and the young trainee. A horrifying scream that will remain burned in their minds for the rest of their lives.

In a blink of an eye, they watched Frog's squirming body melting into the yellow slag pouring down the sides of the pot. Bula heaved, and heaved again, and tried to swallow hard as her whole body shivered in agonizing horror at the site she was witnessing.

Their eyes were fixed on the pot, unbelieving of what had just happened. A horrific smell of burnt flesh seared their nostrils. Reaching for the walkway, Bula pulled herself up towards the stairway to the number four cast house. With hands clasped around his face the young man ran towards the lunch room of the number six blast furnace.

"Dead, Dead!" The screams of the witness filled the entire lunch room. He made a mad dash across the lunchroom floor towards the doorway. He did not notice the large frame of glass ahead, and the shattering of glass could be heard mixed with his screams filling the room. The workers tried to decipher what the senseless man was trying to say.

"Dead, melted, dead, dead!"

Like everyone else caught by surprise by the trainee's behaviour in the lunchroom, Boo lifted his head, awakening from a nap to see the boy disappearing through the window shattering into a million pieces. Boo's face showed a sign of indifference, while the rest of the men gathered at the window to see the boy laying in the sand in the back of a five-ton truck, the boy's body was convulsing as if in an epileptic seizure. His body seemed to have absorbed the fifteen-foot drop through the open floor, but until he was examined no one was really sure of what his mental state would be.

Boo's eyes drifted from the window to the door several times before something in his mind told him that Frog was the one the kid was yelling about. Clutching at the bench with sweating hands, Boo could feel a cold shiver building up throughout the rest of his body. A sweat accompanied by impending fear.

At the stairway leading to the cast house, Bula mustered enough energy to shout above the roar of the furnace.

"Stop, stop you're killing him, you're killing him!" Her finger pointed towards the slag pots.

Slowly pulling at his lower lip, Reese searched the cast house floor, expecting to see Frog sitting somewhere. He had checked the pots. He had seen the gates packed. He had not seen Frog at the start of the cast. What was Bula yelling about? Reese said to himself over and over. 'That damn Frog was not here to poke his gates.' Reese pulled harder at his lips.

Seeing Boo scampering towards number four blast furnace, Salami and Ziggy quickly followed. Reaching Bula, Boo followed the direction of Bula's finger. He did not see anything, but the odour of burnt flesh was stifling into his nostrils. The other men quickly followed Boo's lead. At the number three runner they peered into the number two slag pot. The yellow hot slag with its crust cooling and puffing green smoke drifted with the wind. Salami and Ziggy raised their heads over Boo's shoulder, and there, slowly turning black and melting from the heat was a blue hard hat. Ziggy pointed to the side of the pot where the slag was well crusted and noticed Frog's horned rimmed glasses half submerged. That was all that was left to identify their friend.

"Frog!" cried out Boo. Turning, his face cold and lacking any expression, Boo walked back onto the cast house floor. Across the flowing iron runners Reese stood, his lower lip rubbed red from the constant pull. Their eyes met. There was no need for verbal statements of their hate towards each other. Reaching to the ground Boo picked up a chip-bar and with unbelievable strength flung it towards Reese, attempting to strike it deep into the hated man's body.

Tears covered Bula's face for all to see. Her once hard exterior only showed her vulnerability. Salami clutched at Boo's arm. Ziggy, leaned against him. Revenge at this time would be abated. The chip-bar clanged into the floor when Reese managed to dodge out of the way. The embedded bar wavered to a standstill in the brick floor.

"We have to keep casting, we can't stop." Reese peered into the eyes of all workers standing around unsure of what to do. "Get back to the cast, now!"

Salami and Ziggy dragged Boo from the cast house. Bula dropped to the floor, her head pressed into hands. Some workers began working on the iron runners. Quickly, within minutes the floor was covered with the inquisitive eyes of security and top brass, and of course those who could be of no help at all. Reese paced back and forth nervously, resembling a caged prisoner sentenced on death row.

Once inside their trailer, the boys flopped listlessly into chairs. No words were spoken. Only questions raced through their minds. Salami reached into the fridge and pulled out some beer. They downed them quickly while staring at the door that had been left open. Boo finished the beer and flung the bottle against the wall, while at the same time whispering Reese's name. Boo watched the glass bottle shatter against the wall.

Shadows formed on the trailer walls as the day gave way to the night. A sleepless night! The number ten slag pot rested beneath the moon's golden hue. Off on a sidetrack the night's air slowly cooled the once yellow hot slag into a solid grey mass.

"He's gone," whispered Salami. "Nothing's left to even bury."

"What happened?" Ziggy wiped away nose wetness.

"Happened? What happened? He was killed, that's what happened," Boo responded.

"It could have been an accident," Ziggy replied. "It might not have been Reese's fault."

"Who then? Ours, for being his friend. What did he do to anyone to end up like this?"

"It just happened, Boo. It's no-one's fault."

"Ziggy's right, Boo. It just happened." Salami took a drink to rid his mouth of dryness. "You know Frog, he was always tripping over things, he could have, he could have . . .," Salami did not finish the sentence. All three, swallowed hard and tried to wash away the lump of heart-break with alcohol.

"I'm going back to school," Ziggy spoke up, breaking the silence. "Maybe University or College, I'm not sure, I'm not sure. I just know I'm not going to work the rest of my life in this hole."

Boo and Salami caught each other's questioning eyes. Too much had happened to understand Ziggy's motive.

"Hey that's good thinking." Boo lifted a beer in a gesture of good will.

"A doctor or a lawyer is more your style, Zig." Salami lifted a beer. "Good luck!"

Slowly raising a beer, Ziggy accepted the gesture. Slouching back into the chair, he questioned his statement, but there was no way he would change his mind. 'My parents.' he thought. 'they'll be in their glory; the misguided son has returned.'

Salami opened several more beers. Boo left without questions, hard hat in hand.

From the trailer steps, Boo could see the furnace. The area had been taped off and the furnace was on hold. Up in the control room, cigar smoke circled around Reese's head. The security people and big shots were pumping him for details. They always ask questions of their own people before they seek the truth from the common worker. Slapping the hard hat against a hand, Boo walked through the stove house under the furnace to the track sectioned off.

Red flags stretched out around the grounds beneath the extended slag runners. Useless now for Frog. The pot and occupant were resting out in a dumping slag field alone. Crushing a flag in a hand, Boo walked to the main road. Something was up, this he was sure of. Once again Boo was about to start fighting back. His whole life had been about fighting back.

A year-old Dodge Charger with its metallic brown paint reflecting in the moonlight was waiting for its master. It would have to wait a bit longer for Reese. Reese was tied up at the moment, but Boo was not. Dragging a hand along the smooth sides, Boo's eyes scouted the surroundings. Sliding into the front seat, he disappeared beneath the dash. The engine kicked as Boo pressed on the gas. Purring, the Dodge eased from its parking space and followed Boo's directions. Up and over several tracks onto a service road the low-profile tires gripped against the sand.

Watching a small mound of sand at a distance, Boo gave the car some gas, but it was not enough to crawl over the sand, and the tires dug deep into a rut. Boo slapped the gear shift and the car rocked back and forth but not free. Boo pushed open the door to see Big Bula staring down at him.

"Hey ain't this Reese's car?"

"Yea so?"

"Well don't bother to get out."

Twisting his neck to follow Bula, Boo's eyes widened when her large frame lifted the back end of the car. A touch of gas and it was free from the sand. Without stopping Boo drove up the ramp leading to number seven blast furnace. Unlike the other smaller furnaces, Number seven did not use slag pots. Its slag poured directly into an open pit. Like a view of a molten planet, the yellow slag flowed freely into the pit. Up the ramp to the cast house floor the tires squealed. The dodge slid sideways jumping and straddling the slag runner. Reaching down Boo folded the floor mat between the brake and gas pedal. The door latch clicked open as his foot forced the gas pedal to the floor. Boo rolled onto the cast house floor, his hard hat spinning on the brick floor.

A small smile showed on Bula's face. Her eyes watched the metallic brown Dodge shatter the guard rail and sail through green slag smoke and come to rest on the foreign landscape. 'Bang! Bang!' Gone were the tires bursting into flames, black smoke mingled with the green, and metallic brown turned grey. Bula nodded her head with pleasure, turning away she headed for the gate. With his hands in pockets and eyes skyward, Boo headed down the ramp back into the night.

"Look Reese!" A tall Scottish-looking security guard said. "We're not body guards."

"That guy Boo, thinks I killed his chum purposely." The end of Reese's cigar resembled a wet mop as he continued to chew.

"Still, we can't watch your back every minute."

"Dammit. He's going to get back at me one way or another."

"If he commits an assault, then call us. We'll deal with him then."

"Then will be too damn late!" Reese and the security guard stepped from the stairs of the gate's exit building and out onto the parking lot.

The guard pushed back his hat, frustrated from the night's activity. "I don't think he's going to kill you."

"My car!" Reese kicked up sand where his car had been parked, with arms open in amazement, he turned rapidly anticipating to see it parked somewhere in safety. "I park it here every day."

'Kaboom! Whoosh!' Above the constant sounds of the plant the gas tank of the car exploding sent the trunk lid rocketing towards the heavens.

"There!" The finger of the guard pointed. "I think it's a Dodge. Is yours a Dodge?"

Falling to knees, Reese's cigar limply fell to the ground.

CHAPTER ELEVEN
Best Man

Tommy Jenkins slowly rubbed tense temples, to try and alleviate the pain that was throbbing in his head from the night before. The late-night paperwork he had been working on had not helped matters either, staying up well into the night. After he had finally gotten Reese to go home, and having promised that another guard would accompany him, Tommy still had to get the car out of the pit for evidence. There was certainly something in what Reese had said about the kid in the pot, and his chums. It was not all one-sided. Reese had to have been involved in some way, but what was the connection? Leaning slightly forward in the chair, he stroked off names on the page; Ziggy, Salami, Boo, Big Bula, and that kid that had jumped through the window, he did not have name.

Recalling what he had heard about the raid that the girls had made on the men's locker room, he had to laugh to himself. Tommy tried to imagine Big Bula hugging those naked men. Men that probably squealed like frightened little girls. Well, if he was going to start asking questions, he should start with Big Bula, and at the same time try to discourage her from repeating such escapades in the future. Checking the information sheet, Tommy jotted down where she was working and what shift.

Bula was working the afternoon shift, and her face still had not regained a normal healthy colour. At every sudden noise, that once was just common place, Bula found herself jumpy and nervous, and especially when the sight of a slag pot. Flashes of the previous night's events formed in eyes. When the plant had undertaken to hire women in the workforce, Bula had been one of the first to be hired. Now she was one of the first female millwrights in the plant. When there was a very tough job that needed to be fixed, Bula was given the job, and she often tackled the job with an incredible gusto.

"Bula." Tommy softly tapped her on the shoulder. The tap on the shoulder startled Bula, as she turned around anxiously to face Tommy.

"You got a lot of fucking nerve coming up behind me when I'm working. If I was any angrier, I'd shove this prick of a wrench down your throat."

"I'm sorry," Tommy spoke softly. "I did not mean to bother you. I am concerned about you.

"Cut the crap! What the hell do you want with me?" Bula spit out a piece of chewing tobacco.

"I need any information that you can provide about the accident last night."

Suddenly, Bula's anger seemed to dissipate completely. Leaning down, she picked up tools, and at the same time nodded.

"Yes, I understand."

"Then come with me, we'll sit inside the van and you can tell me whatever you can."

Tommy and Bula entered the security van, and in the quiet, Tommy removed his hat and pulled out a clipboard, paper and pencil to jot down whatever information Bula could provide.

"Are you acquainted with these guys; Ziggy, Salami, Boo and Frog?" Tommy asked.

"Frog, that was the kid that was killed? I heard that guy, Boo, yell out the name." Bula wiped eyes. "I just know of them, that's all."

Over the next little while, Bula related what she remembered about the accident. Tommy tried to write everything down as fast as possible. At times, there were lengthy pauses as Bula held back tears. Although she was still in an emotional state, she did not want to break down in front of some lowly security guard.

"What happened to that kid, I was showing around, ahhhh, Jeff, I think his name was?"

Tommy laid the clipboard on the bench seat then rubbed at sweat building up in palms. Listening to the details of the accident was sending a funny sensation through Tommy. He knew that he had to tell Bula what happened to Jeff. Tommy felt sickened that sometimes terrible things happen to people, just at the time when they're starting to get going in life.

"After Jeff jumped through the window, he landed in the back of a sand truck, which saved his fall. They brought him to the hospital by ambulance and checked him out. Physically he's okay, but later that night his mind seemed to crack. The last report I got, is that he's strapped to a bed and under heavy sedation."

"It's a sad thing . . .," Bula stiffened and stopped speaking in mid-sentence. Her voice became coarse. "Is that all you need from me?"

"Ah yes." Tommy opened the side door of the van. "Thank you."

Standing over six-feet tall and weighing about a hundred and ninety pounds, Tommy, for the first time, found himself standing face to face with Bula, and realized just how tall and big she really was. Thinking of some of the past labour strikes that the plant had, and the trouble that they had with the men, he had wished that Bula would have been on their side.

"One thing more Bula," Tommy said placing a finger on his lips. "I have to warn you about that little raid you and the other women made on the mens' shower. That was a no-no, and if it happens again, there will be demerit points or a straight dismissal for you."

Bula stared deeply into Tommy's eyes and gave a little snicker, though noticed that he was trying to hold back a smile.

About twenty minutes later, Tommy had tracked down Ziggy and Salami working down in the pit. Tommy's questioning was short and direct. Ziggy and Salami answered the questions quickly and with as few words as possible. It was not really something that they wanted to talk about or even remember. They related what they remembered of the incident and that they had arrived on the scene like everyone else, after the accident had occurred. So, there was not really very much that they could say about what happened. For the most part their version was the generic.

When they were questioned about the rumours about some girl getting gang banged, the two became rather cold and withdrawn, and denied any knowledge about it. Ticking off their names off the clipboard sheet, Tommy walked away, reminding himself to get back to them when further questions arose.

Tommy stuck his head into the doorway of the dumping station belt shack. For a moment, Tommy hesitated stepping in until eyes adjusted to the dusty filtered light inside. He glanced downward towards the far end of the belt, which originated under the dumping station, and shook his head. He decided to follow the upward climb of the belt. There were nine miles of beltway here, and he was assured that Boo would be somewhere in there. 'Why could the man not come to my office,' he thought. 'That way I would not have to get dirty.'

"Jeezs!" Tommy yelled. From the other side of the belt came a shovel full of iron ore pellets. The half inch balls caked in dry dust splattered dots against the front of Tommy's uniform. "Why don't you watch what the hell you're doing?"

Boo peeked over the belt and through the dust at a man. Tommy could see only eyes gleaming with a certain expression of pleasure on Boo's face.

"You can get awfully dirty working in a place like this. You should wear older clothes than that."

"I'm a security guard."

"And they got you working down here?" Boo asked lacking interest.

"I'm not working down here. I've come to talk to you. I'd like to ask you a few questions."

Tommy brushed the dust off the uniform, but it was hopeless because the whole building had a layer of dust that floating throughout the air like a sandstorm. Boo was not particularly interested in answering any questions, but was bound to give this guy as rough a time as possible.

"Well then you're going to get dirty. I just can't stop work and answer your questions."

"I don't want to interfere with your work, but do you think you could do both?

"Sure." Boo bent down while Tommy leaned over the belt to peer at Boo. Boo raised himself holding another shovel full of pellets. Again, pellets and dust bounced off the once clean blue uniform. "You're getting in my way."

Tommy coughed while brushing dust off the clipboard. The dust was now pretty-well ground right into the notes.

"Okay, Okay. I'll get out of your way, but I want answers to my questions."

"Sure." Boo continued to shovel up the pellets and dust.

"Were you there at the accident?"

"No."

"Were you there after the accident?"

"Yes."

"Do you know what happened?"

Boo's shovel moved quickly, and he felt an anger building inside, a volcano about to erupt. "Damn right I know what happened. A good friend of mine was killed. Killed by some ass hole that was not doing his job. Go and ask Reese your questions. Let him explain."

"I have to ask everyone questions," Tommy spoke quietly through the dust building up in his mouth.

"And when you get your answers to your questions, then what?"

"We will . . .,"

"Like fuck you will. You'll explain it as an accident, saying that Frog was not careful at his job. Meanwhile, an ass hole like Reese is still incompetent at his job."

Boo shovelled several more shovels of pellets, filling the air with more choking dust.

Most of the time, Tommy was calm and tried to maintain composure, even though he was starting to feel a temper erupting deep within. But, this man was certainly bringing his temper to a boil. "We have to find out what the truth is first, and then we can correct and discipline the ones that acted irresponsibly."

"It's funny that the last accident that happened two years ago, is just now being reviewed." Boo yelled, slamming the shovel against the moving belt. "Reviewing two years later after most workers have forgotten or have been relocated in the plant."

"We can't get matters accomplished overnight," Tommy said, trying to use a calm voice, and at the same time trying to keep his blood pressure down. "We work as efficiently as possible."

"One accident report concluded every two years, that's excellent work!" Boo of course was being sarcastic, and was wishing that he could replace Frog with the guard's body.

"I take it you're not in the mood to answer any more questions." Tommy looked at Boo and understood the glare. "You would not be interested in telling me anything about a girl getting gang banged?"

Boo stared at Tommy for a second, then turned back to the shovelling of pellets. Tommy used the clipboard to fan the air around his face. With a shake of his head he headed back down the way he had arrived. Out of the corner of an eye, Boo waited for the dust covered figure to fade into the darkness, then threw down the shovel and watched the changing weather. He noticed northwest clouds starting to fill with rain, and they seemed to be headed towards Steelton.

The summer had hit its midpoint, and up to now the heat and the nice days had seemed endless. Good things never last forever, and Boo knew too well how life at times had dealt many bad hands. Frog had been dealt one of those bad hands.

. . . .

St. Veronica's Catholic Church, with its high peaked ceiling located down in little Italy, echoed with silence. The alter boys and priest at the front of the church walked around as if they were walking on air. In the very back seats of the church; Ziggy, Salami and Boo watched as the church slowly filled with people. Ziggy's parents walked in with Rita and her parents. Rita glanced at Salami dressed in a black suit. When noticing his sneakers, she pointed at them in disgust. Salami looked, but did not understand what was wrong.

In their vest pockets, all three of the boys were carrying something, something that helped them to drown out their sorrow. Something that provided them with strength so that their sorrow would not show on the outside. From behind a lapel, Boo sipped on a straw leading to a flask in in the vest pocket, a flask filled with liquor. Boo sensed a certain satisfaction of liquor flowing with warmth in throat, warming his entire body.

Eventually the entire church was filled with mourners. The very last to arrive were Frog's bereaved parents. Frog's mother smiled fondly at the boys, and she placed a quivering hand on Ziggy's face. A face that was tear streaked. Ziggy had been trying hard to hold back emotions, though useless. Taking a hard look at Frog's father, Ziggy understood where Frog got his physical features. Frog and his father could have been more like twins than father and son. The only difference was the greying hair and aging wrinkles.

A hymn filled the church and exploded into a crescendo of voices as the church mourners and the choir filled the church with the sound of anguished voices. The boys continued to drink liquid strength. At the very front of the church, resting on a red crushed velvet pillow lay Frog's remains. Inside a porcelain urn were all that was left of their friend. All the remains that could be found were the ashes of his helmet and glasses and particles of grey slag. The remainder of Frog still lay dissolved within the mass of slag, on a lonely track in a field to be forgotten. They would remain there until the emotions of time faded and then the molded matter would be dumped at the end of the slag piles where Frog's remains would rest forever.

The boys had been the first to enter the church, and they were the last to leave. In the secluded shadows of the back entrance, they openly drank a toast to a friend who would be forever missed.

"Look! Look! Look!" whispered Salami.

With a single flower in her hand, and dressed in the same fluffy pink dress worn at graduation, Penelope walked down the long lonely aisle to where Frog's remains lay. Endless tears streamed down flush cheeks as she placed a long-stemmed lily on the pillow by the urn. She placed praying hands to lips then quickly turned and rushed away. A brief memory would be all Penelope would have to cling to. A brief memory of the short-lived time she had spent with Frog.

"I think she really cared for him," Ziggy said, placing the cap back on the flask.

"I wonder if Frog really got laid that night with Penelope," Asked Salami hoping to receive a positive answer.

"Sure, he did," Boo answered quickly with no hesitation. "But, what if she did not use anything, she could be . . .?"

"Hell!" Salami echoed with pleasure. "At-ta boy Frog."

. . . .

Tommy continued to show up during the following week with questions, and more questions that were no different from one day to another. The answers did not seem to be any different either. At least not from the guys. Slowly Tommy started to piece together clues as to what may have happened. There was gossip and rumours from the various workers and conveyed to Tommy. From what Tommy had gathered so far, it had been Boo who had arranged the gang bang, but he could not prove it. Even the girl herself refused to finger Boo. Somehow, he had the feeling that Reese was also involved in all of this. Tommy could not rule out the fact that others were involved as well. But how? There were so many unanswered questions to contend with.

His once clean uniform had taken on a rather dingy look. His wife had complained several times that it was getting harder and harder to get it clean. Tommy seemed to be spending more time in the plant as he became more intrigued with the death of Frog, and the goings on between one girl and several men.

. . . .

Salami's parents had left early in the morning to make sure that relatives found their way to the church in time for Salami's wedding. Boo was laying on the floor with his feet up on the couch, and Ziggy was asleep in an Easy-Boy chair. Meanwhile, Salami had found himself passed out from the night of drinking. He found himself passed out under the coffee table. It was already past ten o'clock in the morning when the three started to awaken. Boo sucked on an empty beer bottle resting on his chest, and Salami was trying countless times to free himself from under the coffee table.

"Holy shit!" Ziggy yelled, holding a throbbing head. "What time are we supposed to be at the church?"

Salami banged his head on the table. "What time is it?"

"Time to get another drink." Boo rolled over on the floor attempting to get up.

"The wedding's at twelve o'clock."

"Well, Salami, it's ten-thirty," Ziggy said reclining back into the comfort of the chair.

The three attempted to move about, but were unable to move about as quickly as they should have. Instead, they continued to drink. In no time at all they began to reminisce about Frog. It was Ziggy that quickly put an end to the sombre mood.

"Frog's dead, gone! We've got to keep going, live our own lives." Ziggy held up a beer bottle. "To a happy life for Salami and Rita."

Reaching out, they clinked bottles.

"It won't be a happy marriage if we don't get to the church," Boo added.

Salami quickly crawled out from under the table and staggered up the stairs to his room.

The three arrived at the church filled with joyous sounds of organ music. Inside, the atmosphere of the church was much different from that of just a week earlier. The three entered the side door of the church and slithered to the front. Sounds of 'oh's and ahs' echoed from those gathered. All three boys looked extremely dashing dressed in tuxedos. Even Salami's hair had been combed for once.

The three listened as the organ music filling the church with the traditional wedding march. Boo and Ziggy left their position at the front of the church and walked back down the aisle to escort the maid of honour and bride's maid to the front of the church. Having made their way back to the front of the church, the couples stood across the aisle waiting for the bride's entrance along the plush red carpet of St. Veronica's Church.

Flashes from cameras throughout the church exploded with light leaving pink dots imprinted in everyone's eyes. Franco proudly escorted Rita, in her long white silky wedding gown, down the aisle. The entire church vibrated with the rousing organ music of here comes the bride. Rita focussed eyes downward towards the floor as she slowly walked down the red carpet, her blushing pink cheeks complimentary to the carpet.

Rita approached Ziggy, her eyes focussed downward to his feet, and horror filled her face at what she saw. Glancing down at Boo's feet, she noticed the same thing. Of all the gall, both were wearing sneakers, untied and floppy. She thought, if Salami was wearing the same, she would surely kick him in the shins.

Salami stepped forward to accept Rita's hand from Franco. She immediately looked down at Salami's feet and then glanced deeply into his eyes. A smile covered her entire face. Salami had dress shoes on. His clothes were neat and hair was combed. Rita could not have asked for more. This was truly a miracle of miracles, she concluded.

Throughout the entire day, from the church to the reception, the partying continued, a good time had by all. As the night finally wore down, the newlyweds made their escape. The couple climbed into the Baby Blue, with Ziggy and Boo climbing in after them. Rita sat very close to Salami in the front seat.

In the back seat, Ziggy and Boo stripped out of their tuxedos into their everyday clothes. They had enough of being dressed up to last them an entire lifetime. It was not easy to change their clothes in the back seat of the old Hudson, and at times legs from the back seat dangled between Salami and Rita.

At the entrance of Number four gate, the Baby Blue came to a sudden stop and Boo and Ziggy tumbled out. The Baby Blue pulled away with its horn blaring loudly. The blaring of the horn mixed with the clanking sound of cans dragging along the pavement. Boo and Ziggy headed into the plant, while at the same time continuing to try and get dressed. Boo and Ziggy toasted everything that came into their minds, and hands clasping imaginary invisible glasses.

"Hey, if it ain't two love birds.!" Porky walked passed Boo and Ziggy. "Your goggle-eyed friend sure put on a show when he departed this world." Porky laughed at the two, knowing their condition.

Ziggy reached out with a fist landing squarely on Porky's jaw. Boo reached for Ziggy as he fell off balance, and the two landed heavily onto the ground. Porky recoiled from the solid blow and clenched fists. He laughed at the two sprawling in the mud of the roadway.

"I won't waste my efforts on the likes of you two." Laughing, Porky walked away wiping blood from lips.

It was their second night shift, and Reese had Boo working on the belts again down at the dumping station. Ziggy was down at the scale-car, not driving it, but cleaning up pellets on the track. Reese would have them working their butts off tonight. He had arranged for Wendle, the general foreman, to evaluate their work. With Wendle's presence, Reese felt a certain pressure would be put on Ziggy and Boo. Maybe just enough pressure to make them turn over the negatives. If they thought they could lose their jobs, maybe a deal could be struck.

Down on the scale-car, Reese had given Porky the order to dump pellets purposely on the tracks more than once. At the dumping station the same order was given to the goons there to overload the hopper. With these so-called accidents, Boo and Ziggy would not have a minute of rest.

"Listen Porky, do whatever you have to do to make Ziggy work." Reese poked a finger into Porky's chest. "I'm going to get rid of those guys as soon as possible, before they get everyone thinking I killed their buddy."

"Don't worry, I've got several scores to settle with them as well." Porky rubbed the sting out of his lips. "I'll do my part, but I better get a promotion soon."

Reese poked a finger hard into Porky's chest. "You'll get a promotion when I'm ready to give you one."

Rubbing his chest, Porky headed down to the scale-car.

Entering the building, Porky could hear sounds of shovelling at the far end. A sinister smile covered his face. "I'll get you Ziggy, my way!"

On the first pass, to fill the bucket for the furnace, Porky overloaded the car, pellets spewed onto the ground. Ziggy listened to the voice on the P.A. from the bucket operator.

"Spilled pellets, number two shoot." Porky laughed. With broom and shovel in hand, Ziggy walked the length of the track to clean the spill. No sooner had he finished cleaning the pellets when again there was a voice on the P.A., and another spill to clean up at the opposite end of the track.

Like Ziggy, Boo was having the same problem. Only, Wendle was there watching and asking questions, and making statements. Boo was not able to get away from working, but was able to eliminate the pain-in-the-ass voice of Wendle. Wendle's voice was high pitched, somewhat like a screaming teenaged girl. Boo blocked out the voice by inserting ear plugs, his long hair hid them from sight. Wendle had not noticed as he continued to talk, becoming frustrated the longer Boo ignored him.

. . . .

"You doing this on purpose?" Ziggy yelled.

Porky ignored him. The car sped past spilling pellets at every bump in the track.

"What the hell you trying to prove?"

The horn on the car blared, as vibrating dust from the steel work framing filled the air. Ziggy swept the pellets into a pile. With every stroke, only rage built up inside. Just less than a month to go and he would be out of here, somewhere down south in a college where every day worries would be grades and women. Ziggy certainly would have no problems dealing with those kinds of worries. He had made his parents very happy with his decision to go back to school, even the boys seemed to understand.

Again, the voice blared over the P.A., but Ziggy paid little attention to it. Most of the time he also ignored the blaring of the scale-car horn. He would just work his way along the track cleaning it and thinking of the great times that he would have at college. Sure, he would miss the guys, but maybe it was for the best. Their high school days were over, and there would always be memories.

At night, the scale-car track seemed like an underground tunnel. The walls always seemed inches away from the car as it passed along the track. If one stood on the deck of the scale-car while it was moving, chances are that his head would be bouncing off the steel members overhead. Porky sat at the controls and flipped the electric controls back and forth as he began to maneuverer under the chutes. Two loads of coke, two loads of pellets, one load of limestone then the procedure was repeated over and over, and over again.

Stopping at an open window in the tunnel wall, Porky stuck his head out for a breath of fresh air. He did not have to lean or step from the car. The brick wall at this point was the closest to the scale-car tracks. Porky looked out to the docks. A self-unloading lake freighter was dumping iron ore pellets between it and the docks. Later that night when Porky stopped for a breath of air, his view of the docks would be blocked by a mountain of pellets.

On this side of the high line were the mountains of pellets and limestone. Only the overhead cranes worked silently in this area bringing bucket loads to the hoppers on the high line. Porky then took the car loads from the hoppers to the furnace conveyer belts. Over and over the procedures continued, never would the hoppers run dry.

From his last run, before a short coffee break, Porky made sure to spill a bit more pellets. Stepping down from the car, his foot sank into a pile of pellets that Ziggy had gathered.

"What the hell's gotten into you!" Ziggy yelled. His broom held part of the pile from spreading out again.

"I stop the car here all the time." A cold impersonal look covered Porky's face. "You shouldn't pile pellets here. Someone could slip and fall."

"I knew you were scum in high school, but now you've gone further than scum," Ziggy stood upright as he spoke directly into Porky's face. "You're Reese's little brown nose-er, his personal ass wipe."

Fists clenched tightly and Porky's face tensed, every muscle in his body tightened. Getting revenge was certainly a foremost thought. In the first year of high school, it had been him and Pudden that had started to chum around with Boo, Ziggy and Salami. But then there came Frog and everything changed. From that time on it seemed to be Pudden and himself against the four of them. They were the cause of some of the events that had happened in school. Pudden and Porky ended up being blamed, and the guys coming out on top.

The guys had pulled some stunts mostly in good faith, never out to hurt anyone. On the other hand, whatever Porky and Pudden got into ended up with someone getting hurt.

Porky attempted to push past Ziggy, only to have the pellets take his feet out from under him. Growling with embarrassment, he picked himself up and headed to the control room.

"Well Porky, it just happens that you were the one that left this pile of pellets. I guess the spilled pile is the cause of your falling." Ziggy laughed, but not happily, his thoughts went back to the pellets, and how he had to clean it up again. Ziggy knew it would be a long night with little rest. And in addition to that, Wendle would soon be passing by.

Down in the coffee room, Porky poured himself a hot cup of coffee. Shaking hands wrapped themselves around the cup. He tried to cool unvented anger. He could not let these guys get the upper hand, even if what Ziggy said was true. It was not his style to brown-nose, but it was one way to get ahead in the plant and to secure a good job. Once there, he could dump his act with Reese. Until he got to that position, he would have to do whatever Reese said. If he could get Boo to give up the negatives, and perhaps force one of them, or hurting them bad enough, then they would have to turn the negatives over.

"Porky," Called the operator, waking Porky abruptly from a daydream. "Porky, the furnace is hungry again."

"Yea, right." With a mouth-full, Porky downed cold coffee. His hands had stopped shaking, but cold sweat covered palms.

Before stepping onto the car, Porky looked both ways, hoping not to see Ziggy. Looking downward at his feet, he noticed that the pile of pellets was gone. The scale-car jumped ahead, its clanking sound seemed to disappear in the tunnel where sounds from the high line seemed to drown out all other sounds. Porky made one complete pass with two loads of pellets, and two loads of coke, and one load of limestone. On a second pass, with a load of pellets, Porky forced the control arm as far forward as possible. Dim rays of moonlight caught his eye as he passed the window. By now the car had gained its full momentum.

Wendle had finished with Boo. He had not gained any knowledge from his attempted conversation with Boo, and he could not pin any demerit points on him either, Boo just kept working.

Stepping into the tunnel, Wendle pulled a pen from the clipboard. He glanced at the next name, 'Ziggy,'. "What names these guys have," he thought to himself. Standing close to the door, he familiarized himself with the layout of the tunnel. Glancing to the left, he noticed a dim red light on the approaching scale-car. 'The light should be flashing,' he thought, and made a note of it.

"Oh, there he is," Wendle said, his voice lost amongst the other sounds in the tunnel.

Ziggy was hard at work pushing the pellets from the track, his back was turned to Wendle. Wendle noticed that the speed of the car was quite fast. He glanced first at the approaching car, which was heading directly for Ziggy, and then to Ziggy working to push the pellets off the track. The horn was not sounding. With pencil in hand, Wendle pointed to Ziggy. His mouth dropped open as he watched the scale-car pass and noticed Porky's face, cold and with a frozen stare. Wendle watched in horror as the car's steel wheels rolled over Ziggy's body which tumbled beneath. Less than a second, less than a moment of thought, and the accident was over. The scale-car continued down the tracks, soon to come to a sudden stop at the end bumpers.

Wendle stared. Without blinking eyes, he glanced at a leg laying motionless on both sides of the rail, completely severed from the rest of Ziggy's body. Wendle heaved uncontrollably as the insides of his stomach spewed from his mouth, dripping from chin and onto work clothes. With every bit of strength, Ziggy clawed away from the rails, leaving behind a flowing river of blood.

Suddenly, a piercing sound drowned out other sounds of the tunnel. With hands holding his body against the wall of the tunnel, Wendle pressed the alarm button by the door. He closed eyes and then opened them again to stare against the wall. No matter what he did, the vision of the flowing river of blood from Ziggy's leg burned into his mind with an itching flame of fire. 'They could fly him down to London, Ontario,' he thought, 'perhaps they could sew his leg back on.' Wendle looked back, and watched Ziggy continuing to crawl. It seemed that the leg laying behind was beyond repair. Wendle stopped heaving, and approached Ziggy, making every effort to assist. All the training for emergencies that he had with the safety committee of the plant and rescue operations was forgotten. At this moment, he was of no use.

. . . .

Boo waited at the window opening of the belt-line, waiting for Wendle to return to continue his report. The freshness of the night air at the window was a welcome change to the heavy dust filling the belt-line.

"Hello, anybody in there?" Yelled Tommy above the noise of the belts.

Grabbing the shovel, Boo began to throw pellets back onto the belts. He was not about to give anyone a chance to catch him dogging it. A heavier cloud than usual of dust filled the air. Tommy could no longer wave all the dust away.

"Boo, can you stop for a minute?" Tommy pushed back the hardhat against the back of the head. Dust gathered on the sweat formed on his forehead. "Shut this damn thing down," yelled Tommy, with an obvious restrain in his voice.

Yanking on the emergency cable, the belt slowly stopped, and the whining of the motors ceased. Boo eyed Tommy with a scornful face. Tommy had no time to beat around the bush, and he sensed that Boo would not tolerate any kind of a long explanation. Just in case of retaliation, Tommy stepped closer to a support column nearby. Tommy thought that the belt separating him from Boo would not be much of a deterrence if Boo really wished to vent anger against him.

"Your friend Ziggy has lost a leg in an accident." Tommy paused and looked into Boo's eyes for a sign of what he might be thinking of at the moment.

"The scale-car was involved. About a half an hour ago, he was taken to the General Hospital."

Boo's hands tightened against the handle of the shovel, squeezing it as tightly as he humanly could, enough to bring out the whiteness in knuckles. There was only a blank stare on Boo's face. No expression of any kind, at least not any that Tommy could make out. Tommy wondered if Boo always kept thoughts to himself, as he did at this moment. Tommy sensed that Boo was the kind that usually kept everything locked up inside. Tommy knew, that sooner or later, he would have to explode from all the pressure of keeping everything inside all the time. He knew that the stress of mental pressure could be fatal to others, and certainly to Boo himself. Tommy had seen enough people explode in the past to know that Boo was as likely to explode as many others have.

"I have no other details. I'll continue my investigation through the night."

Other than what he had told Boo, Tommy had nothing more to say. Boo had not paid particularly much attention to the last words. In his mind, he was trying to piece together facts, even though he did not want to believe such a thing could happen.

Suddenly, to Tommy's surprise, Boo cleared the belt in a leap and headed down the sloping belt-line. Tommy stumbled back, dropping the clipboard and realizing that Boo was not going to attack. Tommy followed, only to get outside to see the security van kicking up fine coke dust into the night air.

"You can't take my damn van, you son of a bitch," Tommy yelled at the top of his lungs. It was no use, Boo had already sped away. At this moment, Tommy had lost all patience and had lost ability to be calm amidst the most explosive of situations. In the past, he felt able to handle almost anything or anyone, but someone taking his personal van, well that was too much.

"You dirty bastard!" he yelled, watching the van speed out of sight into the night.

It was hard, if not impossible to ascertain what was probably going on in Boo's mind, at this time. It was obvious where he was going, and he did not seem to be wasting any time getting there. Not being familiar with the van, and which switches did what, Boo flipped them all until the flashing emergency lights on the top of the roof shone a bright flashing red throughout the darkness. This was quickly followed by the wailing of sirens. Other vehicles in the way pulled off to the side as he approached the security guard at the number two gate who quickly pulled up the wooden bar.

Boo thought that Tommy would probably nail him later for what he had done. But, at the moment, he cared more about Ziggy than for his job or anything else that Tommy and the company could do to him. He thought about whether or not Tommy would understand and let things slide. Even if he did, it was unlikely that the likes of Reese and Wendle would let it slide unchallenged. Boo still had negatives to bargain with. None of these things were important at this moment. The only thing that was important was Ziggy's wellbeing.

At the hospital, Boo leaned against the wall as hospital staff scurried hurriedly along. An attending nurse realized that Boo was here probably to inquire about the accident victim and she walked over to him.

"They are operating on him now," the nurse said, her voice soft and concerned, unlike her physical appearance that gave her an air of toughness. "They'll be bringing him into that room there after the operation." Boo nodded to where she was pointing.

Boo never moved from the spot against the wall in the hallway, and he would not until Ziggy was brought into the recovery room. He watched Ziggy's parents being led into a nearby office. Boo could see that Ziggy's mother was very unsteady on her feet, and in fact could hardly walk. A nurse had administered a tranquillizer, and offered her a glass of water. It was obvious to see the pain that his parents were feeling. 'And what about Ziggy, how will Ziggy take it?' All these questions flowed through Boo's mind as he watched an orderly preparing a bed for Ziggy.

In the operating room, a broken arm and multiple cuts to Ziggy's head were being tended to by one team of attendants. Another team of doctors were working on what remained of an unsavable left leg. Below the knee, the leg had been severed and the knee itself had been crushed. A new cut had been made above the knee, where Ziggy's leg would now end.

Hours later, Ziggy was wheeled into the recovery room. When the attendants had left, Boo slipped into the room and stood in the dark shadows of a corner. There he waited and watched as a concerned friend would.

CHAPTER TWELVE
Go for It

"Goodbye," Salami spoke into the telephone receiver to the voice at the other end of the line. Hanging up the telephone receiver, he looked at Rita scantily clad and lying on the bed. At any other time, and under different circumstance, her body would have sent a surge of sexual desire throughout his entire body. It had been Boo who he had been talking to, and he had just learned about what had happened to Ziggy two days previous. Salami felt a sense of helpless, of desperation, and ashamed of not being able to be there with support. He felt a sense of alienation, a sense of being displaced. Was he in the wrong place at the wrong time?

A lot of events had happened during such a short summer, unlike past summers which had been filled with endless days of happiness and dreams of the future. Past summers held the future, so bright and so promising. Frog was gone, and so was Pudden. Ziggy had almost been killed, and he was married. Suddenly life seemed to be racing by too quickly, and without any prospects for a promising future.

Salami gently shook Rita until she awakened. At first a smile covered her face then quickly vanished when noticing tears in Salami's eye staring down at her.

"What happened?" Rita asked softly, stroking Salami's face and wiping away the tears from his eyes. "Has something happened back home?" Her immediate thoughts were of family.

"It's Ziggy, he's been in a very serious accident, he, he, he's lost a leg."

Rita's hands dropped to her stomach as she tried to subdue quivering muscles. Tears flowed from eyes as she threw arms tightly around Salami's neck. They rocked together, back and forth, crying tears for Ziggy.

"We must go back," whispered Rita in a trembling voice.

"But, your honeymoon?"

"It's our honeymoon, and Ziggy's our friend. Niagara Falls can wait for another time."

Salami held her tenderly, kissing her as only two people in love would. No longer were they the kids of yesterday, they were now a couple, two souls fused into husband and wife and they both felt a responsibility towards Ziggy. Both needed to be with him in his most difficult time.

Boo and Salami waited outside Ziggy's door. He had been moved to a private room on the fifth floor overlooking the St. Mary's River. Boo peered out through the window. Ziggy's parents were still there, they had been there almost every day since that fateful night. His mother sobbed as she wiped Ziggy's face. Surely the crying was not doing Ziggy any good. At the window, his father took in the scenery as his wife cried in burst of tears that must be sending Ziggy crawling up the wall. They never said anything, they just stared and sobbed for hours.

Boo grabbed at a nurse's sleeve, the same chubby little nurse he had met the first night. Mary was about five-five, a bit heavy and in her middle thirties. Most patients feared her, but for most, they knew that it was an act, that underneath the hard look, she cared and understood about what was going on and what needed to be done. Boo felt that she would be the one to help him.

"Nurse?"

"Yes."

Boo led her by the arm to the door window. "Would you look inside please?"

The nurse looked at Boo sternly, and then at Salami. Standing up on tip toes, she peeked through the pane of glass.

"Yes?" She said in a questioning voice.

"They've been in there for a couple of hours, not saying a word, just crying and staring."

"Yea, probably driving Ziggy crazy," Salami added softly.

Standing flat footed, mighty Mary pushed up blouse sleeves and entered through the door, like a female Cagney would.

"Okay, people," She said boldly. "It's time to go, this boy needs rest not a teary old lady that ain't doing him any good." She grabbed Ziggy's parents by the arm and forcibly led them to the door. "Come back when you can do him some good."

Salami and Boo backed away from the door as the nurse pushed the couple out and closed the door behind them. Turning she went to Ziggy's side.

"There's a couple of guys outside waiting to see you," she said as she checked his tubes then tucked in the bed and waited for an answer. "I don't think they're here to cry over you."

Ziggy did not answer. his eyes just staring at the ceiling as if he was counting all the little holes in the ceiling tile.

"I take it your answer is yes." Mary stared for a moment to see if he had nodded but found that he had not. "I'll show them in after I empty this."

"Ahha." Screamed Ziggy's mother when she noticed Salami and Boo standing in the hallway. "You call yourselves his friends. Look what you've done to him. You've killed him!"

Salami stepped forward to say something, but Boo held him back. Ziggy's father held his wife back, preventing her from accosting the two friends who were obviously not responsible for what had happened. He knew better, but also knew that his wife was not in a normal state of mind and should be forgiven. Yet, verbally, she continued to lash out at Boo and Salami.

"My boy is bright, not like the two of you from the gutter. He should of had a good clean job for the summer, but you had to drag him to that plant, and take away the rest of his life." She attempted to throw her purse at the boys. "You've killed him, the two of you."

Ziggy's father pulled her away with the help of an orderly. Boo rubbed the stubble of growth on his chin. He and Salami stepped closer to the room door.

"The old bitch doesn't know what the hell she's talking about."

"Yea Boo," mumbled Salami. "She's a little shook up."

"Okay boys, you can go in, but not too long. He does need rest." Mary held the door open.

Salami followed Boo through the doorway and then to Ziggy's bedside. Ziggy continued to stare upward, refusing to acknowledge the presence of friends. Not a single muscle twitched, and at first, Salami thought that he might have been asleep with eyes wide open.

"You awake, Ziggy?" Asked Salami, leaning over the bed to look deeply into eyes. "He's not even blinking Boo, maybe he's dead."

"Check and see if his pecker's still there." Boo pushed Salami closer to the bed. "Maybe it was cut off too. If so, we should put him out of his misery."

Salami hesitated then reached for the blanket, and lifted it up just a bit. Boo leaned over to look.

"You perverted ass holes!" Ziggy yelled, pulling the blankets up to his neck. "It's still there, just my fuckin' leg is gone."

"Oh, is that all?" Boo lifted hands up in an uncaring manner. "As-long as you get it on, what else matters?"

"What girl is going to go to bed with a guy with a leg gone?"

"Lots," Salami said confidently.

"Name one?"

"Yea, name one," Boo added.

"Ahh, ahhhh, Big Bula."

"See, there you go. One hell of a woman, she would be more than you could handle."

Salami laughed hard and heartily.

"You lousy son's of bitches. My life is in ruins and you bastards come in here and try to make me feel good, you jerks!"

At least they had him talking, reacting mentally and physically. He would have to stay in this mood to be able to help himself. Boo and Salami could not be here every moment to pick him up in case he began to fall back into depression. From the earlier scene with Ziggy and his parents, it was understandable that they would be of no help at all in Ziggy's recovery. A hindrance, if his mother cried every time she was with him. The father and son thing was a load of crap. Talk about baseball and hockey was fine, but when it came to life, there was certainly a communication gap, and a big one at that. A hooker would have more ability to cope and talk about life than a father.

The guys talked back and forth for about an hour. With every question put to Ziggy, his answer was blank. The whole event, as far as Ziggy was concerned, never happened. One minute he was sweeping pellets, and then the next he woke up in the hospital. As Ziggy spoke, his eyes were wet and glistening. Salami felt a little choked up, he wanted to know what happened and then again, he did not.

"I woke up and my head felt like it was floating in space. I knew something was wrong," Ziggy said, swallowing, then speaking in short sentences. "My leg was gone. I knew it. I wanted to look, but my head was too heavy to move. I still haven't looked. I know it's gone, all gone."

Turning away, Boo raised a hand to cover moist eyes. Salami glanced down at Ziggy's leg, hoping to see the whole leg.

"Is it all gone?" Ziggy covered his face with cupped hands.

"Your pecker is still there," said Boo, turning with a forced smile.

Salami gave a short laugh then the room fell silent.

"My toes hurt," Ziggy started to yell as he rocked from side to side. "I can't move my toes, and they hurt."

Ziggy grabbed the stand by the bed with the tubes leading into his arm and shook the bags of solution hanging from the rack. Boo watched the beepers and lines on the monitors increase with every movement Ziggy made. The two felt helpless at the moment, unable to help a friend in need.

"I need a shot, the pain! I can't stand the pain!" Ziggy's voice filled the room, the loudness alarming and could be heard by the nurses outside the room. "Give me a shot! NOW!"

The helpful nurse led Salami and Boo to open door, and with a flick of an upright thumb motioned the boys to leave. There was no resentment on her face towards the boys, she was more concerned for Ziggy and her mannerisms showed it.

"Boo, he's not going to keep feeling his leg when it's not there, is he?"

Boo shook his head as he walked away. Salami glanced back one last time and with a disheartened heart followed Boo. There was no way to help now, and it would be a while before they could bring him out of his depression, if they ever could.

In the many hours of visits that followed, the boys seldom got a laugh or even a chuckle out of Ziggy. He eventually ignored his parents totally, and even attending doctors were rejected. His only communication was with the guys, but slowly that started growing fruitless as well. Injections and pain killers were withdrawn only to be replaced with booze that he begged Salami and Boo to bring him.

Boo worked cautiously as Salami watched the door. Plastic tubes ran hidden under the bed and along base boards, along the electrical cords and all led to bottles of booze hidden around the room. Ziggy selected the hiding places and Boo ran the lines. Hidden from the nurses and the doctors, one bottle hung in the lining of a curtain, and another in the water tank of the john, a water bottle served to hold the mix.

Salami and Boo were proud of their apparatus, though somehow, they felt somewhat guilty about helping Ziggy slide deeper into depression. It had reached the point where Ziggy had the hospital keep his parents and family away. The only friends that were welcomed were Salami and Boo. In addition, many of the girls that at one time or another had had intimate relationships with Ziggy also made their way as far as the front desk. Their flowers of love ended up in other rooms where they did bring a bit of happiness.

At night, dreams haunted Ziggy. Dreams that repeated themselves. He dreamed of a room full of girls giggling and caressing him as they led him to the bed and then pulled his leg off. Leaving him there, alone, the girls then ran away laughing and yelling that he would never sleep with a girl again. Ziggy would wake up in a cold sweat, and would suck on the tubes until the alcohol warmed dulled all thoughts. The next night, the dreams would return, and again Ziggy drank away misery and loneliness.

. . . .

Everywhere Salami and Boo happen to be, it seemed that Tommy would eventually pop out of nowhere. Salami had just come down from the locker room when he noticed the blue of Tommy's uniform go into the General Foreman's office. Upon a closer look through the window, the likes of Reese, Wendle and Porky caught Salami's eye.

They were up to something, there was no doubt about it. Was Tommy questioning Porky about the accident? It did not seem likely. Porky was doing all the talking. Reese must be behind this, maybe he was getting Porky to pour out his guts about every dirty lie about the guys that he could think of. There was something being said, and Salami was not one to turn a deaf ear.

Slipping unnoticed into the hallway, Salami pressed an ear to the hollow wall of the office. The voices were clearer. No-way would Salami misunderstand anything being said.

"They've got a trailer somewhere loaded with stuff from all over the plant; radios, T.V., a stove and a fridge," Porky rambled, as Tommy glanced at the two-way radio on the desk, it was off.

"I've got a guy trying to locate it. Has anyone seen the articles inside the trailer?" asked Tommy.

"Yea, one of the women that works at the canteen was inside."

"Will she attest to this?"

"Who gives a shit!" Bellowed Reese. "If we catch them in the trailer with the stolen property, that's it!"

"It's not stolen property until it is taken off company property."

Reese chomped on the cigar. Porky winced at the thought that the guys had found a loop hole. Wendle recalled the negatives that were beyond reach.

"Those guys have been nothing but trouble since they arrived here. I want them gone, out of my department. I don't care what needs to be done, as-long as they're gone. Understood?" Whined Wendle.

Tommy's eyes shifted away from Wendle, and focussed on the ceiling. With a smooth calloused-free hand, he stroked his chin. "I don't," He spoke carefully. "Take care of people. I protect the rights of the plant and the rights of the worker."

Most of the time, Wendle never spoke in such a manner. He was a momma's boy, but when there were cohorts beside him, he would be as mouthy as any ruffian. Any backstabbing work that needed to be done, Wendle would have Reese do, and in turn Reese handed the dirty work to the likes of Porky, and so that was the way it got passed on from one person to the other.

"Just be there when we corner these thugs with stolen property in their hands," Yelled Wendle, as he stood behind Reese and the desk, pointing a finger directly at Tommy. "Just remember what side you're working on."

Tommy had enough of this little get-together. With eyes still staring upward, he turned for the door. "Just be sure that you don't step out of line too far."

With the door closed behind him, Tommy could still hear Wendle mouthing off. Shaking his head, he headed for the water cooler at the corner of the hall. With Tommy's back to the door at the entrance to the hall, Salami quickly departed as silently as he had entered. For a moment, Salami stood in front of the bulletin board next to the door. With a sway of his head, he noticed that he remained undetected. That was not all that he had noticed. His eyes focussed on the bulletin board, and especially at the transfer sheets posted. There, third from the top was his name and new destination; the slab cast, way over near number one gate.

"Those bastards!" Salami slapped the glass of the bulletin board. "Dirty shit heads!"

. . . .

Salami and Boo sat silently in the parked Baby Blue, only the sound of gulping beer could be heard. Outside, Queen Street buzzed with excitement as hot cars cruised the one-way street. Hot girls walked up and down on both sides of the street enticing the drivers. From their vantage point in the parking lot, Boo and Salami had an excellent view and a prime opportunity to hustle or be hustled.

Boo and Salami's eyes stared outward, but they did not see anything, and their minds drifted back to another time and another place. The summer had passed too quickly, too many events had transpired. Gone were the summer days at the beach, the endless nights spent by bonfires. The guys had not spent one night at the beach, and never again would they have that chance. Frog was gone, Ziggy would never let himself be seen at a beach, and Salami soon found himself at Rita's beck-en call. It was a wonder that he was out tonight at all.

Glancing over at Salami, Boo realized that he was all that was left of the gang. In a matter of several months, the only ones that had ever meant anything to him were all gone. The make-shift family had vanished. Quickly looking out of the front window, Boo gulped down a good potion of beer. 'In a couple of days Salami will be in a different mill,' Boo thought to himself. 'It will be me against Reese and his brown nose-ers. Those bastards were the ones that caused this whole situation.

"What's it like without a leg, Boo?"

"Uh," Boo answered without understanding the question.

"I mean, is it going to be like . . ., will there be any-girl that will go to bed with Ziggy?"

Boo stared deep into the bottle of beer and wondered if he should answer. He did not know for certain that his answer would be correct, or whether he was just hoping that what he said would happen.

"If Rita lost a leg or an arm, I'm scared that I would not be able to make love to her." Salami leaned back into the corner of the seat and placed a hand over eyes. "Shit, I don't even want to think about it."

"Hell there's girls that get turned on with the thought of making out with a legless guy."

Salami peeked through fingers. "Show me one."

A devilish grin began to show on Boo's lips as the corner of the mouth turned down with the squinting of his left eye. Lifting the beer up from the steering wheel he gave a silent toast.

"Better than that Salami, I'll show you half a dozen." Sticking the beer into the pocket of his brown leather jacket, Boo eased out of the Baby Blue. For a moment, he stood at the edge of the sidewalk, look one way, then the other. Resting hands deep into back pockets, Boo headed against the flow of girls walking towards him.

"What the hell!" Mumbled Salami, as he quickly headed to the sidewalk to see what was going to take place.

Salami watched Boo heading to the first intersection, once there, Boo leaned against a street light and began to talk to a girl. Not once did Boo's hands leave his pockets, but the girl did slide one of hers in, then the two began walking further up the street. Salami watched the whole procedure repeat itself. It took a few minutes before what Boo was up to sunk into Salami's head.

"Hot damn!" yelled Salami, he slapped the side of his leg as he hightailed it across the street.

Fifteen minutes later, Boo and Salami stood on opposite sides of the Baby Blue grinning at each other. Behind them ladies of the evening paraded in full garb.

"Is this enough evidence for you Salami?"

"I'm convinced." Salami's grin faded a bit. "Is it enough for Ziggy?"

"Shit! He could handle a few more. But for now, these loving ladies will satisfy his needs."

Roaring from the parking lot, the Baby Blue resembled a compact version of a paddy wagon. This collection was headed to a customer.

Once at the hospital, the ladies were escorted up the emergency exits unnoticed by hospital staff. One by one the colourful ladies dashed across the hall and into Ziggy's room. With the last girl, Salami and Boo slipped into the room. The party had already begun, music was turned up, ladies lined the bed, sipping on the tubes leading to the alcohol.

"Salami, we're not needed here," Boo said lifting hands and shrugging shoulders. "Just call out Ziggy, if you need any help."

Ziggy did not reply or even attempt to move as Salami and Boo backed out the door. It was hard to tell if Ziggy was accepting the gifts. Outside, they leaned against the wall and faced each other. Smiles came to their faces as laughter blurted from their mouths.

"That's better than a harem, better than any orgy I've seen."

"What orgies have you seen Salami?"

"Well . . ., well, I'll have this one to talk about and I want to be part of it!"

Laughter broke out as if they were children clambering up and down the halls. They acted out what they expected was happening in Ziggy's room.

"Oh . . ., Oh . . ., that feels good," whined Salami as he rubbed hands over his chest. "Oh, Oh,"

With lips pressed against the wall, Boo cried out. "Do it again, again, one more time."

"What are you doing?" Nurse Nightingale loudly asked. Gone was her charm that she usually showed to Boo and Salami. "The crazy ward is two floors up!"

In mid-action the two froze, Salami with hands shaped around imaginary boobs, and Boo with lips stuck to the wall. The tap of the nurse's foot echoed in the silent hall. The guys relaxed and attempted to stand cool.

"Well, I think something is terribly wrong with us," Said Boo reaching to put a hand on her arm and lead her away. "We should talk about it, maybe you could help us."

"Yes, yes come." Salami gripped the other arm, but neither one of them could move her from her stance.

"Stand right there," She said firmly before easing Ziggy's room door open. She turned around to face the two and gave them a disapproving look. "You two meant good, but it's the wrong time, it's too early."

She burst quickly into the room, and as quickly as she burst in, the ladies of pleasure burst out, departing from their assigned tasks. If only patients left the hospital as fast as these girls did. Outside, by the Baby Blue, Boo slipped one of the girls a folded amount of money. "What happened? What went wrong?"

The tall brunette shook her head, and pressed a hand to a heaving chest and gasped for air. "No matter what we did, we could not get his pecker up."

"Then he pressed that buzzer that calls the nurses," Said another lady pulling at a twisted sweater.

"He called the nurse?"

All girls nodded in agreement. Salami leaned heavily against the Baby Blue.

"Shit-tin bastard." Wheeling around, Boo lashed out and kicked repeatedly at the white walled tires.

After Boo dropped off Salami, he drove the Baby Blue several times down Queen Street. Each time he drove down the length of the main drag, he would reach the end of Queen Street, approaching directly into number two gate of the steel mill. Boo stared at the gate and then revved the car's engine, spinning a hundred and eighty degrees, he headed the Baby Blue back to the downtown section of Queen Street, only to head once again towards the grey linked fence of the Steel mill.

Something had sparked in Boo, something touched off a nerve that drew him towards the plant. Even though it was his day off, there were no particular reason for him to go to the plant. What had happened tonight at the hospital might have egged Boo on, to carry out what was toiling in his mind. A cold sweat formed on Boo's forehead. He wiped the sweat away with the back-hand as he boldly walked towards number two gate.

Inside the security booth an aged guard scarcely noticed Boo walking by. When the guard raised his head, Boo quickly nodded. In return the guard waved him through. Slowing in pace, he held a breath and looking back, Boo realized that he had not even faked punching in on the time clock. The guard's head jerked from a restless snooze.

Boo's white knuckles forming on clenched fists pressed deeply into jacket pockets. He tried to keep his walking pace steady, but he found himself walking faster. In no time at all the corrugated clad buildings of the blast furnaces came into view. The night shift always seemed to be a haunted shift. Buildings loomed tall and dark, and people were scarce outside of buildings. The sound of a working mill never seemed to stop, but tonight, Boo twitched at every little sound, even though other sounds were more deafening at eighteen decibels.

Boo quickly faded into the shadows of the high line as his silhouette crept along walls of mountains of iron ore pellets and limestone. Overhead, the huge cranes moved silently as if floating on air. On this nondescript night, Boo would be just part of the landscape, insignificant to the operators working in their own secluded world.

Like most large mills and plants, every unused space became a garbage site of unwanted tools and discarded hardware. Unlike other places, this space between the mountains and the wall held an assortment of garbage. Feeling with hands in the dark, Boo gripped tightly on a cold steel bar. Like the cold of winter, the chill of the bar penetrated the skin of his hand. It sent a chilling sensation flowing up his arm as sweat streamed down the corners of squinting eyes. Boo brought the bar close to his face and through the darkness inspected its form.

Had this bar been formed from the sweat of the workers, from those that had lost a part of themselves or lost their lives producing this discarded piece of steel? Boo brought the five-foot bar close to his chest and continued to ease along the wall, knowing that this bar would be used once more before being discarded along with the rest of the garbage in this plant.

. . . .

"Porky, did you see Ziggy on the tracks before the accident?"

"No!" Porky answered coldly and directly.

"There you go Tommy. It was a plain accident," Reese said through the heavy smoke of the cigar. "It's impossible to see from that car. Ziggy should have been paying closer attention."

Tommy sat on the uncomfortable bench next to Reese's desk, showing no emotions as he asked questions. The replies that he received were harsh, and there was a revealing bite to each reply. Several times Tommy asked Wendle about the accident, and Wendle repeatedly said something about having more important things to do. Wendle suggested that Tommy's questions be referred to Reese and Porky. Only one statement had been made by Wendle and that was, 'It had been an accident and he had arrived after it had happened.' This was all he had said and would say.

"Do you think it's a good idea to send Porky back down on that job?" Tommy tapped the clipboard as he spoke. "The recall of the accident might hamper his reflexes and his ability to function safely down there."

"Hog wash!" yelled Reese through clenched teeth chomping on the soggy cigar. "It's his job, and he can handle it. Right Porky?"

"Yea, yea sure."

Tommy peered up from a bent head and studied Porky's roving eyes. Outside, Porky seemed quite strong, but on the inside, Tommy felt that he was hiding something, and eventually he would break. Tommy hoped it was before Porky caused of another accident.

"Was the bell or the horn working? Was it sounding at the time of the accident?" Tommy stood and looked directly into Porky's eyes.

"Of course it works. I always sound it."

Porky's answer did not vary in tone. Tommy felt that the words were rehearsed and were expressed without any real feeling. It was hard for Tommy to be able to blame anyone for the accident, or find any specific cause for the accident. Wendle said he had not seen anything, and Ziggy would not even talk to Tommy. The report would be based on whatever Porky said.

"I don't have any further questions," said Tommy folding the clipboard. "Reese, if you feel Porky can handle the job, and he wants to do it, there's no need for me to oppose you."

Reese and Porky watched Tommy disappear along the cat walk before they faced each other. A cold sweat could be seen soaking into Porky's shirt, while hands trembled in pockets.

"If he finds out it was not an accident, it's me that will be charged with attempted murder." Porky started to raise his voice. "I'm the one that hit him!"

"You just do as I say. Keep your mouth shut outside of this office." Reese swung around in the chair and turned away from Porky. "You'll get your just reward when I'm rid of the last one of those jerks."

"It was not you that was driving that scale-car."

"Just get to work!" yelled Reese. A ring of smoke drifted over his head in a steady stream. The constant puffing was an indication that Reese's nerves were certainly on edge.

Trembling in Porky's hands moved into arms and shoulders. The harder he restrained the more he shook. It seemed as if an explosion was building inside his head. Porky swayed as he stood there. Knowing that Reese had finished saying all that he would say, Porky bolted from the office and headed down to the scale-car to work. Perhaps that would take his mind off all that was happening. Or would it?

Sitting in the scale-car, Porky outlined pick-ups and the order in which they had to be done. To the back of him there were two loads of pellets. Two loads of coke where the car now stood, and then two loads down at the far end to the front of him, in the area where he had hit Ziggy.

Staring ahead into the dark, all he could see were the dim lights lining the tunnel. The vision of the accident had not yet formed in his mind, and he did not feel any emotion. He did not feel anything like he thought he should. The trembling and cold sweat were still present, but Porky felt he could handle the job. Slowly the car inched backward down the tunnel for the first load of pellets. Porky increased the speed with confidence that nothing would jump out at him.

At times, when he was young, there were monsters that jumped out from the dark. From inside the closet, from under the bed. In the morning when he woke, he found the shadow in the corner were his pants. The closet was empty. Under the bed the dust revealed no footprints. A slight relieved grin covered his face as he recalled silly childhood fears.

In no time at all the two loads of pellets were gone. The load of coke was waiting at the other end as well as the limestone. Porky's cold sweaty hands moved the car lever past the two notches then into the faster speed of the third notch. Ahead a faint night light filtered through the only window of the tunnel. Heading down the tunnel, Porky would take a deep breath as he passed the opening.

Fifty yards from the opening the scale-car had gathered its full speed, and Porky felt nothing about the accident. He stared straight ahead, siting upright in the seat. Angles of steel above whistled as the car sped by. Only inches from his hard hat the webbing gave the tunnel a closed-in feeling.

In the dark, Boo leaned against the outside of the tunnel with hands wrapped tightly around the steel bar. The wall behind Boo vibrated against his back, and he knew that the scale-car was close. Through the window the bar slid at a thirty-degree angle and it came to rest on the framing of the tunnel ceiling. Porky's eyes widened and his chin dropped when realizing that the speed of the car was too fast. He could not move his hand and he could not duck. A loud thud vented from the opening and the cold steel bar was yanked from Boo's hands and slid along the width of the opening then clanked and dropped to the ground.

Opening eyes, Boo followed the curve of the once straight bar. At the curve it gleamed in a wet dark colour. In Boo's chest, a burning sensation crawled up into his throat. The last of stomach fluids gushed forth as Boo fell forward against the mountain of pellets. Inside, the scale-car bounced heavily against the wooden bumpers at the end of the tunnel, and its wheels forever spinning forward. From the night light filtering through the dust at the one opening, a weak light danced on a round spinning object. A frightened glare filled Porky's face.

Under the cover of the darkness, a curved bar slipped silently beneath the waters of the harbour. Boo heaved dryly, and all the colour drained from his face. Gone were life's happy lines, gone.

Soon, Tommy would be at the scene, one incomparable to the first. The old tunnel would continue to stand unchanged with its dim lights and its dust never changing. Repeatedly, the accidents would be relived in the voices of the ever-changing workers.

With beard hairs protruding from his face, Boo resembled a man lost within himself. Lost he had been. For several days, he had stayed in the trailer. He had not gone to see Ziggy, and Salami had not been to the trailer. Though people wished to talk to Boo, such as Reese, Wendle and Tommy, no one had found him. Rumours would turn out to be the truth, but no one knew for certain.

Sitting in a chair with his hair a mess and his eyes red, Boo guzzled back a cold beer. Thoughts of guilt raced in his mind. Somehow, he did not feel any sorrow for Porky. It was as if it was his destiny, with Boo being chosen to carry the deed to an end. Arguing with himself, he tried to convince himself that it was more a matter of revenge for what had happened to Frog and for Ziggy's mutilation. Revenge for Ziggy, yes, revenge for Frog, no. To have full revenge, Boo would have to inflict pain upon Reese. Boo shook his head vigorously, trying to extradite such thoughts from his mind. It was wrong, he should not have done such a thing. He flung the beer bottle against the trailer wall and watched it shatter. Foam oozed down the faded wood panels.

Suddenly the trailer door burst open and Salami tumbled in, forcing the door closed. Sweat dripped from his brow, and his eyes stared at Boo in utter bewilderment.

"What's wrong? I thought I was too late. I thought Reese was here smashing up the place. You look like shit!"

"Ah . . ., just a rough night."

"You heard about Porky?"

Boo nodded to Salami.

"Everybody's been looking for you. Rumours have it that you had something to do with it."

"Rumours?" Said Boo, brushing back sweat soaked hair. His voice was low and expressionless.

"Well, there's also other rumours," Salami Spoke up, as he straddled a chair and eased himself down. "Big Bula grabbed me by the arm on my way in tonight. Damn near tore it off. She heard from someone, that Reese and some bums, along with plant security found out about the trailer."

"No big deal. We'll just move."

"Well, we better start now."

"Why?" Boo asked inquisitively, squinting eyes.

"Some rat is going to show them where it is, sometime tonight."

"Big Bula know who the rat is?"

"No, but I have no reason to doubt her."

"Me either, let's get the hell out of here!"

The boys had no time to waste. The afternoon shift had started and within hours, Reese and the informer would be pouncing on their prey. Boo started to jack up the trailer from the blocking. Salami headed for a float and a truck. Within minutes Salami jockeyed the truck back with the float lining up under the trailer. Boo swung wild with the sledge hammer, knocking the jacks from their position. Heavily the trailer settled onto the float. Under the strain, the dust covered blue Ford jerked ahead. The guys were pushing their luck trying to move with daylight still prevalent.

No sooner had the truck began to roll smoothly, when their eyes spotted the red lights of the security van coming around the corner of number six blast furnace. The lights were not flashing, and the speed of the van was slow but the inevitable had happened. Boo focused on the side view mirror, behind them another van was closing in.

"Either we get caught or we make a run for it," Salami said, looking over at Boo. "There's a lot of power in this old Ford."

"There's no evidence if we get away." A grin came to Boo's face. Not as noteworthy as before, but a devilish grin all the same.

The look was enough for Salami. He geared the truck and its wheels grabbed deep into the muddy earth. Blue smoke puffed from the tail pipe. With all its heart, the Ford pulled from its depths with all the energy it could muster. The wheels turned, forcing the trailer and float to squeeze between the furnace wall and the van. In the rocking van, Reese grabbed for security, his eyes calling for help. Tommy gripped the steering wheel, his face cringing at the scraping sound of the trailer dragging along its side.

"Is it them?" yelled Reese, almost swallowing what was left of the cigar. "Is it?"

Tommy stared straight ahead when he replied, "Shall I get out and see?"

Reese spat onto the floor. In back, Wendle covered eyes with baby-soft hands. When the scraping sound stopped, Wendle peeked between fingers, only to see the second van force its way past. The chase was on when Tommy finally managed to turn the mode of transportation around. In and out of tight spots the vans followed the guys through the older part of the plant where the roads were narrow. When the guys reached the main road leading to number four gate, they had managed to gain enough speed to stay ahead of their pursuers.

"Go Salami, go!" Boo yelled, raising a fist into the air. His yell was of pleasure and excitement. Salami steered joyfully with one hand, while resting the other arm casually out the window.

With a rattling bump, the truck and trailer bounced over the first set of rail tracks before the bridge to number four. With confidence Salami turned hard to make the turn onto the bridge. The second set of tracks resounded the same as the first. Only the truck righted its way onto the bridge. Behind them the trailer bounced then slid in the opposite direction of the float. A loud crunch was all Boo and Salami heard as the length of the trailer bounded itself against the walls on either side of the bridge. A perfect roadblock that no one could have planned better.

Tommy slammed on the brakes as the van skidded to a screeching stop, facing the door of the trailer. On the other side, the old blue Ford bounced roughly along the slag road leading out past the slag dump. Once outside the service gate, the guys and the truck would disappear.

Boo roared with laughter. Salami whistled confidently, his arm resting comfortably outside the window.

CHAPTER THIRTEEN
Two Can Play

It felt somewhat weird coming into work the day after Salami made that daring escape. Boo walked alone with only the thoughts of what had happened the day before, and what might have happened if they had been captured. Surely, Tommy would track him down and ask him more questions, but it did not matter what questions he would ask, Boo's answers would be the same, uninformative.

Walking slowly towards the locker rooms, Boo felt out of place, as if he did not fit in these surroundings, and as if everyone was avoiding him. In a way it was probably true, his only friends had been Frog, Ziggy and Salami. Starting today, Salami would be at another part of the plant and on a different work shift.

Stepping out of the locker room in work clothes, Boo lifted his head skyward. The wind seemed to be carrying the smell of fall, and the sky's colour did not have that usual summer warm blueness about it. Instead, only wisps of grey clouds dotted the sky. Already, the afternoon sun lay deep in the west, creating long shadows in the forest of steel. Boo enjoyed the winter, and at this moment he wished that the cold freshness of the winter's snow would cover the ground.

"Boo," called out Tommy, breaking Boo's concentration. "I would like to talk to you, ask you a few questions down in the main office."

Glancing down the long flight of stairs towards Tommy, Boo nodded with agreement. Tommy waited at the bottom as Boo slowly took his time descending down the steel grated stairs.

Holding the wooden door open, Tommy followed Boo into the office. There in front of Boo were gathered what looked like a trigger-happy firing squad. Several security personnel, some big brass from the clean offices downtown, and of course there was Reese and Wendle. The heavy stench of Reese's cigar lingered in the air, and Boo wished that it had been a stick of dynamite he was puffing on.

"Have a seat Boo," said Tommy in a most pleasant voice. He then joined the others on the one side of the room, leaving Boo sitting there alone.

"We would just like you to answer a few questions for us." None of this seemed to mean anything to Boo. Flipping over several pages, Tommy licked the tip of a pencil and ticked off the first question. "Were you working the night that Porky was killed?"

Folding arms, Boo shook his head no. To the following questions about Porky, he also answered no. Boo stared straight into the faces of the men. He noticed Wendle pulling at his sweaty collar. Reese puffed rapidly every time Boo answered no. All the other men seemed to be preoccupied, they either twiddled their thumbs, or rested their heads in their hands to hide tired eyes. Boo realized that they had the same attitude as he did, indifference.

"Do you know anything about a car in the slag pit of number seven?"

Again Boo answered no. This time Reese jumped to his feet yelling, and pointing the cigar towards Boo.

"Damn right you do. You're the bastard that put it there. I know you did."

Scratching his chin, his face revealed a look of contemplation. Slowly Boo answered in a way that made fun of Reese. "I don't think it was me. Then again I was not there to see me do it. Were you?"

"I know damn well you did it. I'll get proof . . .,"

"That's enough Reese. Sit down. I'm the one investigating the incidents that have happened lately, so I'll ask the questions," Tommy said in a low voice. He did not seem to get excited. The others were startled to reality, yet resumed their past-time once Reese sat down.

"This is just an informal meeting to gather information. Not to accuse anyone."

Boo grinned widely at Reese who stuffed the soggy end of his cigar into a foul mouth. Wendle leaned forward towards Reese and mentioned the matter of the negatives. Reese mumbled, 'not yet', then turned to stare at Boo.

"Do you know anything about a trailer?" asked Tommy, ticking off another question.

There was a moment of silence before Boo answered. "Yes." Ears perked up and eyes widened. "I think there's one for sale at Root River Trailer Park."

"You, lousy son of a bitch!" Reese yelled as he threw the cigar towards Boo. "You were there. You stole that trailer then tried to leave the plant with it. You and that Salami guy."

Boo ducked as the cigar flew passed his head, and then gripped hands tightly around the metal brace of the chair ready to swing if Reese came after him. Seeing the other security personnel holding Reese behind the table, Boo regained composure and gave a typical devilish grin.

Tommy seemed cool and collected throughout the questioning. On his face were lines of disappointment in the way this meeting was unfolding. "I think we should call this to an end." Feet shuffled and chairs moved but soon stopped when Tommy spoke. "Is there anything you would like to say or ask Boo?"

"Yea," answered Boo. The men stopped in mid-motion. "I'd like to know how fast the investigation is going on the death of Frog, and the accident to Ziggy. Or are they not as important? Is it being hushed up because it may have plant personnel involved?"

"That's ridiculous!" Spoke up one of the men in the clean-cut suit. "We don't hush up anything."

"Crap!" yelled Boo, rising from the seat. "Why was no statement made to the public. A reason for the death?"

The room fell silent. The men cast their eyes to one-another, hoping the other would answer.

"Just as I thought, you're hiding the facts." Boo knocked the chair from his path to the door. Tommy followed.

"Boo," called Tommy from outside the building. "I did not investigate Frog's accident, but I was there when Ziggy was hit."

Stopping, Boo waited for Tommy to catch up. "So what are you trying to tell me?"

"I was pulled off of Ziggy's case. But, if you're willing to tell me what you know about the two accidents, I'll keep an ear open and see if the cases are being dealt with by the book."

"And what's your reason for the interest?"

"I like to see things done fairly. There's good and bad people on both sides. I just want to see the truth come out on top."

Boo agreed, and began to tell what he knew about the accident. He made sure that Tommy was clear on the fact that the safety standards were deplorable. Lack of safety could have caused the accidents, but safety took second place over production. Foremen let things slip, just so they can get the maximum tonnage of iron out.

"Since the first day we started in this place, Reese has been on our backs. The stakes had built-up, and Reese was pushing hard to get rid of us. Maybe, any-way he could."

Reaching into a pocket, Boo pulled out several pictures. "He was also working his way to the top of the ladder any-way he could."

"What's this?" Tommy took the picture and examined it carefully.

"Reese arranged a get-together between Wendle and this girl for a future favour. I just happened to be there at the time. If he arranged this, then he would be able to arrange other things. Think about it."

Boo walked away, leaving Tommy staring at the picture. New thoughts were forming in Tommy's mind. There were new questions, and a different perspective on the incidents that had happened. As Tommy walked away, he shuffled the pictures between fingers like a deck of cards.

Bulging in a shirt pocket, Boo carried pictures of Wendle and Linda. He passed these out to everyone who passed by. There was not a conversation as he handed them to interested people. He knew sooner or later, that the word would reach Reese and Wendle. Boo would have the upper hand after the pictures started to circulate. The anger that Reese and Wendle would show was exactly what Boo hoped for. If Tommy could not set things right, then Boo would, and this would be the start. Boo had handed out about fifty pictures by the time he walked across number six cast house floor towards number four.

The loud hissing sound of the furnace drill pierced Boo's ears as he stopped at the stairs and looked over the cast house. All eyes were on the shaft of the drill penetrating to the molten iron within the heart of the furnace. At any moment an explosion of sparks would shoot forth in a dazzling spectacle. As the drill backed out, the trough would fill with molten iron. Boo descended the stairs and stopped when Reese, from the other side of the trough, noticed him. With a cold hateful stare, Boo glared at Reese, enticing him to come forth in anger.

Stepping forward and spurting out angry words, Reese attempted to cross the main runner. From behind a hand clutched his green jacket, just as the furnace spurted sparks and smoke shooting skyward. Shaking his head, Reese realized what Boo had intended for him to do. Stomping a stubby foot on the cigar, Reese strained to see through the smoke. When he could see, he noticed that Boo was already gone.

"I'll get you, you bastard!" Blurted Reese, as he bit the end from a fresh cigar. No doubt the circulation of the pictures had put

Reese in a bad light. If Wendle went down, Reese would be sure to follow. "I'll make you pay."

"What did you say Reese?" asked one of the workers.

"Uh.... nothing."

. . . .

Sitting in bed, Tommy held a file out in front while eyes studied the wording on the front. File number 313, Motonovich. The next file showed file number 235. Tommy tried to picture the likes of Frog in his mind. He could not. The face was just a number to him. Ziggy Motonovich he had met. At the thought, he shook his head in sadness.

For the past two hours, Tommy had been going through the two files trying to piece together what had happened. Everything that was written on the pages were different from what Boo had told him. He was not able to understand the difference. The question that Tommy was trying to avoid was, was there an upper management cover-up.

Turning in a light sleep, Tommy's wife opened one eye and focussed it on the pondering man. Bracing herself on an elbow, she glanced at the clock on the bed-side table.

"It's one-thirty dear. Are you going to worry yourself over those accidents?"

"What time?"

"Never mind the time. What about those files?"

"I just finished reading them." There was a distant look on his face. Only a look his wife could understood and she knew he wanted to talk about it.

She raised herself up and leaned against the headboard close to him.

"What's puzzling you most about these accidents?"

"That's just it. They seem like just accidents. No foul play or even a planned accident. But, there's an underlying feeling that something is being covered up. It may not be the same thing in both accidents, other than the same people are involved. One way or another."

His wife was not following what had transpired. Until Tommy explained what had happened, she was somewhat in the dark. "If everything points to an accident, what's the catch you're looking for to show that it was not?"

"Four chums, all started at the same time, same place, same crew. Then within two and a half months, one is dead, one is mutilated and one is transferred. And one is trying to fight back against what he says are the ones that caused the accidents."

"That's the guy they call Boo?"

"His name sure fits. He's a spooky guy in many ways. There's not much information in his employment file. No next of kin, no home address or phone number. Anyway, he says Reese should have had the rails fixed on those overhanging runners, and that the pots are supposed to be checked before cast, but were not."

"And the other accident?"

"Boo came right out and said that Reese and Porky, the other guy killed in the area, were the ones that planned the accident."

"Was the last accident an accident?"

"I've got a feeling it was also planned."

"Boo?"

"Yea, revenge." Tommy dropped the files onto the night table then folded arms. There was a sad look on his face. In his mind, he wondered if he should pursue the matter any further, since they were not his cases.

"Are you going to prove the others were not accidents?"

"If I do, I'll have to prove the last one was not an accident. Everyone's head is going to roll."

"Including some security people."

"Yea," answered Tommy in a low voice. He eased under the covers as his wife placed arms around him.

She was a tall woman and almost as slender as Tommy. She was the kind of woman that stood behind her man. "Well dear, if it's a matter of everything going wrong, you should set it right."

Tommy flicked the night light off. In the darkness, his eyes searched the shadows for answers. What he had not told his wife about, were the pictures that Boo had given him. He felt he could not discuss it with her. If he set out to uncover anything about the accidents, this would be a good place to start. He would confront Wendle, and get more information on this girl Linda. As sleep slowly became dreams, Tommy planned priority moves for the next day.

. . . .

Reese sat in an old beat-up car he was using until his was replaced. Along with him were several thugs that once helped him lay a beating on Boo. With all the windows rolled down letting the flow of smoke escape into the darkening light, Reese kept an eye on the road leading towards number four gate. Under the approaching night sky, Reese was going to carry out his revenge against Boo. All that was holding him up were the other thugs that were bringing a tow truck. In the vast parking lot stretching away from the view of the security guard, Reese had planned to tow away the Baby Blue.

With the tow truck behind, Reese drove slowly towards the Baby Blue. Reese did not speak, only pointed with the cigar, making his intentions known. In a matter of seconds the front end of the car lifted from the ground and eased from its berth. Eyes scanned their surroundings, when no-one came into view, the three vehicles headed down Goulais Avenue and out to a secluded part of town.

Waving a hand out the window to slow the tow truck down, Reese pulled off the main dirt road onto a cleared path. Out here they were beyond the view and out of hearing range. Standing between the Baby Blue and the lights of his car, a smile covered his face from ear to ear. From behind, the thugs gathered with their hands leaden with bars, with pipes and sledge hammers, like vultures preying on a helpless victim.

Glass shattered under the explosive blow of the sledge hammer. Reese hooted with joy as the others joined in. The once beautiful classic Blue Hudson, within minutes became nothing more than a mere piece of scrapped metal. Gone was a life time of memories. Gone was the character of the car, and the boys that rode in her. She had met the fate of her owner under the hand of the same person. Like Ziggy, the Baby Blue lay lifeless, unable to continue as it once had, mutilated.

Standing back, Reese admired the destruction. From a bottle of Canadian Club, he drank with satisfaction. In the glow of the headlights, the bottle passed from one hand to another as the late hours of the night dwindled. In an hour or so, Reese planned to be at the gate when the afternoon shift ended. Hidden from view, he would watch Boo become devastated at the sight of the once proud Baby Blue. Meanwhile Reese gloated as he admired what remained of the Baby Blue.

Boo had become uncaring of work and his job. This night was no different as he headed to the gate early. He also would punch out early. No longer had position in the work force or the lost wages become something to worry about. All that was on his mind were the facts that he was alone, friendless, and the matter of revenge weighed heavy in thoughts.

Tommy glanced at his watch when he saw Boo emerge from the passageway tunnel. Ten-thirty the watch indicated. Walking from number seven furnace, Tommy quickened his step as he headed towards number four gate.

"Boo! Boo! Wait up," called out Tommy. He stepped into a run when noticing that Boo was not waiting.

"You could have waited. I'm not a young man anymore." Gasping in mouthfuls of air Tommy kept pace with Boo. "I'd like to let you know, that I'm going to investigate all the accidents on my own."

Boo's face was blank, as if he did not hear what Tommy was saying. He had not even acknowledged Tommy's presence.

"What do you expect me to do, jump for joy?" Boo barked back. He shrugged shoulders. "Your conclusions won't bring the past to a new living form. It can't erase what's happened."

"Your friends can't come back. But maybe justice will prevent others from falling into the same situation." Tommy waited for an answer that did not come. "Your convictions on the accidents may be true, and I might be able to prove it, but I'll also have to prove what happened in Porky's accident."

"That must of been some gory accident to clean up after."

What Tommy had expected Boo to say was far from what he heard.

"Aren't you going to punch out?" Said Tommy as the two passed the clocks.

"What . . ., yeah." Boo backed up the few steps and placed the time card into the digital clock.

Tommy now knew that Boo was thinking deeply, not just playing it cool the way his mannerisms showed. If only he had not suspected Boo as the one that killed Porky, he could begin to like him. As it was, it was hard to understand Boo, hard to get into his thoughts. Though Tommy knew in his own mind that Boo committed the act, it would be hard to prove. There was a lack of evidence. If it was as suspected, Reese and Boo would be going at each other, and the situation could become more ticklish.

Standing at the gate, Tommy watched Boo head along the sidewalk of the parking lot. He wanted to follow and continue trying to talk to him. At present, it seemed useless. Stopping near the end where the Baby Blue was parked, Boo slowly glanced around. When his attention became more acute, his movements became more disturbed. Stretching his neck, Tommy watched and anticipated that something was amiss.

Screeching around the corner, the tow truck pulling the Baby Blue attempted a U-turn. Quickly jumping out, an evasive man released the cable holding up the Baby Blue. As wheels left rubber on the pavement, the once car of many pleasures lay motionless behind the fleeing tow truck. Tommy watched Boo stand motionless, his eyes fixed on the Baby Blue.

From a block away, Reese watched Boo walk to the middle of the intersection, beneath the glow of security lights. Reese kept his car running and in gear, in fear that somehow Boo would give chase. Boo had not noticed anything or anyone around. His thoughts were on the car, his face was a blank emotion. Tommy began slowly walking towards the car and Boo.

Boo placed his right hand on the front fender of the car and caressed its full length. Once at the back, he bent down and pulled a knife from a pocket. Thrusting an arm up under the back the knife point pierced the gas tank. Stepping back, Boo watched the gas flow evenly beneath the car. When the flow trickled to drops, Boo lit a match and tossed it towards the Baby Blue. A vacuumed roar of flames reached skyward lighting up the starless sky as Boo walked away under its hue. Tommy stopped half the distance of an intended walk and watched in amazement, oblivious to the fact that Reese and his cohorts had retreated down Goulais Avenue to disappear in amongst the side streets.

CHAPTER FOURTEEN
Where's the Gang

The laughter and screams of little children could be heard outside the door. An aged grandmother was speaking in an Italian dialect as Boo rapped on the door a second time. Salami opened the door slowly, while at the same time was trying to hold back a yapping little poodle with a foot. The little girl in Salami's arms was crying as she pulled at Salami's curly blonde hair with sticky hands.

"Hey Boo. How you doing? Come on in."

"Not bad," replied Boo. "You don't look like you're doing too well."

"When I got married," replied Salami. "I thought it was supposed to be just the new bride and groom. And, here, I ended up with a whole family that ain't even mine!"

Boo walked from the hallway into the living room and gave the place a once over. It seemed that Rita's younger brothers and sisters had turned the living room into what resembled a battle ground. Rita's grandmother attempted to herd the kids around as if they were lost sheep. Boo acknowledged Rita, who waved from the kitchen. Rita seemed to have lost her attractiveness, and as she stood in the kitchen wearing a maternity dress, with her hair in rollers, Boo noticed only a look of discontentment covering her face.

"I heard about the Baby Blue," spoke Salami sadly. "Have you told Ziggy yet?"

"No, no." Boo slumped into the nearby arm chair and stared at the dog that was yapping at his feet. With a swift kick he sent the dog scurrying under the couch. Giving Boo an okay sign, Salami nodded with pleasure.

"They just came over and stayed, even the old bag of dirt," lamented Salami, in a voice that was loud enough to be heard by the grandmother. "It's okay, he added, she doesn't understand English. I enjoy married life, but not the trimmings that have come along with it. We're going to move to the other side of town."

Boo sat quietly in the arm chair, and Salami noticed that Boo had changed from the guy that he had known in the past. In a lot of ways, he expected that he had changed in Boo's eyes as well. Suddenly, it seemed as if they no longer had anything to talk about, nothing to share and nothing to laugh about. No doubt things had changed a lot, and that both had done a lot of growing up this summer. The old bag and the kids seemed to hang on every word that was said, and Boo felt as if they were a jury about to pass judgement on Salami's actions.

"What have you been up to Salami? Besides married life that is."

"Hell, nothing much, Boo. I go to work and then come home, and then do it all over again. There doesn't seem to be any time to go out and do anything."

"Supper's on the table!" yelled Rita from the kitchen. "Boo, please come join us."

No sooner had the words faded when the living room emptied, including the grandmother. Boo looked around the kitchen and made up his mind.

"I can't stay, thanks. You understand Salami."

"Hell, yea! If I could leave, I'd probably leave with you." Salami walked Boo to the door, and watched as Boo slowly made his way down the front walk.

"Hey, Boo!" Boo turned and stared at Salami. "If you need anything, I'm good for it. We're still friends, you know?"

Boo nodded, then walked backwards down the side walk with hands deep in pockets. He watched the door close and Salami disappearing behind it. He stared at the door for a moment and felt as if it was a door closing on him forever. Salami was a good buddy, yet he had not been there when Boo needed him. Like when the Baby Blue was destroyed. A cold September wind blew across the vacated street and Boo lifted the coat collar, and walked slowly away from Salami's house.

. . . .

It was about six o'clock when Boo walked past Penelope Snidermost's house. In the dimming light of evening the house looked equally dim. It was certainly a far cry from the night the party was held. During his reminiscing, Boo did not notice the continental that was pulling into the drive. He stared blankly towards the house while standing on the sidewalk. For a moment, Penelope hesitated before continuing to walk towards the door with her parents. She had noticed the figure standing on the sidewalk. She recognized Boo immediately, and crossed the lawn, walking towards him.

"Boo!" She called, startling Boo out of a blank spell. "Are you all right?"

"Ah . . ., yeah, where did you come from?"

"Here, I live here."

"Penelope," yelled her father "Get back here this very minute." His voice was stern, a voice that was not to be questioned.

"I'm pregnant, I'm carrying Frog's baby." No sooner had she spoken the words when she turned around and walked towards her father, obeying his command.

"That damn Frog did it!" exclaimed Boo to himself, as the door to the large house slammed shut. "At-ta go Frog!" yelled Boo towards the house, raising a fist in the air in a salute to Frog's memory, and to his successor who was at this very moment growing within Penelope. With a happier gait, Boo continued walking down the sidewalk towards Ziggy's house.

. . . .

Boo rapped twice on the door with the knocker, and waited until the door opened. Boo faced Ziggy's mother. Her smile turned into a sour frown when she saw Boo. At first glance, Ziggy's mother reminded him somewhat of a cultured woman. The way she dressed and mannerisms, seemed to reflect the upper-class position in life that she held. But, one would never know it the way she stared at Boo.

"You have a lot of damn nerve to come back to this house!" she yelled in a high pitched voice. "Especially after the way you treated Ziggy, with all those floozies and all those hoses for booze."

Boo was caught by surprise by the way in which she yelled at him, and even before he had the chance to say good evening, or to ask to see Ziggy. The smile that covered his face vanished quickly, and he felt a stab of pain cut deep into his heart from the words that Ziggy's mother was yelling at him.

"I order you to stay away from this house, and from Ziggy, and if you're standing here a minute from now, I'll call the police." With a sound that pierced his ears, the door was slammed shut in his face.

Pretending that he was leaving, Boo walked along the pathway till reaching the hedge surrounding the house. The curtain in the door's window returned to its normal position when Boo was out of sight.

Raising himself up on toes, Boo peeked into the lit room of the house. He felt the pain aching in fingers as he strained to hold onto the window sill. He noticed that the inside door to the room was closed. Forcing the window open, he raised himself up and dragged himself through the window and into the room. Ziggy was laying in bed, watching and laughing as Boo clumsily climbed through the window. It did not matter to Ziggy if the action was funny or not.

Boo smelt a pungent odour of dry sweat defiling the room. The air was stale, so he left the window opened as he stood by the bed. Their hands gripped warmly with solid grip. As Ziggy raised an arm to greet Boo, Boo noticed the red blotches covering his arm. Red blotches that had a distinctive pattern that ran the full length of the forearm. They were the needle tracks following the veins that protruding from the skin.

"Hey man, you shooting?"

"Prescription, pain killers."

"You give yourself shots?"

"Yea. The doctor can't come by all the time." Ziggy strained as he attempted to sit up. All life seemed to have been sucked from his body. Boo noticed the yellow stained sheets, yellow from sweat and spilled beer. Staring at these caused Boo to avert looking at Ziggy.

"They're all prescription shots," said Ziggy, swaying his head back and forth. At the moment his head felt as light as his thoughts.

"Ziggy I have bad news," spoke Boo softly.

Ziggy's face turned cold as he spoke.

"The bad news is down here and the pecker don't work either." Ziggy pointed to himself. "What can be worse than that?"

Boo paused for a moment, staring deep into Ziggy's eyes. "Reese smashed the Baby Blue."

"Big deal!" retorted Ziggy, reaching under the pillow to pull out a beer. "In the garbage can there's another beer."

Reaching into the garbage can, Boo pulled out the beer, and popping watched warm beer foam from the spout.

"You don't care about the car?"

"Hell, what do I need a car for. Never mind an old one like that."

"You've got to get out of this spell you're in. You'll die in here if you don't get out."

"Hey I'm already dead!" shouted Ziggy.

It was the sudden opening of the door that startled Boo. A crazy woman came towards him flinging the end of a broom. It was enough to make Boo scramble to avoid being hit.

"Get out of here you mutilator, you murderer!"

Although it was not at all funny, Ziggy laughed heartily as he tossed beer all around the room. He laughed with glee at the sight, as if this show was being staged entirely for his pleasure. A random swing of the broom handle knocked the beer can from Boo's hand, and shattered a nearby picture of the four guys together, the frame sitting on Ziggy's bedside table. As the broom handle swung towards Boo, he dived out through the open window and landed beside the broom protruding from the ground. The very last thing Boo heard was Ziggy's boisterous laughter as his mother slammed the window shut and drew the curtains.

Under the present circumstances, Boo felt that it was useless for him to try and help his disabled friend. A friend who was now disabled, not only in body, but also in mind. Boo wondered what was worse, Ziggy's mother or the man's present affliction.

As the days passed, Boo's appearance was deteriorating. His once shaven face was now covered with the scruffiness of a beard that was starting to form, and grey lines appeared around his eyes. His hair remained uncombed, and Boo looked as if he had not slept for at least the past several days. Going to work had become just a routine process, and his meetings with Tommy every time he entered the plant seemed like a ritual. There were always questions that were asked, and Boo would always give the same answers. Tommy continued to be persistent in his questioning, no matter what.

"Boo, you have a minute?" asked Tommy sitting next to Boo on the bench.

Boo did not reply. Obviously, he was not going anywhere, except perhaps to the cast house floor on number six where they would be casting very shortly. Leaning back, Boo let Tommy proceed with his questioning again.

"Boo, with your testimony, and the evidence that I've uncovered, I think the blame for your chums' accidents can be placed on the true culprits."

"Get to the point," Boo responded sharply.

"In view of what took place, before and during the accident, justice might very well consider your actions as part of temporary insanity."

"Insanity?" Boo yelled. "You think I would at any time be insane?"

Tommy stared deeply into Boo's cold brown eyes.

"No, I can't say I could." Tommy knew that he was trying to be too helpful, but he did not know why he wanted to help this man. "Then it could come down to your word against mine?"

"Yup." Boo grinned confidently.

"I did do a lot of my own investigating, and in a way, I believe you. I'm going to Security and Administration with the pictures and a witness. I think there'll be charges and most likely dismissals. That girl in the picture, Linda, she will testify that Reese set up that little get-together between her and Wendle. It all comes down to favours granted on down the line."

"You do what you have to do." Boo stood up and put on an asbestos jacket. "I'll survive, going one on one. It just happens that the survivor, is not always the winner."

"Cast Time!" yelled a voice over the P.A. system.

Pondering what Boo had said, Tommy jotted down the last statement. He knew that if Boo came out on top, the survivor, he would pay for his achievements by losing his friends. If Reese came out on top, what would Reese loose? 'Reese would not lose anything,' thought Tommy. 'so what Boo was saying, was that he would be the survivor!'

CHAPTER FIFTEEN
Memories

For the past couple of days Tommy had been keeping very close tabs on the activities of both Reese and Boo. If there was something, that was going to happen, he wanted to be there when it happened. Today, Tommy was hanging around the number four blast furnace and after examining the work sheets, he felt sure that something was going to happen today. As Tommy examined the work sheets, he noticed that Boo was on with Reese for the afternoon shift.

Ducking around the drill control room on number four, Tommy watched Boo emerge from the number six blast furnace. Near the trough, Tommy saw Reese walking out of the shadows to face Boo. The cigar that Reese usually chomped on was gone and he stood as close to Boo as he possibly could. Boo was much taller than Reese, and his chin only reached Boo's chest.

Reese spoke quickly and forcefully, hoping to intimidate Boo. "Tonight's the night we have it out, you son of a bitch," Reese yelled. There was an unprecedented anger in Reese's voice as he stared coldly at Boo.

"After the first cast is over, it's you and me in the electrical room. Only the winner is going to come out alive."

Reese disappeared into the shadows as quickly as he had appeared. Only the thunderous roar of the number four furnace filled the air as Boo stood there with Reese's words ringing in his ears. Boo stood alone for a moment and then proceeded to walk to the office to check the work sheets. Having done so, he headed out towards the locker room. Boo did not seem to be particularly bothered by anything that Reese had said, because he knew that in a fight it would be him that would emerge the winner. But he also new that at no time could Reese ever be trusted to fight a fair fight.

. . . .

The level of chatter increased as men of different proportions milled around the locker room. Men clad only in towels walked to and from the showers. As the number of men increased, so did the chatter. For about an hour and a half, between the three to eleven shift and the eleven to seven shift, the room full of bodies seemed to be in a state of chaos. In a short period, the aisles would be empty and the lockers would be silent. For now, the smell of human sweat filled the air. In a short while, the men would be heading home or to their jobs.

As the last man left the Welfare Room, only silence remained. A cool September wind blew through the open window above the lockers. It would not be long before the impending Winter would bring its cold blast of arctic air. The summer was eventful, but as the Fall of 1979 arrived, it was obvious that life had changed. The times would never be the same again.

A stream of light filled with dirt beamed down upon the shoulders of a lone man sitting silently on a hard bench worn with age and use. Dressed in work clothes, and with boot laces untied, eyes glanced at the concrete floor. He reflected on a different place and a different time. Raising his head, an expressionless face glanced from locker to locker. His eyes seemed to anticipate something that was there, but was not. Closing eyes, he gently rested his head back against the locker.

Longish brown hair, cut in a shag style, rested on the shoulders of the six-foot one-inch body, weighing a hundred and seventy pounds. His clean cut face and deep brown eyes were accented by a moustache which extended down to the corner of his lips giving him the essence of a loner. He sat alone with hands resting on his lap, facing upward in a questioning manner. He opened glossy wet eyes and scanned the entire length of the lockers, as the smell of sweat disappeared. A smile came to his lips, but faded as quickly as it had arrived, his thoughts seemed to depart from his body. No-longer were there lockers, or the clanking of the steel mill.

Lowering eyes, he bowed his head downward. Above him, a beam of light rested gently on slumped shoulders. He sat on the green painted bench, and felt the cool September wind whispering above him. Clothes moved in rhythm with the wind blowing gently above the lockers. Around him empty lockers stood waiting to be occupied.

There was a time before this, a good time. His thoughts gravitated towards those times as the cool wind above the lockers gently caressed the darkening night's sky. He wished for the wind to carry him away.

. . . .

Boo checked the torpedo shaped clay gun as he stepped onto the cast house floor. This was the clay gun that he was assigned to take care of. After the cast was over, the gun would be swung into the trough and placed at the spout, where the molten iron flowed. Inside

202

the clay gun heat drying clay would be forced into the hole until it was sealed. Boo's job was to fill the gun after each cast.

With a steel bar in hand, Boo poked at the spout of the clay gun until the hardened clay fell clear of its opening. Boo tested the plunger, forcing the remaining clay out. Opening the back lid, Boo broke into its cavity several chunks of clay. He pressed the plunger forcing the clay to the front of the spout. Normally the gun would consume about twenty chunks of clay. Boo had placed three into its chamber. At the lid, Boo shoved one more chunk of clay into its opening and packing it so that it would remain there, then he locked the lid shut. At the controls, Boo moved the plunger to its most forward position. The gun was ready for the cast.

Putting on the asbestos jacket, Boo sat on the bench and waited for the rest of the workers to get ready for the cast. Minutes later Reese walked out onto the cast house floor.

"Cast time," yelled Reese. Then he took his place off to the side where Boo and the operator sat. "Let's go Tony."

Tony approached the controls and started the air drill. Within seconds sparks started to fly, sending a shower of colours out over the cast house floor. Reese paced back and forth as the cast continued. At every twist and turn he would see Boo's grinning face, sending shivers up and down his spine. Reaching for a cigar, he shoved it into a foul mouth and started to chew on it. It did not seem to calm the nervousness he was feeling.

Noticing a motion from Reese, Boo adjusted the position of the last iron torpedo from a remote control lever. Reese was under the impression that Boo would most certainly decline any order that he gave.

The last of the slag spurted from the hole in the furnace and behind it new forming iron spewed forth. The cast was almost at its end, and Reese thought about the meeting that was soon to happen in the electrical room between him and Boo. He had everything planned down to a tee this time. In the darkness of the room, Reese's brown nose-ers waited anxiously to use their rubber hoses as weapons on an unsuspecting Boo.

"Plugger up," yelled Reese above the roaring of the starving furnace. With a hand, he directed the clay gun into the trough. Seeing the downward motion of Reese's hand, the operator pressed the plunger button that forced clay into the furnace.

Boo sat motionless on the bench.

"Plugger up, plugger up," Reese yelled repeatedly, while crimson red iron oozed freely from the furnace. "Plug up the damn thing!"

A devilish grin came to Boo's lips. From across the cast house floor, Tommy Jenkins watched the commotion.

"Pull it back out," yelled Reese to the operator. "The tip of the clay gun is melting. Refill it and try again!" Reese looked around for the clay-man that was supposed to pull the release chain so the operator could bring back the gun. "Pull that damn chain Boo!" Boo just grinned at the fuming Reese. "Boo, you bastard!"

Globs of melting cast iron fell from the clay gun's nozzle. Reese pulled several times before the gun released. Unexpectedly the iron exploded in the hole. No one was safe on the open cast house floor. Tommy dropped to the floor as sparks shot over him. Boo grinned like the Cheshire cat, as sparks exploded past the opening. Unlike others, he was protected by the operating room. Tommy shielded himself and listened to the shrill of the emergency sirens ringing as everyone evacuated the area. Tommy counted heads and found that only one was missing. Tommy could only see Boo on the far side of the trough.

Was it an accident? Had Boo something to do with it? These questions raced through his mind. He had witnessed the whole thing. He had not seen anything out of the ordinary, and most of his suspicions and evidence was melting away. 'Was Boo the only survivor?' thought Tommy?

. . . .

The dark black sky filled the night as grey smoke and steam billowed upward from the factory. Red hot slag flowing from one of the four blast furnaces illuminated the night sky. The road past the railroad tracks, along number four furnace, was brightened as if it had been daytime. A steady stream of men walked the half mile distance from the number four gate. It was the shift change, and along the pathway, somewhere between number seven and number five blast furnace, workers walked to the welfare building nestled among smaller factory shops.

Tonight the air possessed a certain burden as men brushed silvery graphite off their already dingy clothes, others coughed sporadically, an industrial cough, the kind that never seems to go away. Men on the graveyard shift walked up the brick walled stairway on their way to the locker rooms.

Rows upon rows of lockers, painted repeatedly with the company's dark green colour, stood like soldiers all in a row. Sweat permeated the air as steam filled the shower rooms. Work clothes filled the baskets hanging over the lockers throughout the room.

Men; young, old and middle aged, chattered in English and Italian. Of the two, Italian was the more common language of most workers who had settled in the steel town. Boo's thoughts were carried away by the cool September wind blowing gently through the windows above the lockers. He wondered, as he had done so many times before, why had the times changed. It had been a nicer time when the Baby Blue would cruise Queen Street, with Ziggy and himself sitting up front. He remembered Salami bugging Frog in the back seat about Frog getting laid before he went blind.

THE END

OTHER TITLES AVAILABLE FROM
MOOSE ENTERPRISE BOOK AND THEATRE PLAY
PUBLISHING
Visit our web site at www.moosehidebooks.com for complete title listings.

NOVELS

     Steeltown
     Steeltown Blues
     Roosevelt Street
     Executor of Mercy
     A Print of a Man
     Sky Flyers
     Assault of a Princess
     Assault
     Basement Bargain Price Leafs for Sale
     Five Star Investigations
     Rusty Butt (Treasure of the Ocean Mist)
     Arrow Boy
     Big Bobby Boom (and the Marble Mayhem)
     The Sidewalk
     Time Warriors
     The Letter
     Reflection
     Guilt in Accession
     Déjà vu

www.ingramcontent.com/pod-product-compliance
Lightning Source LLC
Chambersburg PA
CBHW020559250626
47154CB00004B/1283